JOAN LENNON

PUFFIN

PUFFIN BOOKS

Published by the Penguin Group
Penguin Books Ltd, 80 Strand, London WC2R ORL, England
Penguin Group (USA) Inc., 375 Hudson Street, New York, New York 10014, USA
Penguin Group (Canada), 90 Eglinton Avenue East, Suite 700, Toronto, Ontario, Canada M4P 2Y3
(a division of Pearson Penguin Canada Inc.)
Penguin Ireland, 25 St Stephen's Green, Dublin 2, Ireland (a division of Penguin Books Ltd)
Penguin Group (Australia), 250 Camberwell Road, Camberwell, Victoria 3124, Australia
(a division of Pearson Australia Group Pty Ltd)
Penguin Books India Pvt Ltd, 11 Community Centre, Panchsheel Park, New Delhi – 110 017, India
Penguin Group (NZ), 67 Apollo Drive, Rosedale, North Shore 0632, New Zealand
(a division of Pearson New Zealand Ltd)
Penguin Books (South Africa) (Pty) Ltd, 24 Sturdee Avenue, Rosebank, Johannesburg 2196, South Africa

Penguin Books Ltd, Registered Offices: 80 Strand, London WC2R ORL, England

puffinbooks.com

First published 2008
1

Copyright © Joan Lennon, 2008

The moral right of the author has been asserted

Set in Baskerville MT by Palimpsest Book Production Limited,
Grangemouth, Stirlingshire
Made and printed in England by Clays Ltd, St Ives plc

British Library Cataloguing in Publication Data
A CIP catalogue record for this book is available from the British Library

ISBN: 978-0-141-31917-9

For my mum, Jean Lennon, who would have had those Kelpies dressing warmly, using good reading lights and eating vegetables before they knew what had hit them.

I'd like to thank Kathryn Ross and Lindsey Fraser, my agents, and Yvonne Hooker, my editor, for their help – there's many a creek up which (paddle-less) I would certainly still be without you! Special thanks to Lindsey and my sister Maureen for hand-holding provided above and beyond the call of duty, during the ridiculously difficult year in which this book was being written. And thank you also to Sally and Colin for letting me write in their spare bedroom while various of my sons restructured their garden, and Tyrella Nash at Milton Cottage for the very productive times I spent there, writing with one hand and guzzling her cooking with the other.

Contents

There are places they call 'liminal' — where the divisions between present, past and future are thinner than normal. Even the walls between universes aren't always up to scratch. Things blur and leak into each other in places like that. Connections are made between peoples and times that are against all the rules. Things . . . break through, good things sometimes, but not always. Sometimes the things that break through are evil, and relentless, and driven by terrible hungers.

The Western Isles of Scotland is a place like that.

Dark worlds, bright worlds, worlds (like our own human one) that are peculiar combinations of both — so many realities include this stretch of islands and seas and sky, heart-breakingly beautiful at one moment and deadly the next, full of softness and hardship and terror, and a hundred shades of purple and green, blue and grey.

In the sixth century, on the island of Iona, there was a boy called Adom. In the twenty-fourth century, in a suburb of Greater Glasgow, there will be a girl called Jay. And in the universe of the G there is Eo, a young shape-shifter-in-training. You'd think there couldn't be three more different specimens of life in existence, and yet they do have two things in common.

One — they all live in the same place, in this landscape of chance and change, where the tides are powerful and strange, and the walls of a thousand worlds are thin.

And two — they don't always pay attention.

Professor Pinkerton Hurple's Answers to Your Most Pressing FAQs appear in boxes scattered throughout the text. They are taken from an ongoing manuscript which the Professor is writing, and which he keeps with him at all times. It is on the subject of pretty much everything. The pages have become quite disreputable-looking over the years, marred by paw prints, stained with rabbit blood, and almost all with the edges thoroughly chewed. (Composition isn't easy, even for a mind as agile and at the same time cram-packed as the Professor's.) It is only with the greatest reluctance that he has allowed access to his unfinished masterpiece, but as it's anybody's guess when the work will finally be published, he could hardly have expected us to wait.

1 *Eo*

A basically human shape is the default appearance of the G. In fact, before they reach fully trained adulthood, human is all a G *can* do. So it wasn't surprising that Eo should look like a boy, since his training still had a long way to go. (His full name was Eo Gofer-Baroque, but that is another story.) According to his current teacher, Professor Pinkerton Hurple, the point at which Eo's training would finish was actually *receding* rather than getting closer.

'It's hard to believe that anyone *could* know less at the end of a lesson than they did at the beginning – but *you* manage it. If it weren't so AGGRAVATING, it would be an interesting phenomenon.'

At fifteen, Eo gave the impression of being a master of self-confidence and complete bone-idleness – at one and the same time. Having said that, he often did *plan* to be attentive, but then he forgot partway through. The things going on inside his head were so much more interesting.

Any self-doubts he had, he kept well buried. If the work threatened to become difficult, he didn't wait around to find out. He slid out from under such things as neatly as possible, with charm and his own personal brand of deviousness.

Some of the time, Eo pretended to be more stupid than he really was, just for the fun of it – particularly during lessons with Professor Hurple. He enjoyed watching the Professor's fur get all bunchy with irritation. The Professor was a ferret and his emotions clearly showed in the state of his coat. A more dapper beast at the beginning of a lesson would be hard to imagine; by the end, he was dishevelled and unkempt and fit to be tied – and Eo would have had an enjoyable afternoon, learning not a lot.

Confusingly, Professor Hurple was not a G. He couldn't shape-shift. He actually *was* a ferret (though an exceptionally intelligent one, as he was quick to point out), coming originally from the early twenty-first-century Scotland of the humans. How he came to be in the G universe at all is a story in itself, but not one that Eo had yet managed to wheedle out of him. (Of course, *all* ferrets are astonishingly good at squeezing through the tiniest cracks or down the most unobvious holes, and all ferrets are enormously curious, so finding a way from one universe to another is not the challenge to them that it would be to most life forms.) And although Professor Hurple had never *been* human, he had, as it happened, spent more time in their company than any of the G themselves.

He had also read a great deal, which helps.

Why would the G need to be educated at all, you may ask, since surely all they have to do is shape-shift *into* something else to know everything about it, from the inside out, as it were. In fact, the truth is exactly the reverse. *Before* a G can shift, they have to know as much as possible about the life form they are changing into.

For example, a G can't become a clam (at least not for long) without knowing about clam predators, or what to do when the tide goes out, or even (if so inclined) how to tell girl clams from boy clams. But, not surprisingly, individual G then find themselves more comfortable in some shapes than in others. And the more time they spend in that form, the more they learn and the deeper their understanding becomes. Then, as specialists, they pass on their knowledge to trainees. For example, Eo was taught about pack dynamics, how to organize herbivores and the joys of digging by Hibernation Gladrag, currently Head of the G and, most of the time, an extremely handsome Border collie bitch. (Eo paid *close* attention to these lessons because he quite fancied shifting into some kind of canine, and also because every time his teacher smiled he remembered she was capable of ripping his throat out.)

Very few of the adult G chose to spend time as human, however. This could be because they got enough of it as children, when human was all they *could* do. Or it could be because, as a species, they rated fun as the highest goal and being human was often just not fun enough. So the G tended to use the shape only for formal occasions or boring ceremonies or rare moments of unpleasantness with other universes. Which explains why, when a Professor of Human Studies was needed to teach a young G, they were grateful to be able to turn to Pinkerton Hurple.

FAQ 998: Do the G have horrible, embarrassing parents like mine?

HURPLE'S REPLY: The G like their young, and are always friendly to their own particular offspring when their paths cross, but not to the point of letting this interfere with their own pursuits. Parenting is seen as pretty much a communal affair. Take our friend Eo, for example. His parents were both ocean birds most of the time – usually gannets – so they were frequently far out to sea, riding the Atlantic storms and diving at wing-ripping speed into frantic shoals of fish. On the upside, this means that when they **were** around, Eo was in for some fabulously exciting bedtime stories. On the downside, there was always the danger of one or other parent absent-mindedly trying to shove a fish down his throat.

Today, Professor Hurple had decided he was going to teach Eo the fine art of triangulation IF IT KILLED HIM. 'Him' could refer to pupil or teacher – or both – in this case, but whichever way, *Hurple was determined.* He was convinced that mathematics was essential, the key to whole swathes of human experience, and Eo was going to be introduced to those swathes come hell or high water.

(It could be proposed that all the events that followed happened as a result of Professor Hurple's obsession with mathematics. And his being a ferret, of course, since most mathematicians will not normally eat rabbit unless somebody cooks it first.)

Eo was receiving this part of his education on one of the most beautiful of the G islands. It was as close to being the centre of G society as any place could be, an unofficial capital, for the simple reason that it was green and pleasant and had beaches of the finest silver. In terms of practical triangulation, the view from its shores offered a number of distant mountain peaks to work out the height of, but to a ferret there were much more interesting problems to solve.

'Now, pay attention, boy! As you can hear, I have placed a beeper –'

'Ooo – what's a beeper, sir?'

'It's a thing that beeps – what do you *think* it is?!'

'Just checking, sir.'

Professor Hurple narrowed his ferrety eyes suspiciously. He never quite trusted Eo when he started calling him 'sir' in that oh-so-innocent tone of voice. Still, *I will not be distracted!* he thought to himself.

'I have placed a beeper,' he repeated more loudly, 'down a tunnel in this deserted rabbit warren. I will give you the length of the tunnel – you may use the horizon as observable from this point – and I would like you to use the principles of triangulation, as explained on *a number* of previous occasions, to work out the exact depth at which the beeper may be found. Do you understand?'

Eo nodded earnestly. 'Yes, sir! Yes, I do . . . except for one thing.'

Hurple sighed. 'Well?' he said wearily. 'What is it?'

'The beeper. You said it was a thing that beeps?'

'YES?!'

'Well . . . it's stopped.'

What the Professor said next was, thankfully, in Ferret, thus saving Eo's tender ears. Still, it was quite a safe guess from his tone – and the instantaneous fur muss-up – that he was not best pleased.

'Wait here,' he snarled (in G this time), and disappeared into the warren.

Eo grinned contentedly. Old Hurple was certainly good entertainment. He even had some interesting things to say, sometimes. Eo quite liked maths, though it seemed to involve more work than should be absolutely necessary. He lay back on the grass while he waited for the ferret to re-emerge, and looked up into the blue autumn sky.

The clouds were fat and frisky before a brisk wind, and the tide was on its way out, so the smell of fresh mud and seaweed was strong on the air. Eo rolled over on to his stomach and squinted out to sea, watching the way its colours changed themselves restlessly from bright aquamarine to blue-black and back again.

It was one of those moments when Eo felt good about life in general, and being Eo in particular. There wasn't any real reason, beyond it being such a nice day – it just happens like that sometimes.

After a bit, though, his feeling of well-being began to leak away. He started to wonder a little uncomfortably about what had happened to the Professor. Even an exceptional ferret can sometimes forget other commitments while underground. Not that Eo minded – he never minded not having lessons – but he didn't want to have to spoil the mood of the day by needing to worry about his teacher . . .

He frowned, and put his ear to the ground. Sure enough, there were muffled scuffling noises to be heard, and then a short screech. Then silence. Eo chewed his lip. The scream hadn't *sounded* like old Hurple's voice. But still . . . If he were an adult, it'd be no problem – he'd just shift shape, into another ferret maybe, and scuttle on down there. Find out what was what. But he wasn't, and he couldn't. All *he* could do was dig down from where he was (and he didn't even have a shovel) or else go and find an adult G someplace and get *them* to help. He didn't like to leave, though. He didn't really know *what* to do, so he decided to do nothing for a while longer. That sometimes worked.

Eo had just reached the point of *having* to make a decision when, to his great relief, the Professor re-emerged from the tunnel.

He was looking dreamy and content, in spite of being in dire need of a good grooming. His muzzle in particular had some pretty incriminating red marks round it. He seemed surprised to see Eo.

'Ah . . . yes . . .' he said, and stopped.

'Are you all right?' asked Eo.

9

Hurple burped. 'Pardon me,' he said. 'Yes, I am quite all right, thank you for asking. I did, however, make one slight miscalculation. I believe, earlier, that I stated this warren was deserted. I was wrong. Then. But I'm right now!' He grinned a little sheepishly at Eo and then gave himself a shake. 'Right,' he continued, trying to sound a bit more like a proper Authority Figure. 'Did you bring your bag with you, boy?'

Eo nodded. School-age G needed sturdy and capacious bags with strong straps. There was no telling what your tutor might want you to carry around or bring to lessons. (Especially if the tutor in question couldn't carry things very well himself because of not, for example, having any hands.) In Eo's case, his bag had more of the Professor's work in it than his own. The ferret never liked to be without his great work, *Professor Pinkerton Hurple's Answers to Your Most Pressing FAQs*, and was quite capable of breaking off in the middle of a lesson – even the middle of a sentence! – to get down a new idea that struck him.

'Here it is, Professor,' said Eo.

'Good. Excellent. It is my intention, at this point, to get into your bag for a period of, uh, meditation. That doesn't mean wasted time for you, however. You may continue with your essay on "Demon Incursions from the Dark Worlds" for Supernova Tangent. She mentioned to me only this morning that you were not progressing with it as diligently as she could have wiiiii–'

An enormous yawn interrupted him. Ferrets fall asleep after a meal, in the same way that rivers run downhill and the sun rises at dawn.

'She was not at all sure you'd been paying attention when she explained the special dangers of this time of year to you. Again. You may refer to my manuscript if you need any really *strong* quotes. Don't forget to consider the moon . . . don't forget . . . eclipse . . .' Hurple could barely keep his eyes open.

Eo suppressed a grin, and held the mouth of his bag open invitingly. In a blink the ferret was inside, curled up and snoring on his own manuscript and the boy's notes for his essay. Eo didn't care. He had no intention of progressing in his understanding of *anything* today. With a chuckle, he folded the top of the bag over, picked it up carefully and headed down to the shoreline.

At no point up till then had anything *irrevocable* happened. There was nothing actually dangerous about a teacher falling asleep or a pupil skiving. And what came next might seem pretty insignificant too, particularly if you think only big actions have consequences.

Or that only cruelty on a large scale is actually cruel.

Eo laid his bag down on a soft bit of the beach, then tiptoed away to look for rock pools. And almost at once he found a beauty. It was a perfect little world of miniature seaweed and red sea anemones like clots of blood, darting transparent fingerlings, at least one small crab, a few snails and a colony of shrimps with their long feelers and their perpetually prissy expressions (Eo disliked shrimps). It was like a little zoo, or his own private collection.

Eo drew his hair back from both sides of his face, knotted the two pieces behind his head and told it to stay there. One of the convenient things about G hair was that it always did as requested, come high wind or water.

It was fascinating, for a while, just to watch the inhabitants going about the place, aware that they were unaware that they were *being* watched. But after a bit,

Eo was gripped by the temptation that comes, sooner or later, to all zoo owners and collectors – the temptation to *interfere*. To find out what would happen *if* . . .

He started with just shifting his weight a little, so his shadow fell across the rock-pool world, cutting off the sun. This made the inhabitants pause for a second, but it was the sort of thing clouds did all the time so they forgot about it almost at once. Then he tried dropping rocks, just small ones, out of the blue on to their heads. That got them agitated! Then he had another idea – he looked about him for a stick . . .

Every G had tuition on the dangers of demonic entrance – living where they did, it would have been criminal negligence otherwise. Just because the main pillars of G existence had always been pleasure and the satisfaction of curiosity didn't mean they were reckless or stupid. They knew better than to walk round a standing stone widdershins, or sleep on a faerie mound, or whistle rudely at sea.

Eo had very recently been reminded of all this. The lecture from Supernova Tangent was the same one she gave every year. It described – in painstaking detail – the way certain things could combine at certain times, things like phases of the moon, lunar orbit, whether or not an eclipse was imminent, what Festivals of the Dead were near at hand. When even a few of these things happened together, the walls of the worlds became even thinner, and the chances of a rip between one world and another increased. When *all* of them happened together, it was wise to be very, very careful indeed not to do anything that would attract the attention of the dark realities and the endless hunger of their inhabitants for souls to feed on.

FAQ 246: I get that demons from other worlds are attracted to the energy in souls, and that's what they feed on. And that they're always trying to get into other people's worlds to find some. But then why is there so much mention of riddles and challenges and forfeits in stories involving demon breakthroughs? When they make it into another universe and then catch somebody, why do they mess around with all that? Why don't they just get on with their meal?

HURPLE'S REPLY: You're right – there does seem to be a practically genetic leaning in demons of all kinds towards gambling. Playing chess with Death, swapping riddles with sphinxes or poems with the Blue Men – there are as many variations as there are stories. (Though obviously victims who are killed immediately wouldn't get the chance to tell stories.) Some scholars believe that dallying and delaying like this serve a culinary purpose – the sudden upsurge of hope generated in the victims' souls is thought to intensify the flavour. Others think that it has to do with cosmic balance – if, like cats, demons were not constrained to play with their food, they might wipe out entire populations. Whatever the reason, it certainly adds to the general tension of inter-dimensional interaction!

But Supernova Tangent was not a thrilling lecturer, and Eo had heard it all before and his attention wandered . . .

He didn't make the connection between what he'd been told, and sitting by a rock pool on a sunny day, casually tormenting the occupants. It amused him to shut off the sun. He enjoyed sending them meteors out of the blue. It made him laugh to create a miniature maelstrom with a stick, to see the little shrimps being swept backwards round and round, waving their tiny legs ineffectually and then staggering across the sand grains afterwards like old women in a high wind until he stirred them up again. He didn't notice he was stirring the pool counter-clockwise. The word *widdershins* didn't even cross his mind. He didn't notice that the sun really *had* gone in, though his body shivered a little. He didn't hear the way the wind was picking up, or see it flinging bits of foam off the waves and shredding them over the expanse of low-tide sand. He was so intent on the captive world before him, so caught up in the exercise of power, that the changes going on behind his back didn't register.

Until he suddenly realized that all the sounds of *his* world had stopped. It was as if a giant bell jar had been shoved down over him, cutting him off. He banged the side of his head, desperate to ease the pressure in his ears, to no effect. He turned, and froze.

A gigantic whirlpool of powering black water had appeared, towering over him out of nowhere, balanced impossibly on the wet sand. It was black like a hole ripped from a moonless sky, or out of the dark depths of the sea, full of grotesquely swirling women's faces and the bodies of men and flailing horses' manes and hooves.

He noticed *that*.

2 *The Challenge*

Kelpies!

Eo felt his heart lurch with dread as he realized what he was seeing. The faces in the vortex were clearer now, too eerie and elongated to be beautiful, yet riveting – animal- and human-shaped, horses, women and men. They swept past, some half-obscured by foamy hair, others pinning Eo with their eyes in the instant before they were whipped away again. They seemed to be crying out to him in the silence, yearning for him, drawing him . . .

Eo took a step closer. And another. Then, without warning, the side of the whirlpool split open, vertically, in an explosion of white noise that threw him on to his back and tore all the breath from his lungs. Out of the rip plunged a gigantic white mare, lean as a predator, with muscles that showed like bunched steel as it galloped on to the beach, bucking and screaming and biting the air. Then, just as suddenly, the vortex sealed itself again.

Wheezing and rasping, Eo pulled himself up on to his knees. He barely registered that the pressure in his head had eased and he could hear again. He no longer noticed the immense column of water whirling its frantic cargo so close beside him. Crazed by terror and Kelpie mesmer, he was utterly focused on the horse.

The huge mare thundered to the far end of the beach and reared round, flailing its hooves in the air and screaming a triumph. As its front legs hit the sand again, Eo could feel the ground shake, and then it was powering towards him and he had staggered to his feet, and at the last second the horse stopped, stiff-legged, showering him with grit. It stared down at him with black, blank eyes, and spoke.

'So small,' the Kelpie said. 'So utterly insignificant. And yet the life in it . . . luscious! I can almost taste it already . . .'

Eo stood there, watching helplessly as the great head began to lower towards him, the lips pulled back to show sharpened white teeth. With an enormous effort he tried to raise an arm to cower behind.

Flecks of foam flew from the Kelpie's mouth. Three drops fell on Eo's bare forearm. He watched in horror as his skin began to blister, as the acid in the spit started eating into his flesh. For a moment he was too shocked to feel anything at all. Then the pain hit and Eo, screaming, collapsed in a heap on the sand.

All over the island and beyond, in ever-widening circles, G were dragged out of whatever was absorbing them by their awareness of his distress. Sooner than seemed possible they began to arrive, in so many forms – birds, beasts, creatures of the sea – then morphing

FAQ 444: What is mesmer and how does it work?

HURPLE'S REPLY: Mesmer is the ability to slide past a person's normal defences and go straight for the most scramble-able bits of the brain. These include your memories and your hormones. The resulting mental chaos is overpowering but, fortunately, it doesn't last all that long.

Species like the Kelpie (who have learned how to hardwire straight into two basic areas of intense interest in the humanoid brain — love of horses and love of, er, love) use mesmer to devastating effect on their victims, causing them to forget their loyalties, their loves and every scrap of common sense. The question, 'Why does this totally incredibly overwhelmingly gorgeous stranger want to kiss me?' should be answered by, 'Because he/she is a soul-sucking demon and it's been a long time since his/her lunch.' But it rarely is.

That's mesmer.

into human as the seriousness of what they faced became clear.

And as they changed, the Kelpie began to change too. Slowly, grotesquely . . . For the G, each shift is a single, continuous, effortless swing into the new form. But *this* was painful to watch, a horrible lurching, limb by limb, from a horse to a tall, tall woman, pale-maned, with long feet and hands and a skin so white it was almost transparent, like the skin of something that lived in the cold depths of caves and could not imagine the sun. When her transformation was complete, she stood before them all in a woman's shape, but tall as a thundercloud, merciless as an iceberg, and with a set of mind-boggling curves that defied gravity and several other laws of physics. The G in human form are a spare, slight people. Compared to the Kelpie, they looked like a flock of children, yet they pressed forward, trying to get close to the boy.

With one white foot she pinned the barely conscious Eo to the sand and swept the G with her dead black eyes.

'I am the Queen of the Kelpies,' she hissed, 'and he is *mine*. He opened the way and his soul is ours to feed on, according to the Rules.'

Interactions between the worlds were governed by 'the Rules'. No one knows who first spelled them out in words, or when the species of the various universes agreed to be bound by them. But bound they were. There may be ways to make the Rules work for you – whole encyclopedias had been written on the subject. But the Rules themselves must be followed through to the end. With a sigh, the crowd of G fell back.

FAQ 1,116: What do the G do about clothes when they're shifting from one shape to another?

HURPLE'S REPLY: Feathers, fur, scales and shells are all part of the form a shape-shifter might take, but clothes are not. To deal with the inconvenience of moving to and from a human shape, caches of one-size-fits-all robes are dotted all over the Western Isles. The G themselves are not particularly bothered about nakedness but would be the first to admit that the human shape is extremely badly insulated.

The Queen laughed. It was a sound like razor shell on roughened rock. Still laughing, she was reaching a long white hand down towards Eo –

– when a large dog loped up, pushing past the legs of the G. It panted to a halt, dirt all over its nose, tongue hanging out of the side of its mouth. (If Eo had been conscious of anything outside his own pain, the sight of that muddy nose would have made his heart sink. Only the extremely foolish, or the pathologically brave, dared interrupt the present Head of the G while she was digging out rabbits.)

'Rrrr?' the dog growled.

One of the G stepped forward and whispered into the animal's ear. A look of embarrassment crossed its face and it at once began to blur upwards.

'I do beg your pardon,' it said as she became human. 'Rude of me not to have changed for company.'

Someone passed her a robe. With a murmured thanks, she pulled it on over her head, and turned to face the Kelpie once more. Two other G, male, one middle-aged like the Head, the other young, came to stand beside her. (Since no one was much interested in the bother of politics, the adult members of G society took it in turns to form a very basic government – one to be in charge, called the Head, and two to assist, called Designated Companions.)

'I am Hibernation Gladrag, currently Head of the G.' She gave a slight bow. 'And these are the Designated Companions – Market Jones and Interrupted Cadence.'

'You *name* your Lackeys?!' sneered the Queen. 'Then you are even more of a fool than you look. I have no interest in your introductions – I'm leaving now. The brat's mine. Unless . . .' A new, slightly mad light flickered in her black eyes. 'Unless he'd like to choose a Wager . . .?'

There was an almost visible shiver in the crowd of G. Everyone knew how addicted the Kelpie were to gambling.

'The boy is in pain,' Gladrag said firmly, 'and in no condition to consider that. We will first deal with the damage you've done him.'

'Don't trouble on my account,' said the Queen. 'He's in perfectly good enough condition for *my* purposes.'

Hibernation Gladrag continued to gaze calmly at the Queen, waiting, as if the Kelpie hadn't spoken. The moment lengthened unbearably until, with a tiny shrug, the Queen stepped aside.

Eo was immediately surrounded by G, shielding him from the Kelpie's sight and therefore from the full brunt of her mesmer, but it didn't seem to help. The boy was still broadcasting anguish.

'Why doesn't it stop?'

'Why isn't he healing himself?'

'Where's Abalone?'

One of the first things Gs learn is medical maintenance – how to shift the shape of any *part* of themselves if it becomes damaged. Eo should have immediately blocked the pain pathways to his brain and set about healing the wounds the Queen had inflicted.

But nothing was happening.

'I'm here.' Pentathlon Abalone was the closest the G had to a medic, and he'd taught practically every member of the crowd their maintenance skills, including Eo.

'Why isn't he healing?' came the anxious question from all round.

Abalone bent over the boy and examined him carefully. He shook his head. 'These are not natural wounds. Healing them will not be simple. I fear . . . Eo, can you manage the pain? That at least should not be affected. Try.'

Abalone had a soothing, familiar voice, and it was this more than anything that got through to Eo in his blind distress. He stopped panting and whimpering, and began to work.

'That's right. You remember. Start at the source of the pain. Follow the pathways to the door of the brain. That's it. Now shut the door. You can do it . . .'

Every G on the beach felt the relief when Eo succeeded. It was so great for Eo himself that he went wobbly again, falling back into the arms of Abalone in a half-faint.

The Queen was pacing impatiently. She stopped in front of the Head and snapped, 'I hope these *repairs* aren't going to be lengthy. My people have been abstemious long enough. I'd hate to keep them waiting more than need be.'

'Been having trouble breaking through, eh?' muttered the G called Market Jones.

The Queen didn't deign to look at him directly. 'Tell your Lackey to mind his manners,' she snarled.

Gladrag inclined her head. 'Market, behave yourself,' she said solemnly.

Market made an elaborate bow, and then murmured to the other Companion, Interrupted Cadence, 'So hard to get good Lackeys these days.'

The Queen resumed her pacing.

'*Souls . . .*' they heard her mumbling, '*so many souls . . . I smell their souls . . .*'

'How vulgar,' commented Market.

'Are you unwell?' Gladrag asked politely.

The Queen swerved suddenly and loomed over the Head of the G. '*I won't wait any more!*' she half-snarled, half-wailed. '*He's mine – hand him over!*'

She focused her attention and, at once, Gladrag could feel her throat beginning to close up.

'Nggg . . . ggg,' she said – and then Interrupted Cadence thrust himself between her and the Kelpie.

'No stomach for that Wager you mentioned? Of course you *know* you'd lose,' he snorted. It was only partly a snort – the rest was a sort of nervous squeak – but at least he'd broken her attention. He could hear Gladrag dragging the breath back into her lungs behind him.

When he looked round at her, however, she and Market both were gazing at him in dismay. Then the Head rallied.

'Er, yes, that's right,' she croaked, trying to give an impression of calm, while behind her back she was making wild open-handed gestures. 'Why don't you, um, make my day.' A ginger-haired G clutching a book (entitled *Encyclopedia of Demonic Entrance: The Rules, and How to Make Them Work for You, Volume One*) pushed through the crowd and succeeded in thrusting it into the Head's flailing hands. Gladrag heaved a silent sigh of relief. 'If you'll excuse us for just a moment . . .?'

The three went into a huddle. Market and Interrupted immediately began to squabble with each other in low voices.

'Are you out of your tiny mind?'

'I didn't see *you* doing anything – that was your Head she was strangling, or didn't you notice?!'

Gladrag was leafing through the book with what was meant to look like only casual interest, but was in fact becoming more and more of a desperate trawl. The others paused, watching anxiously as the blood drained from her face.

She waved the book at them. 'It only goes up to J!' she hissed.

'What!?'

'What I *said* – this book stops at J. "Kelpie" starts with the letter K, or had you forgotten!? The information on Kelpie Challenges must be *in Volume Two*!'

She turned and mimed frantically at the G who'd brought the book. He blanched, and fled in search of Volume Two.

'But . . .' Interrupted was whispering to Market, 'it's not a problem, is it? Because we all *know* that stuff. We were tested on it enough as kids. Right?'

'Of course I knew it *then* – but I haven't exactly been revising ever since. Have you?!'

Interrupted shook his head mournfully.

'Time's up!' blared the Queen. 'Let him choose a Wager, or let me take him as he stands!'

'OK. Right. He can choose,' shrilled Gladrag. 'But you can't interfere with him – you can't use your mesmer on him! He must be *free* to choose!'

'And *you* must not prompt him!' said the Queen, and she grabbed the (in fact useless) encyclopedia out of Gladrag's hands and tossed it away.

Gladrag bowed her head and then turned to the silent crowd. 'All right. Send out the boy . . .'

Eo had been lying still, keeping his eyes shut. At least one part of his brain was desperately hoping the whole thing was just a bad dream. If it was, the dream wasn't over yet . . .

'Come on, boy,' said Abalone. 'You heard her.'

Reluctantly, Eo opened his eyes, and squinted up at the faces surrounding him. There was no sign of his mother or father, but he knew he shouldn't be surprised. The sprats were running in the South Atlantic and no natural power on earth could travel so far so fast. It would take them several days at least to return, even with parents' terror and gannets' wings. Totally irrelevant facts about the migratory patterns of schooling fish rose to the surface of his mind, and sank again.

He staggered to his feet, the crowd parted – and Eo had his first glimpse of the Kelpie in her human form. There was no mistaking her – even without the sudden blast of her mesmeric power hitting him between the eyes. If anything, it was worse now. The Queen may have been magnificent as a horse, but as a woman she was more than any fifteen-year-old boy should have to face.

He came close to fainting again.

Everyone was staring at him – he could feel the intensity of all those eyes, making his skin creep. But he couldn't have turned and looked back at any of them to save his life. Not with the Kelpie Queen there before him, so close she filled his eyes, his brain . . .

If only she'd hold still!

But the Queen wasn't moving. What made her seem to be writhing voluptuously was the way her robe swirled round her body, sliding over her curves like waves round a shape on the shore, obscuring, revealing, caressing. Her mane of pale hair stirred about her face and shoulders as if it were alive, and her black eyes bored into him like cold fire.

It wasn't just the occasional flash of flesh that had Eo spinning. His brain lurched and his thoughts were as helpless and out of control as eddying shrimps. The Queen was speaking, presenting the Wagers he was to choose from, as was required, but low and *fast*, too fast. She was also pacing again, so that every time she turned her back on him he couldn't quite hear what she was saying . . .

'A way opened between the worlds can be closed at the price of a soul. That price may, however . . . the Recognized Wagers. These include the Riddles Three as laid down . . . Single Combat with a Champion of my choice . . . Race of Twelve Peaks, the Seventh Tide, the Rock Hurl . . . must decide WITHOUT FURTHER DELAY!!'

The final words ended on a shriek that made every G on the shore jerk in fright. Eo's eyes showed white all the way around and he was panting again like a stressed cat. The Kelpie's words whirled by in his mind, again and again, and he tried desperately to grab hold of their meaning. He *had* to understand – he had to *remember* what he'd been taught – where had his brain been in those lessons?

He could hear the voice of his Health and Safety tutor, Extraneous Chrome, explaining patiently for the umpteenth time, 'Now, young Eo, I'm sure neither of us wishes to go through this material too many *more* times, so let's pay attention, shall we . . .?' He'd scraped through that exam – just – and then promptly forgotten the lot.

The thing with the rocks . . . Single Combat . . . the Riddles Three . . . the Seventh Tide . . . Get a grip . . . get it right . . . Look at the choices, idiot . . . What am I good at? . . . I'd be useless at the combat, and racing, and hurling . . . Not terrific at riddles . . . What was the other one about? . . .

He tried pounding his forehead with his fists in the hope of shaking the knowledge out, but it didn't work. He couldn't remember!

'I'm sorry . . .' he babbled. 'I'm not sure . . . The Seventh Tide?' He looked round at the G for help. He saw, instead, horror.

'The child means "*What* is the Seventh Tide?"!' Gladrag started shouting.

'*The child chose!*' screeched the Queen.

'It was a request for clarification!'

'*It was a choice!*' The triumph in her voice was terrifying.

The faces in the vortex grinned wildly and mouthed,

'*A choice!*'

'*Chosen!*'

'*The Tide! The Tide!*'

Without understanding a word of what had happened, Eo could tell he was doomed.

3 *The Throw of Hibernation Gladrag*

Memory is an unpredictable thing. It is perfectly happy to desert us at some vital moment and then come strolling back, all rested and relaxed, when the emergency is over.

This is exactly what Eo's memory did to him. The choice was made; the die had been well and truly cast; and now that it was altogether *too late* the information he'd been looking for came flooding back.

The Seventh Tide . . . I've just agreed to the Seventh Tide! Different from all the other Wagers, the outcome of the Seventh Tide involved more than the individual victim. He had walked straight into a disaster, the best the Queen could have hoped for.

She was watching him now, gloating, enjoying the way his fear for himself was being overlaid with guilt.

'There is only a little time left,' she announced in a loud voice, 'till the turn of the tide, when the Wager will begin. No one is to approach the Challenger, for good or ill, until that moment.'

Reluctant but unable to resist her, all the G drew back, until Eo was left alone, isolated in a little circle of empty sand. He was rigid with terror and despair now, and hardly seemed to notice what was happening around him. The Queen turned and glared meaningfully at the Head and her Companions.

'If you will excuse us just a second?' said Gladrag, and the government went into a huddle.

'What just happened?' whispered Interrupted Cadence, looking across at the boy.

Gladrag sighed. 'He raised the stakes,' she answered hoarsely.

'I'm not sure I remember the details of . . .' said Interrupted tentatively.

'The Seventh Tide is probably the most complicated of the Wagers – and we have to hope that we can make that work for us . . .' said Market. 'Because – correct me if I'm wrong – *please* tell me I'm wrong – the forfeit is a *permanent* way in.'

'You're not wrong,' murmured Gladrag sadly. 'If we lose, the Kelpies would be free to enter our world at will . . .'

Everyone knew of worlds that had been lost to the Kelpies. They were the stuff of nightmares, tales told in the cold and sober hours of the night, and there were no happy endings to tales like that. Worlds lost to demons did not often come back to the light.

There was no time to consider the horror of that prospect, for just then the red-haired G, whose face was now practically the same colour as his hair, rushed up with another volume from the encyclopedia, practically throwing it at the Head. The Companions clustered desperately round as Gladrag flipped pages.

'*Kelpies* . . . *Kelpies* . . . *Kelpie Challenges* – here it is – *The Seventh Tide!*' She ran her eyes down the page, speed-reading. 'OK . . . OK . . . right . . .'

She put her finger in the book and spoke to the Companions. 'What happens is this. Each side has three throws. We could use the beach, from here where the grass starts, on out to sea, to throw on. You need to imagine that as a stretch of time, from the beginning of history, near us, to the far future furthest away.'

'I accept.'

As one, the three G jumped. They hadn't remembered what acute hearing Kelpies have.

'I – I beg your pardon?' stuttered Gladrag.

'I accept your proposal,' said the Queen. 'The beach will make an excellent playing field. Now we need to decide on which world.'

'Er . . .'

'To which world will we send him? I'm sure you wouldn't want to take any unfair advantage, so *this* world won't do. The Kelpie world perhaps?'

The vortex speeded up visibly and its inhabitants' excitement grew.

The three G shuddered and shook their heads.

'Someplace *neutral*, then,' purred the Queen.

'The boy is young and can only take human form as yet,' said Gladrag. 'Perhaps, then, the human world would be the best choice?'

The Queen's smile was slow and satisfied. It made Gladrag wonder if somehow she'd been tricked, but she couldn't think what other world she *could* have suggested.

She turned back to the others and lowered her voice to a whisper.

'So, the lad gets thrown to six different times in human history, staying where we throw him from one turn of the tide to the next. During each Tide, according to the Rules, he may receive one thing –'

'It doesn't have to be a thing – that's right, isn't it?' interrupted Market. 'It can be people too – champions – powerful warriors.'

'That's right – or wisdom, even – anything to help him when it comes to the Seventh Tide. The Final Challenge. When he enters the Dry Heart.'

'He has to go to *the Island*?!'

'I told you it was a *final* challenge . . .'

Among all the isles of the G, only one was called 'The Island'. It was the one place that, when they were birds, they avoided flying over; as creatures of the sea, they never swam the waters round it, or hauled out on the black rocks of its shore. It wasn't an *evil* place – not evil the way the Kelpies were, for instance – but it wasn't a good place either.

It was just very, very . . . *other*.

'OK, OK. What happens there? Inside the Dry Heart, I mean.'

'No one can say,' said Hibernation.

'What's that supposed to mean? Are you trying to say . . . no one comes back?' quavered Interrupted.

'Oh yes. A few have come back. They just can't say, afterwards, what happened to them. It has that effect, I guess.'

'Great. So no help there,' said Market. 'But there must be some clue as to what the lad's supposed to be *doing*?'

'Oh yes, that's *crystal* clear –' and Gladrag read from the text: '*You must thread the mazes with no path, pass the rivers with no water, find the Centre and mend the Dry Heart . . .*'

'What?!' spluttered Interrupted, but Market butted in.

'So it's not just killing Kelpies?' he asked.

'No.' Hibernation shook her head. 'The Kelpies are in there too, somehow, and they try to kill you, so killing them first is a good idea. But the *Challenge* is to mend the Heart.'

All three G looked across to where the pathetic figure of Eo was standing in his little circle of empty sand.

'We *have* to get him some help,' murmured Interrupted.

'No argument,' said Market. 'When it's our turns to throw, we need to be aiming for times when we know he can find heroic warriors or clever tricksters or amazing weapons to help him do whatever it is he's supposed to be doing in the maze and river place, while not being killed by Kelpies.'

'And while we're aiming for all that, *she's* presumably aiming for times *without* heroes or handy-dandy piles of anti-Kelpie weaponry lying about,' said Interrupted drily.

Gladrag gave him a rueful smile.

'Stop looking for a way out – there *is* no way out!' the Queen sneered. She had been pacing up and down on her long white feet, growing more and more impatient with all the whispering and delay.

'We were explaining the Rules of the Challenge, for the benefit of our colleague here,' said Gladrag, ignoring Interrupted's bleat of 'My *benefit? You had to look it up in a book!*' 'He is not entirely familiar with –'

'*My* people know *all* the Rules. There is no such thing as an *ignorant* Kelpie. I would trample on him – I would gouge out his eyes with my hooves – I would drip acid into his ears and pull out his intestines with my teeth!' She thrust her face towards the Companions, showing off her teeth – all of them.

'Well, I'm sure he'd resolve to do better after that!' said Interrupted Cadence with only a hint of a quaver in his voice.

Gladrag smiled thinly to herself for an instant and then spoke.

'So that we're *all* clear, this is the summary of the Challenge,' and she raised her voice so everyone (including Eo) could hear, and read: '*The Challenger will be sent to six times, and spend in each time the length of a tide. With each Tide he will be given a gift – a weapon or wisdom or the services of a champion – and these gifts must be given freely and without duress. And these gifts he may take with him for the Seventh Tide, to the Dry Heart, to aid him in the Final Challenge – to thread the mazes with no path; to cross the rivers with no water; to find the Centre and mend the Dry Heart . . .*'

Gladrag looked up. Every eye was fixed on *her*, so no one else noticed Professor Hurple making an extremely brief appearance. He stuck his head out of Eo's bag, gasped the equivalent of '*Crikey!*' in Ferret and disappeared back inside again.

Which is why Hibernation Gladrag was moved to say to Eo, 'And don't forget to take your bag, child.'

'What? Why? What for?' The Kelpie was instantly suspicious, and Market and Interrupted both stared at their Head in surprise.

'To carry whatever objects he may be given,' Gladrag answered mildly. 'It's only sensible.'

The Kelpie's eyes darted from face to face suspiciously. Then she lunged suddenly, grabbed the bag and shook it violently upside down. A half-eaten apple, a bundle of scruffy papers, Eo's essay notebook, some odd bits of string, some junk and one ferret fell out. But Hurple didn't just *fall* out – he crashed, hard, on to the sand. An enormous sneeze from Gladrag at just the same moment covered the sound of the Professor's breath being knocked out of his lungs. He lay there limply, playing possum. At least that's what Eo hoped was happening. But what if Hurple was hurt? Unconscious? What if he was –

'As I said, a bag in which to carry the gifts of the Tides,' said Gladrag to the Queen. Then, turning to Eo, she continued, 'Collect your things. Take your bag. And put your collar on, child.' Her voice managed to cut through the panic in his mind. 'You heard me sneezing just then. It's getting chilly.' She returned her attention to the Kelpie. 'We're a delicate people. Why, just last season . . .'

Eo had just enough presence of mind to do as he was told. He hurriedly stuffed everything back into his bag and scooped up Hurple, while Gladrag was distracting the Kelpie with some truly revolting details of her last cold. He draped the Professor carefully round his neck, reassured by the warmth, worried by the lifeless way he hung there.

'But you don't want to hear about that,' Gladrag interrupted herself abruptly.

The Queen jerked round wildly, unsure of what had

happened. But there was nothing in the feeble little figure of Eo that suggested treachery. The Kelpie felt she was being tricked, but couldn't quite see how. Just exactly what kind of threat was a child wearing a fur collar likely to pose?

She glared at the crowd but found no clues there. Nothing but a sea of blank G expressions faced her – some deliberate, some the result of not having a clue and some stemming from being in a state of near-catatonic shock. The Queen's eyes narrowed to slits, but she still couldn't see through to whatever their deception was.

Finally she gave up.

'I am tired of your squirming,' she said in a voice thick with menace. 'Let the Challenge begin.'

'No,' said Hibernation Gladrag. 'Not *quite* yet.' The Head of the G turned her back on the Kelpie. She walked calmly to the nearest cluster of her people and spoke to them quietly – so quietly no one else could hear. From there, the word went out through the crowd, a wave of whispers, until everyone knew what they had to do. Throughout the crowd, hair of every colour and texture coiled itself serviceably out of the way and, grim-faced, the G began to leave.

The danger was old and unremitting. The souls of the G were so full of life that demons of every variety never gave up hope of breaking through to such a luscious world. So the G were prepared. If the first line of defence was breached, there was a second plan, a contingency plan – a worst-case plan.

Change! Scatter! Hide!

Spreading out across the isles, the G would find forms

that were camouflaged, changing into the unnoticeable shapes of life that are easy to miss. One more sprat in a shoal, or limpet on a rock. A midge among millions, or a mouse snug among the heather roots. But what about the children of the G, who hadn't yet grown into their shape-shifting abilities? On the backs of dolphins and whales, they would be taken and laid away in secret caves, in a self-induced cold sleep. They would lower their heart rates and slow their breathing until they were as near to rock as a living thing can become. In this state they would wait, and hope for a miracle.

The G practised these plans regularly and with some care, to be ready for the worst-case scenario no one ever believed they would see. With a word, Gladrag had set the plan in motion. This is not a drill. This is not a drill.

In a shorter time than seemed possible, the crowd of G had gone. The beach and the cropped grass of the dunes were empty. Only when Eo and the three were the last remaining, did Gladrag turn her attention back to the Queen of the Kelpies.

'Let the Challenge begin *now*,' she said sweetly.

The Queen looked as if she were about to explode but there was nothing she could do. There was nothing laid down in the ancient Rules to control the movement of bystanders. Her own people were contained, but the slippery G . . . The Head's expression was bland and blank. For a long moment they stared at each other, but it was the Kelpie who broke the contact first.

With a snort, the Queen turned on her heel and stalked back across the sand. When she was right underneath the looming slanted side of the vortex she paused and then, without warning, thrust her hand into the maelstrom. It must have been the G's imagination that made them think the gigantic phenomenon flinched away from her touch. And the scream they heard could perhaps be explained by some law of physics that governs the interruption of water moving at impossible speed and under unbearable pressure. But it seemed much more as if the vortex screamed like a creature whose flesh had been torn. The figures within shrieked violently as well.

The sounds made the Queen smile.

With a casual twist of her hand, the stuff she was holding began to spin and form itself into a funnel which she balanced on her palm – a perfect tiny copy had been spawned, identical to the huge vortex whirling above it. For a moment the Queen played about with it, leaning it this way and that and watching it right itself like a gyroscope, admiring her new toy.

'We call it a Traveller,' she said, still dallying with it.

Then, as if by accident, she let it fall.

As soon as it hit the ground the Traveller began to grow, until it was as tall as the Queen herself. She nodded, satisfied, and flicked her fingers at it. As the Traveller started to move, the three adult G found themselves frozen to the spot, unable to escape in any way. But the thing wasn't interested in them. It was Eo it wanted. Closer it came, and closer, until the very edge of the Traveller touched him. Eo screamed in terror and the onlookers groaned, but even then it didn't take him all at once. Instead he began to be drawn out, thinner and longer, as if he were paint dissolving in water that caught and swirled and dragged him in, dragged him round.

Even his cries for help became thinner, like a distant wailing, and then he was gone.

In the silence that followed they could hear the Queen chuckling to herself. She snapped her fingers and the Traveller returned to her, shrinking as it came, until it was as small as when she first formed it. She scooped it up from the sand and showed it to the remaining G. They clustered around, needing to look but sick at the thought of what they might see . . .

A tiny Eo was trapped inside, whirled round and round, his face distorted with fear, his hands clawing at the invisible barrier, his body stretched impossibly backwards around the contour of the minute maelstrom. With a sudden jerk, the Kelpie Queen tipped the Traveller into Gladrag's hands.

'Your throw,' she said.

Gladrag yelped and almost dropped it.

'Careful!' warned Market Jones.

Hibernation nodded, holding the thing gingerly now in her two hands, as if it might break. She couldn't stop staring at it and the tiny terrified face that kept swirling past.

'*Your throw!*' The Queen's voice grated. '*It's TIME!*'

Market Jones leaned close to the Head of the G and whispered to her from behind his hand. Gladrag closed her eyes for a moment and then nodded. Interrupted Cadence was practically jigging up and down on the spot with anxiety.

'I don't understand,' he half-whispered, half-wailed. 'How can we know when – *where* to throw it?!'

'*NOW!*' shrieked the Queen. '*The Tide is turning – can't you tell?! NOW!*'

39

'Best guess,' Gladrag muttered – and threw.

The tiny vortex glinted in the morning sun as it arced from her hand and then fell towards the sand . . .

. . . and disappeared.

For a moment no one moved. Then the distant, indifferent cry of a gull broke the silence. The G stirred and looked at one another.

'Is that it?' croaked Interrupted. 'Is there nothing more we can do? Do we just *wait?*'

Gladrag had already started to nod when the Kelpie Queen laughed scornfully. 'Why wait when watching's half the fun?' she shrilled. She reached into the main vortex, making it scream again as she dragged away a part. She smashed the piece flat between her long hands, then spun it out like pizza dough till it was about the size of an Extra Large.

'A window on the worlds,' she purred unpleasantly, and flipped the disc on to the beach, where it lay, shiny and vibrating slightly.

The G looked from the Queen to the disc and back again.

'Er,' said Hibernation. 'You're staying? I mean, aren't you going back in, er, there?' She nodded at the Kelpie vortex.

'You'd like that, wouldn't you?' the Queen sneered. 'You'd like me to just leave you on your own, hatching up some cheat. Well, I don't choose to do so. I think I'd rather just stay. Settle in a little, don't you think – since it all, in a very few tides, will be mine . . .'

She turned her back on them and studied the thing on the sand intently. The G took a step closer, trying to see over her shoulder, but she turned on them like an animal guarding a kill. 'Mine!' she snarled. 'Mine!'

They reared back, shocked by the look on her face.

Then Market Jones reached for the encyclopedia. 'What was it I read?' he murmured, as if to himself. 'It was under Unfair Advantage . . . Rules of Forfeit . . .'

The Queen frowned, unable to remember any such section, but unwilling to call his bluff. For a long moment she hesitated, then, with a poor grace and no apparent care, she reached one more time into the body of the maelstrom and repeated the process. She flung the new disc up the beach, well away from hers, and turned her back on them again.

The G rushed over, peered into the disc, and gasped.

Inside the Traveller . . .

It was terrifying – a whirling boneless blackness. Eo couldn't feel Hurple round his neck. He couldn't breathe. He should be drowning in the freezing dark but eternity passed and he was still alive, still aware . . .

It was only when the Traveller finally spat him out that unconsciousness, kindly, came.

4 *The First Tide*

'*God forgive you – do you never pay attention?! A* beast *could write better than that!*'

'*Gently, Brother. Maybe God meant him to be thick of head as well as thick of arm. He can row my boat for me even if he can't get his wits round Holy Writ!*'

Adom felt his face flare red all over again.

I'll be hearing those words on my deathbed, he thought to himself. *I'll be old and grey and every morning I'll wake up to the Holy Father jeering at me in my head.*

He didn't notice the way anger was making him pull too hard, skewing the curragh off course.

'ADOM!'

'Pay attention, boy! Follow the boat in front, can't you?'

'He practically had us on the rocks there –'

The brothers were all of a twitter, but the Holy Father hadn't even looked up. If he were any other old man, Adom would have sworn he'd nodded off in the warm sun, but Columba was not like any other old man. He was *Columba* – the Holy Father, the stuff that saints are made of. Why should he care about Adom?

And yet he'd brought Adom back from the edge of death, all those years ago. How could that not *mean* something?

Adom was the youngest of a large family, a bit of a late surprise to his parents, but there had always been comings and goings between the farms of his older brothers and sisters, so he was never lonely. It was a life he knew well. He could so easily have just stayed a part of it all – if it hadn't been for Columba.

He'd heard the story a hundred times, of how ill he'd been, and how his family had given up hope.

'Then we heard a holy man was come to the village to preach and heal, and we carried you there, as one last chance.

'We laid you down on the ground, and the good man kneeled down beside you and prayed silently for a while. Then he made the sign of the cross on your forehead and was about to rise and move on – when you grabbed him! You grabbed hold of his hand with your two little ones and you held on to him like a dog with one bone. You didn't *say* anything. You just held tight and *stared*.

'We didn't know what to do – we couldn't loosen that grip for fear of hurting you! But the Holy Father only smiled, and said, "Let go of me now, little man. If it's God's will for you, when you are well once more and grown, I will take your hand again. Eh? How would that be? Sleep now, my son."

'You let go of him then, peaceful as could be. And

when he marked your forehead with the sign of the cross a second time, you were already asleep.'

'And I got better?' Adom would prompt.

'You did! Before the week was out, the fever had left you, and it wasn't long after that you were up and about as if you'd never been so ill at all. Of course, the Holy Father left long before then, and with the world so big we may not ever have the blessing of his presence here again. But yours is a different story. He set you apart, that day.'

It was a good story.

But when, at age fifteen, he left behind everything he'd ever known and journeyed to the great man's monastery on Iona, it was as if the story had never happened. There was no special welcome, not even any kind of *acknowledgement*. The Columba who had saved him – *he* might have remembered Adom. But not this gaunt, silent old man.

He barely saw the Holy Father that first summer, so caught up was Columba in his vigils and fasting and wrestling matches of prayer with God. Adom *did* see a lot of Brother Drostlin, though, the monk in charge of the boys and novices. And Adom was even *less* special to him.

'Lazy. And stupid.' That was his verdict on the new recruit. And the reason was simple: weedy youngsters half Adom's age were learning in days and weeks what months of Brother Drostlin's beatings failed to teach *him*.

It had never occurred to Adom what the hardest part of his new life was going to be, because he had never had to deal with the written word before. You didn't need to read to plough your scrap of land. You didn't need to know how to write to catch enough fish to feed your family. Books and book learning were the province of the Church, part of its magic. But for Adom, it was a magic for which, it seemed, he had no aptitude. He could not make the letters speak to him. His hand was perfectly capable of everything else he'd ever put it to – but it *could not* control a quill.

But I'm not lazy! Adom yelled inside his head. *I'm not stupid! Why can't I do this? I don't understand!*

Some days it felt as if the world had become very small, crushingly small, no more than the square of table before him and the tormenting symbols that inhabited it. It may be that the summer felt that way for the Holy Father as well. Whatever the reason, one fine autumn morning, Columba burst into the scriptorium, where Brother Drostlin was, as usual, berating Adom for his laziness and inattention.

'God forgive you –' he was saying – 'do you never pay attention?! A *beast* could write better than that!'

And Columba's voice, sounding positively jovial for the first time in months, broke in with, 'Gently, Brother. Maybe God meant him to be thick of head as well as thick of arm. He can row my boat for me even if he can't get his wits round Holy Writ!'

Not fair! Not true! Adom cried out silently. The injustice of it was so enormous he was numb to everything else – the escape from the hated books, the excited bustle of preparations, the last-minute inspection of the curraghs and oars, all passed in a blur.

And now he was on the water, on the way. Columba's journeys to preach and heal were the stuff of legend, and here he was, a part of it all.

A part. Set apart. Who believed *that* any more? He knew he was nothing. He was just a pair of strong arms . . .

It was late in the day when the curragh finally turned towards shore. They pulled into an inlet, where a river flowed into the sea and there was a shingle beach to drag the boat out on. And, further back in the hills, the welcoming smoke of a settlement could be seen, hanging above the trees.

'Where are we?' Adom asked one of the brothers.

'Don't you know, boy?' he said. 'That's the hall of the Bard up there, just beyond the village. Bard Devin. Surely you've heard of him?'

Adom shook his head.

'Don't know much, do you? He came out from Ireland at the same time as Columba. They were friends in the old country, you know. They still are, only they don't meet so much these days, of course. Oh, we'll get a warm welcome in Devin's hall, don't you worry – and likely a tale or two as well! There he is now!'

The figure approaching them from among the trees could not have been less like Adom's idea of a bard. Devin was not an impressive sight. He was short and wiry and ordinary-looking, more like an underfed farmer than a poet and speaker of truths.

The brothers were nervous about him, though.

'How did he know we were coming?' they whispered among themselves.

'They say he has second sight.'

'*I* heard the animals speak to him,' another shrilled. 'Birds, especially – they tell him what they see.'

He's a sorcerer?! thought Adom.

It was hard to believe, especially when you saw him next to Columba, with his great height and his imposing beak of a nose and his charismatic, hooded eyes.

Adom blinked. Had he just seen the little man *slap the Holy Father on the back*?!

There was no time to wonder, though. Brother Drostlin found plenty of things for Adom to do, getting the curragh hauled up above the tide line and their gear to the Bard's hall, and then helping to see that everyone was fed and cleaning up afterwards. It had been a long, hard day and Adom was dropping in his tracks by the end of it. All he wanted in the whole wide world was to lie down and go to sleep . . .

. . . until Devin stood up.

The moment the Bard opened his mouth all Adom's tiredness was forgotten. Along with the others, he was immediately spellbound, frightened and inspired and soothed by turns, and laughing till he got side-ache at the ribald bits. The Bard could make his listeners feel anything he wished. Adom saw to his astonishment that even *Columba* went where the stories took him!

When the tale-telling was over, Adom's head was whirling. And then, as the company lay down to sleep, one more astounding thing happened. Adom and the brothers clustered close to the fire but Columba set himself further off, away from the comforting warmth, with his head on his pillow of stone and only the thinnest of cloaks over him. When Devin saw this, he tutted audibly, marched over and, without a by-your-leave, tucked a warm woollen blanket around the saint.

And if that wasn't amazing enough, Columba let him!

Next morning, Brother Drostlin woke up cross. He didn't like Columba suddenly going off on 'adventures' again, and he didn't like being forced to rub his sanctified shoulders with peasants, and he didn't like *change*. These were not feelings he was going to share with the Holy Father, of course, but that was no reason he shouldn't pass on his discomfort to someone else . . .

Which was why Adom found himself trudging back down to the shore. He'd been in trouble from practically first light. By mid-morning he'd acquired a cuffed ear and a stinking bucket of ox tallow, with orders to reseal he seams of the curraghs 'for the safety of the Holy Father'. Adom had no desire to be responsible for the drowning of a future saint, or of himself for that matter, but the picture of Brother Drostlin going down for the third time had a certain appeal.

Adom sighed pitiably (which is hard to do when you're trying your best not to actually breathe), turned, tripped on a stone and almost glopped tallow all down his front.

Idiot! he chided himself, since Brother Drostlin wasn't there to do it for him.

He made the rest of the journey with due care and attention, not stopping till he reached the edge of the trees. Here he paused for a moment and looked out over the bay. The curraghs were still safely there, long upside-down humps on the pebbles. The tide was well out -- probably on the turn – revealing an expanse of mud and seaweed-encrusted rocks, with the river snaking through in its own little gully. The sky was clear and there was a brisk wind from the water.

That'll help with the stink, thought Adom approvingly, and he was just about to start off again when he saw something else. Partway between the curraghs and the river there was a wet, dark shape. It didn't look right for a rock or a tree stump. *A seal?* wondered Adom. *A beached baby whale? Meat?!*

He was already running forward, the bucket forgotten and a hefty stone in one hand. The pebbles crunching under his sandals were too loud! And then he was slipping and splashing across the muddy stretch, the rock raised, ready. In his mind he'd already killed the beast, whatever it was, he was the hero of the day, there'd be another feast, and more stories, and . . .

Oh no, it's heard me! It's moving! It'll get away!

He slithered to a stop. There would be no feast tonight. His prize groaned and lifted its head – it was a waterlogged boy.

The stone dropped from Adom's fingers and he ran forward.

'Heaven save us – are you all right? I thought you were a seal – were you swept off a boat? Can you stand? Can you walk?'

The stranger seemed to be about his age, or maybe a little younger. He was alive and his big eyes were just opening, but at first he didn't seem to be aware of his surroundings. Then, all at once, he dragged in a sudden desperate breath and grabbed hold of Adom's habit with both hands. A spasm shook his body.

'Where is this?' he croaked. 'Who are you?'

'Easy, easy.' Adom gently detached himself from the stranger's grip. 'You must have nearly drowned.'

The boy looked at him with his over-large blue-grey eyes.

'I should have,' he said wonderingly. 'I really should have. I guess it's not in the Rules for me to drown in the . . . what did she call it? The Traveller.' He gave Adom a sudden blindingly cheerful grin and staggered to his feet. 'My name's Eo. What's yours?'

'Um, Adom,' said Adom. 'Here, you've got something tangled round your neck . . .'

It looked pretty much like a hank of seaweed, but when Adom reached out a hand to unwind it, it sneezed. Adom leapt back and yelped, before realizing it was just some sort of wet weasel.

It sneezed again, and then shook itself, splashing salt water into Adom's face.

'*Hey!*' he spluttered.

'Professor!' cried the boy. 'You're all right!'

The animal chittered rudely back and then tried to get inside the bag the boy had with him, until he opened it, and it flowed inside.

'Sorry,' said the boy. 'He's, um . . . a bit shy.' The bag bulged crossly. 'Can you tell us, please, where are we?'

Adom nodded. 'Let's get you off the mud first, though,' he said.

He helped the boy up, and they stumbled to the rocky beach and on into the trees, before sitting down on a fallen log.

'Please,' the boy asked again. 'Where is this? *When* is this?'

Adom gave him an uncertain look. 'It's about mid-morning,' he said, glancing at the sun. 'And we're quite near the dwelling of Devin, Bard of the Shores. I'll take you there when you're able – I know he'll shelter you.'

There was a blankness on the boy's face that made Adom pause.

'Devin the Bard – you'll have heard of him?'

He shook his head.

Not from round here, then, thought Adom to himself, handily forgetting that he hadn't known of Devin before yesterday himself.

'Are you a bard too?' the boy asked tentatively.

'*Me?!* No, of course not. I'm Adom. I'm a novice – or I will be, anyway. I'm from the monastery on Iona.' *He's bound to have heard of that!* he thought. 'I'm here with Columba.' He sounded a bit smug, even to himself.

The boy looked as if he were still puzzled, but before he could speak the weasel thing exploded out of the bag, shouting, 'Columba?! Did you say *Columba*?! *There's* a bit of good news! So, let's see, that means we're sometime in the sixth century, not on Iona itself, no, the beach isn't right for there – too shingly – but we can't be far from it.'

'Saints and Angels – a talking beast!' Adom staggered back, caught his heel on a root and sprawled on to his rear end in the leaf litter. Frantically he made a sign against the evil eye, then one against demonic possession, and then a sign of the cross, just to be on the safe side.

The animal turned his fierce little eyes on Adom and tutted. 'Don't be foolish, boy. There is nothing demonic about me. It's a little-known but not impossible fact that Joseph the Holy Carpenter himself kept ferrets, and if so, Jesus almost certainly might have played with them when he was a boy. There is a story I could tell you of how James, one of the lesser disciples, blessed all ferrets with the possibility of speech, but I think this is neither the time nor the place.'

There was a stunned silence. Adom lay there, with his

mouth hanging open, barely breathing. The animal turned his attention to his left shoulder and began to give it a much-needed grooming. And the strange boy looked from one to the other, obviously wondering what the next step of *this* was going to be.

'Who *are* you?' whispered Adom at last.

'Oh. Well, like I said, I'm Eo, and this is Professor Hurple. I'm a G – you know, one of the shape-shifting people – and he's a, um, ferret. As you can see.' The boy gave an uncertain grin. 'And we're looking for some help against the Kelpies – demons who are trying to take us over. You mentioned somebody called Columba. Who's he?'

'Who's *Columba*!?!' The ferret and Adom both turned on him in amazement.

'He's only the greatest holy man in the whole world – he's only practically a *saint*!' spluttered Adom.

'Yes,' cried the Professor, 'but more to the point, he's also *the most famous Kelpie-killer of all time*! Probably. One of them, anyway. Imagine Gladrag managing to land us on *his* doorstep! If only we could convince him to come with us, to be our champion in the Dry Heart, why, we might even have a fighting *chance*!'

Eo gave Hurple a troubled look. It was so abnormal to have to be really serious about something, so hard to stay guilty and afraid now the Kelpie Queen wasn't hanging over him. It was a G's nature to *enjoy* adventure!

Adom was back on his feet by now, though he was keeping a careful distance. There was a *lot* he didn't understand about all this, but one thing was more important than the rest.

'Are you *sure* you're not demons?' he said.

Eo stared. 'I *told* you – I'm a *G*! The only reason we're here is *because* of demons!'

Adom shook his head. 'You'll have to tell me the whole story,' he said. 'I don't understand at all so far. Tell me *everything*.'

Eo hesitated.

Then, '*Well?!*' the ferret snapped suddenly, making both boys jump. 'Get *on* with it! You –' he turned on Adom – 'sit down properly, and pay attention. And *you* –' he turned on Eo – 'get telling! We haven't got all day. The tide won't wait, no matter *what* you think!'

Eo was insulted. 'When did I *ever* say I thought that tides *waited* . . .?'

'GET ON!'

And, for a wonder, Eo did as he was told.

Adom was a riveted audience, though there was a good deal of what he was being told that still made absolutely no sense to him. When the boy finished, the ferret named Hurple gave him a small nod of approval.

'Succinctly done,' he said, causing Eo to blush with embarrassed pleasure.

But Adom was still troubled.

'It's a wonderful story,' he said. 'Truly – but . . . it isn't really *proof* that you're not demons.'

Eo stared. 'Do I *look* like a demon to you?' he asked, disgruntled.

'Well, it wouldn't be very smart of you to look like one if you were, would it? I mean, I wouldn't be likely to take your word for it if you had horns and lots of jagged teeth and stank of brimstone.'

'You'll have to wait till he's older if it's teeth and stink you're after,' grunted Hurple sourly.

Eo sighed. 'You're not helping!' He turned back to Adom. 'Look, trust me –'

'Never trust anyone who starts a sentence with "trust me",' muttered Hurple under his breath. 'Sorry, sorry . . . Listen to what the boy's saying to you, Adom. He's not nearly as dim as he looks.'

A glance passed between the two boys, the comradeship of the under-appreciated and unfairly maligned. But Adom was still uneasy.

'If only there were some sort of test . . .' he murmured, biting his lip anxiously.

Then he noticed something that had in fact been niggling for his attention for some time. It was music – pipes, and people singing – and it was coming from the settlement further up the hill.

'That's it!' he exclaimed, jumping up. 'The people are gathering for the Holy Father to bless them and heal their sick. And since everyone *knows* a demon cannot bear a blessing, that's what we're going to do.'

'What?'

'Come on!'

As they came to the edge of the clearing, however, Adom paused. He looked out at the settlement, less sure now.

If they *were* demons, should he be leading them straight into a group of unsuspecting folk?

Hurple seemed to guess his thoughts.

'We're hardly going to do anything hellish in full view, at midday, surrounded by a gaggle of holy men, now are we?' he said reasonably. 'To be properly eldritch we'd

54

have to wait till after sundown and, oh, I don't know, pick you off one at a time, probably.' All the time he was speaking, the smells from the cooking fires were drifting tantalizingly past his nose. That rabbit in the warren seemed a long time ago now . . .

'Come on – I'm starving!' said Eo. 'Is there time to eat before we get desecrated?'

'*Blessed!*' said Hurple and Adom in chorus.

Eo shrugged. 'Whatever,' he said. 'Is there?'

And suddenly Adom was hungry too.

'Come on, then,' he said with a shrug, and led the way.

The people were still gathering. The ones bringing sick and injured with them came last of all, having to travel slowly and with care. The Bard's people and the monks moved about among the crowd, greeting and making welcoming gestures towards the cooking fires. A piper was playing a tune that Adom knew from home, at least he was until Brother Drostlin fussed over and made him stop.

Too vulgar for such a holy occasion, Adom mimicked the monk sourly in his mind.

Eo's sky-coloured eyes were wide with curiosity. He was taking in the scene with great concentration and enthusiasm.

'Maybe we could get your lot to *convert* the Kelpies,' he suggested suddenly.

'Don't be daft. You don't convert demons – you kill them!' Adom scoffed. Then he stopped, uncomfortable at the thought that it might be a demon he was speaking to. The idea of Eo and the talking ferret having to be killed was becoming more and more . . . unthinkable.

Suddenly he straightened up. 'There he is!' he said in a low voice. 'Columba!'

Eo and Hurple looked about expectantly.

'Where? Which one is he?'

'*There!*' Adom pointed, amazed that they had to be told. The Holy Father was a head taller at least than the men around him, but even without his height he stood out in any crowd. Adom wondered why they couldn't see it. 'Over there!'

There was a short, appalled silence. Then, 'But . . .' said Eo, 'he's *old!*'

'There's irony for you,' murmured Hurple. 'She was *so close*, our Gladrag, not more than, what, ten years too late.'

'What are you talking about? What's a Gladrag?' said Adom.

'Hibernation Gladrag is the Head of the G – that's Eo's people, remember? She will have had first turn to throw the Traveller, and she evidently tried to fling us to the time of the great Columba, who, *as we all know* –' and he looked down his snout meaningfully at Eo – 'is one of history's most renowned Kelpie-killers. Only problem is, she flung us just a bit too far. We've missed Columba the Warrior of God and instead we just have Columba the Old Man.'

Adom was shocked right down to his sandals. Were they really turning their noses up at a saint?! Did that mean they *were* demons, after all?

'What are we supposed to do *now*?!' said Eo. 'If the old man can't help . . .'

'Well, he can't *fight*, that's obvious, but maybe he can give us some advice . . .'

'Look, I don't know what your problem is here, but sit *down* and I'll bring you something to eat. Assuming you can eat *food*, and not just *souls*.' Adom shoved Eo down on to a rock at the edge of the crowds and stomped crossly away.

'*Watch out!*' said Hurple in a much quieter voice. '*I think we're drawing attention . . .*'

'So?' said Eo.

'*Don't be stupid!*' Hurple hissed. He was getting really agitated now. 'I can't think of *any* period in human history where a talking ferret isn't going to be in big trouble. And I for one don't fancy spending every new Tide being burned as a messenger from hell or stoned as an abomination or dissected as a freak of nature or bored to death on a string of chat shows – so start treating me like a normal ferret!'

Eo blinked. 'And that involves . . . what, exactly?' he said tentatively.

Hurple tutted impatiently. 'Just pick me up and carry me around. I'll do the rest. Look out!'

'A fine animal.'

Eo managed to grab Professor Hurple, swivel and fall off his log in one uneasy motion. From the ground, he looked up into the face of the man they called the Bard. His eyes were laughing, though he was trying hard to keep the rest of his expression polite.

'I'm sorry to have startled you,' he said. At exactly the same moment Eo heard a tiny strangled whisper from under his chin – 'Not so tight!' – and he adjusted his grip on the Professor, while struggling upright again.

'Sorry!' he said. 'Um, I mean, thank you. Yes. He's

very . . . pretty.' At which point Hurple bit him on the thumb. 'OWWW!'

The Bard tipped back his head and laughed out loud.

'I think "handsome" is the word you wanted!' he said. 'This is clearly no mere jill but a noble dog, one of the wisest of his kind.' He started to move on, then stopped and looked at Eo more closely.

'I've not seen you before – have you travelled far?'

Eo nodded.

'Has anyone offered you food?'

Eo nodded again. 'Yes . . . Adom. He's –'

At which point Adom came bustling back. 'You can eat later,' he said. 'The Holy Father is about to begin. Excuse us, Bard –' turning to the man – 'they have come to be blessed, and it's time now . . .'

'Off you go!' Devin said cheerfully. But a moment later he thought, *They? That's an odd word to use . . .*

Adom was already showing Eo where to stand in the line, then stepped back.

'I'll be watching,' he said. 'God speed.'

Eo peered nervously down the queue as Columba began his progress. The people seemed so grateful for the old man's attention, so *awed*! It didn't make sense to him – maybe it was a cultural thing? – but really, he couldn't see what all the fuss was about . . .

. . . until Columba was standing before him, putting out his hand and looking him in the eyes. Suddenly Eo understood it all. The Holy Father was no less old than he'd thought, no less decrepit-looking, but the *greatness* was still there. It had nothing to do with vigour of muscle or agility of mind, or even depth of experience – and

58

it had everything to do with native power. It flared out of his grey eyes and welled from his touch in ways that Eo was unable to find words for.

'Bless you, boy,' was all Columba said, but Eo couldn't at that moment have asked for more. In fact, he almost forgot Hurple, sitting in his hands and also needing to be given the all-clear as far as being demonic went.

Just at the last moment he remembered, and squawked, 'Holy Father, will you bless this beast?'

Columba turned back, smiled at the adoring boy with his animal, alert and expectant in his hands. He sketched a cross with his thumb on the animal's furry forehead and moved on.

And nothing happened – neither Eo nor the ferret began to scream or dissolve in smoke or show in any other way the kind of major discomfort hellish things usually manifest when touched by holiness.

Adom stirred. He hadn't realized he'd been holding his breath. *Well, that's a relief,* he thought. *I'm glad they're not demons, not even the beast.* And it was true. But that didn't stop the twisted feeling in his gut.

'The crowds can always light him up.'

Adom jumped. It would seem he wasn't the only one watching. Devin the Bard hadn't gone far. Any interesting gesture or turn of phrase or snippet of conversation was grist for his mill. He had seen how Adom's face changed from tension to relief, but hadn't lost the troubled look round his mouth and eyes.

'I've always found jealousy to be a crippler in my line of work,' he said conversationally. 'I imagine it must be the same in yours.'

Adom gave an outraged gasp. 'I'm not –' he began, but the Bard had already moved on.

Adom scowled. Was that what it was, this worm inside? Jealousy? Was he jealous that Columba had smiled at Eo and not at him? That Eo and the talking animal had been given the full measure of the great man's charm and, and, *greatness*, and he, Adom, who lived and worked with him every day (well, in the same general vicinity, anyway) – *he* got *nothing*?

It was a lot to swallow. Adom gulped hard, and went to collect his new friends.

No one seemed ready to speak at first. They got some food and returned to the cluster of rocks to eat, separate from the crowds but still nearby.

Then, when their hunger was dealt with, the three exchanged looks.

'My!' murmured Hurple, and flopped down on his tummy in a patch of sun.

'Well!' said Eo. 'I mean . . . well!'

'So, um, congratulations!' said Adom.

'What?'

'I'm glad you're not demons,' Adom explained.

'Oh, right. Well, we did *say*.'

'I know. Sorry.'

'Never mind. And sorry from us too, for not understanding about, you know, *him*,' said Eo.

Adom sighed. 'That's all right,' he said. 'What happens now?'

'Now?' Hurple scratched vigorously. 'Well, I can't say I know *exactly* how the "Gift of the Tide" thing is supposed to work, but it seems pretty obvious that we've arrived in the perfect place at the perfect time to acquire the perfect champion . . . the perfect . . .' He turned suddenly on Eo. 'He was standing right there in front of you – why didn't you *ask* him?!'

'Are we allowed to ask? Then why didn't *you* ask him?' Eo protested.

'Because *I'm* not supposed to be able to *talk*! I'm the dumb animal, right?!'

Eo muttered something rude under his breath.

'Oh, well,' said Hurple grudgingly. 'I guess it wasn't exactly the moment, was it? We'll need to meet with him more privately. Set that up for us, will you, Adom? Tell him it's important.'

'*ME?!*' squeaked Adom. 'You expect *me* to walk up to the Holy Father and say, "You have to meet with this boy and his beast 'cause I'm telling you it's important"? Just like that!'

'Yes. Is there a problem?' asked the ferret innocently. '*Is there a problem?!*'

'*ADOM!*'

It was probably the last voice on earth Adom wanted to hear just then. It was Brother Drostlin's.

'I don't believe *for a moment* that you did a proper job on that caulking, and *already* you're back up here stuffing your face and playing about with . . . playing about –' He seemed at a loss for words to describe anything as lowly as Eo. 'The Holy Father wants to leave at the turn of the tide. He wants be a good few leagues further north by moon-rise.'

'But he *can't!*' blurted Eo, just as Adom exclaimed, 'But *why?*'

Brother Drostlin began to quiver ominously. 'You dare – you *dare* to question the wishes of the Holy Father? You *dare!?!*'

His outraged voice went swooping up to such an unbelievably high note on the last words that it made Eo giggle. He didn't mean to. It was just nerves, of course.

Brother Drostlin didn't think it was very polite, however, so he belted him.

One blow more or less was nothing much to Adom, but it was a new experience for Eo and not one he particularly enjoyed. Adom hustled his new friend away before anything worse could happen, down through the trees to the shore and the forgotten, but still stinky, tallow bucket.

'Don't worry. We'll speak to the Holy Father when he comes to the boats,' Adom reassured them as they went, but Eo wasn't listening.

'He hit me! He *hit* me!' he kept squeaking, until Adom turned on him.

'Are you trying to tell me no one ever hit you before?!' he asked incredulously. 'How do you learn anything?'

'I bite him from time to time,' Hurple offered.

Adom shook his head. The G world sounded too good to be true. In the meantime . . .

'Here, you can help.' He cobbled together another brush out of sapling branches and handed it to Eo. 'The sooner this is done, the sooner we can be ready to grab just the right moment and ask Columba for help.'

Hurple took one sniff of the stuff and retreated to the edge of the trees, while the boys got on with the job. And the reason they both needed to completely wash themselves and their clothes in the sea afterwards had everything to do with their zeal for labour, and nothing at all to do with any silly tallow-flicking fights . . .

The afternoon was wearing on when the first of the brothers started to return to the shore. The mood they brought with them was cheerful. Two people had been healed on the spot and several others were expected to get better soon.

'*He* should be coming down as well any time now,' Adom whispered to Eo and the ferret. 'Now, you must speak to him as soon as he's here – *before* he wants to get into the boats – he hates to hang about.'

But it was easier said than done. At first Brother Drostlin had the Holy Father's ear and no one else dared approach. When the monk was finally finished, a crowd of latecomers rushed up to Columba, begging his blessing before he left. Then there was a homily – far too short to be a proper sermon, which was expected to go on for several hours, but still long enough to be eating up a lot more of the remaining time. The two boys tried to work their way up to the front of the listening congregation, but were caught by Brother Drostlin, who dragged them away by the ears.

'This isn't *working*!' hissed Hurple through his teeth, as they huddled disconsolately by the boats. 'How can we ask him if we can't *get* to him? The tide is practically on the turn, the Traveller is going to be back to drag us away any minute and we're still without a Gift to take with us.'

It was Adom who came up with a plan.

'If *you* can't come to *him*,' he said, 'then what we need is for the Holy Father to come to *you*.'

'How?'

'When the demon thing rises up out of the Otherworld to claim you, all you have to do is call out to Columba to save you – *and he will*. I know he will! How could he resist? It's not as if it's the first time he's dealt with Kelpies. Ask anyone, they'll tell you. And can you think of any *better* way of getting his attention? Not even Brother Drostlin could distract him if something like that was happening!'

'Well . . .' said Hurple.

'It might work,' said Eo thoughtfully. 'I know he'd be our champion if only he knew we needed one.'

'It's cutting it very fine, though,' said Hurple, rubbing an ear with his paw. 'And what if he refuses to help? What if he just stands there and says, "Not today. I'm not in the mood"?'

Eo stared down at him. 'You've met him. Can you seriously imagine him saying anything like that?'

Hurple looked embarrassed. 'No. No, I can't.'

'Then that's what we'll do,' said Eo firmly. 'It won't be long now.'

Which was when Adom realized, suddenly and with a great sinking of the heart, that it was about to be over. The G boy and the talking beast were going on to face unimaginable dangers and excitements and strange new places and times. And *he* was going to go back to rowing and Brother Drostlin and the horrors of the written word . . .

They'll be in good hands, he thought, though the words tasted sour. *For such important affairs they need the best.*

Hurple was becoming more and more agitated now, wreathing round Eo's neck like a hoop.

'It's coming! It's coming!' he squeaked.

Columba had his back to the boats, saying a final prayer. Adom and Eo edged closer, ready for the moment when he turned round, casting nervous glances over their shoulders, fearful of what would come out of the sea.

But Columba didn't turn round. He went on praying, and the crowd stayed kneeling before him, heads bent, unseeing. Only Adom and Eo and a frantic ferret had eyes for what was about to happen to the peace of the afternoon.

First the pressure came, so that the far fringes of the crowd shifted uneasily, while nearer the epicentre, penitents clutched the sides of their heads and moaned. Even the tall figure of the saint swayed a little. Then . . .

'What's that?' whispered Adom, squinting against the sun. 'Is that *it*?'

There was . . . something . . . a disturbance in the bay . . . It was growing, and beginning to move. It was heading towards them – it seemed full of purpose – he could see it more clearly now –

The Traveller. How could something so silent seem to scream? It was the height of a man and moving at a tall man's pace and aiming straight as an arrow. At the slight figure of Eo.

'RUN!' shrieked Adom, shoving him hard up the stony beach. 'Columba will save you!'

But Eo couldn't hear him. Everything seemed to be happening at once. The vortex speeded up and clipped Adom as it passed, flinging him aside like a bit of unwanted junk. He landed hard on his side, and a sickening pain in one arm tried to tell him he'd done himself serious damage. But there was no time to listen. He scrambled to his feet and set off after Eo, trying to scream at the praying man to turn around, to *save him* – but making no sound.

Eo was sprinting forward in panic, his hands stretched out towards the saint – he was almost there – but the stones underfoot were treacherous and he slipped, still moving forward as he fell.

Suddenly, there was a grinding wrench of perspective in Adom's head. He saw, with horrible clarity, through *Columba's* eyes as the man swung round to face the shore. An impossible unnatural maelstrom had appeared, spiralling towards him from the water, and it had spawned a creature, claw-handed, open-mouthed, that lunged forward, trying to catch hold of his robe, catch hold of him and drag him down into a whirling hell . . .

With a silent roar of holy defiance, Columba struck, sweeping aside what he thought was a demon. Then, raising his arms and his voice, he tried to pray, fighting against the deafening silence that threatened to choke him.

Eo landed some distance away on the hard pebbles and lay there, winded. Columba didn't see how the vortex swerved away from him, seeking only Eo, but Adom saw . . .

He threw himself forward, ignoring the screaming protest from his damaged arm, reaching for Eo to pull him back, to bring him to safety . . .

It was too late. His hands met Eo's as the G boy's body was dragged into the Traveller.

Adom could have let go – he should have let go – but he didn't. It had all gone wrong – it was all his fault –

What Columba saw was horribly impossible. First the demon and then the boy were stretched and thinned as the vortex pulled them inside. The last thing to be seen were the soles of Adom's worn sandals, sucked from the stones and into the wall of water. At the same instant, the vortex itself blinked out of sight, and there was nothing left.

'God help us,' whispered the saint in horror.

5 *The Throw of the Kelpie Queen*

Back on the G beach, Gladrag, Jones and Cadence were struggling. Using the viewing disc was like looking down a hole into another world, and at first the three kept lurching back and clutching each other every time they tried, feeling as if they might be about to fall in. The viewpoint appeared to be hovering a few metres above Eo's head, showing anything that came within a circle of a couple of metres centring around him. Everything was oddly foreshortened from that angle, of course, and they got to know the different characters that entered the circle mainly as clumps of hair with noses sticking out the front.

What they were able to *hear* also centred on Eo, though the audio range extended further, beyond the circle of what they could see. What was peculiar, however, was the way they could only hear something when Eo was paying heed to it. When his attention wandered, the speaker's words blurred into white noise. It was an interesting insight into the selective hearing of the young, but maddening for the G on the beach. The words, 'Why can't the boy *pay attention!?*' were heard on more than one occasion, with a range of adjectives added on.

They knew the exact instant the Queen realized Hurple wasn't just a collar – there was a furious hiss and the look she threw in their direction was pure venom. She didn't actually say, 'You'll pay for this!' but there was no doubt that was what she was thinking.

The G shivered, and returned to their vigil.

It was impossible not to get excited when Columba was mentioned, though, like Eo and the ferret, they were worried about how old he looked.

'He's got white hair!' whispered Gladrag. She sounded devastated. 'I threw too far!'

'Don't let *her* know,' muttered Market urgently, tipping a nod towards the Queen. 'Act like the thing landed *exactly* where we wanted it to.'

So, as the day wore on, the G did their best to appear confident and chipper. They were successful to some extent – the Kelpie Queen was clearly irritated and suspicious – but they would have been more convinced themselves if Eo had managed to wrest an actual *commitment* from the saint.

'We're not getting everything, of course,' they reassured each other. 'We can only see what's immediately in the wretched little circle. There may be all sorts of things we don't know about going on where we *can't* see!'

Then the afternoon was nearly over, and out to sea there was a last golden light on the water, and the white flash of gull wings on the wind, and a few high clouds. Where *they* stood, though, it was different. The tall vortex dominated the beach, drawing the eye and oppressing the spirit. The waves fell heavily at their feet, as if the effort to do so were almost too much.

Suddenly, without warning, there was nothing to see on the viewing disc any more – it had blurred over into blank greyness just before Eo was reclaimed by the Traveller. The last thing they saw was the boy reaching out for Columba, desperate for the saint's help . . .

The three G stepped back from the disc and stared at each other. Then, as one, they looked out to sea.

'Is it time yet?' whispered Interrupted. 'Is it the turn?'

Hibernation Gladrag pulled an odd-looking device out of her robe.

'I'll check,' she said.

Market's mouth dropped open. 'You have a Tide Turn Calculating Device? *With* you?!' he said, amazed.

'Don't be ridiculous. I borrowed Sanskrit Macmahonney's when I was speaking to everybody back there,' said Hibernation absently, twiddling another knob and then squinting at the much too tiny display screen.

The turn of the tide is like the furthest point in the swing of a pendulum – a time of weightless pause before gravity and movement kick in again. Surprisingly, this pause is not entirely uniform in length. It can vary slightly from one tide to another, so if, for some reason, it is important to know the exact second . . . then it is essential to own a Tide Turn Calculating Device.

(Kelpies, and indeed most species of faeries, demons and the eldritch, don't need them. They are instinctively aware of these moments because they are part of the ebbing and strengthening of the barriers between the worlds, a pattern of change – *and opportunity* – which goes on all the time.)

'Not yet . . .' Gladrag muttered.

'But what's going to happen?' twittered Interrupted Cadence. 'When does the next throw happen – *how* does it happen . . .?'

The answer exploded out of the sea and flicked towards them at terrifying speed. It was disorienting, the way the Traveller got smaller as it came closer, so that it seemed to be moving towards and away from them at the same time. Both Market and Interrupted shrieked and ducked, but Hibernation forced herself to stand firm. Letting the Calculating Device drop to the sand, she lunged – and grabbed the vortex out of the air with both hands.

'Gotcha!' she crowed.

Market and Interrupted clustered round, trying to see what was in it. Tiny faces showed, moving so fast they were gone before the eye could focus. Bodies came behind them like the tails of comets, elongated round the curve of the vortex.

'There's definitely two of them in there now.'

'We did it! Did we do it?'

'Does the second one look like a Celtic saint monster-slayer?'

'Well, who else could it *be*?!'

'It *must* have been Columba –'

'My throw.'

They hadn't heard the Queen move, but suddenly there she was, right behind them, smiling her slow, predatory smile. All three jumped like guilty children, and then tried to pretend they hadn't, which widened the smile by several teeth.

'My throw,' she repeated, holding out her hand. It was long and white, and there were no lines on the palm.

Without a word, Hibernation gently tipped the vortex on to her outstretched hand. She made no attempt to steady it; nevertheless it spun without a wobble, balanced as if rigid with fear on its point. The two faces could still be glimpsed, whipping round and round, tantalizingly distorted. The G forgot about the Calculating Device, the moment of the turn, *everything*, in their desire to read the Traveller. With a private sneer, the Queen watched them squinting, leaning closer, closer, until –

– with a spurt of sharp sand, she spun round on her heel and threw the Traveller, up and over the inter-tidal waters, far, far out to sea.

'Struth!' said Market Jones.

The Queen sneered, a study in smug satisfaction, and strolled away.

The G were appalled.

'Are there still champions that far into the future?' gasped Cadence.

'Are there still *people* that far into the future?' said Market Jones.

Gladrag scratched her ear, only remembering at the last moment not to use a hind foot, and stared out to sea.

'Where *are* they?' she murmured frantically.

Where, indeed?

Inside the Traveller . . .

Colder than a stone cell, and even a starless night wasn't as dark as this. Adom could only pray he still had the boy Eo in his grip, for his frozen fingers felt nothing. And then he didn't pray for that any more, as all his soul was caught up in longing for one thing, for the motion to stop, the sickening whirling, make it stop, dear God in heaven, make it stop . . .

6 *The Second Tide*

'Look, we *know* you can do better than this!' Her father waved the report in Jay's face, barely missing her nose. 'You just have to make an effort. You just have to *pay attention!*'

Her mum took the report disk from him by one corner, as if it might bite.

'Look, darling,' she said calmingly, 'you *know* you have to work harder than other people. It's not a punishment – it's just a fact!'

'It's not like we don't know how that feels, Jay!' her father waded in. 'Your mother would never have got her job as a neural technician without higher marks than the competition.'

'*Substantially* higher,' murmured her mum.

'That's right. And the same for me. Let's face it – there are only so many jobs available to people like us – unless you *want* to be somebody's minder? Is that what this is about? You've decided on the noble career of making sure somebody *important* gets to work on time? *Is that it?!*'

Jay shook her head sullenly.

'We're O-class, Jay! And in spite of a lot of rubbish to the contrary, that's always going to be a major disadvantage.'

'Which can be overcome,' prompted her mum.

'Which can be overcome, yes – but *not* the way *you're* going about it, is all I'm saying!'

Of course, it *wasn't* all he was saying. The lecture was only beginning. But that was all that Jay actually *heard*. This was the stage at which she normally stopped listening.

'Now, let's not say any more about it,' said her mum at last.

If only. Jay heaved a weary sigh to herself.

'Your father's on rotation at the forest and I have my neuro-tech conference – and I want you to *promise* me you'll work hard while we're away. At least three units a day. You need to be caught up by the time term starts again. Right?'

Jay said she would. She said she'd be good. Her parents left, trying to look as if they believed every word, her father to his work for the Kelp Forestry Commission and her mother to the Annual Convention of Neural Technicians. Jay then got as far as opening a homework file titled 'World Government Section A(a)(i)' before giving it all up as a bad lot. She grabbed a bag and headed out into the Tubes of Greater Glasgow.

Greater Glasgow was huge, but it didn't cover much ground. This was because the vast majority of this vast city was underwater. The monumental rise in sea level was ancient history, and the world's enormous population had been almost exclusively sub-aquatic for generations.

Living quarters, industry, food production, transportation – everything that used to happen on land now happened beneath the waves.

At school, they were taught about the centuries of climate in turmoil, the millions dead, the extinction of species – but it was just words. The human population had more than recovered its numbers by Jay's time, and society had adapted to the restrictions of living in an element that was basically hostile. And if some of the old images of chaos and death *did* come back to haunt you in the night, they were easily patched away. Anxiety, anger, sorrow, over-excitement – they were all managed by tranquillizer patch. With people living so closely packed together, it was argued that there wasn't room for a lot of uncontrolled emotion. Breaking a window in a fit of rage didn't just mean an unexpected glazier's bill – living underwater meant that if someone decided to let off steam with an axe, it was quite likely to end in drownings.

There was no shortage of statistics for the levels of violence in the olden-day societies, and all those land-based cities just seemed to be willing to accommodate it. In the twenty-fourth century, things were tighter, cities more densely packed, and their inhabitants surrounded by an element for which they hadn't exactly evolved – well, it made sense to keep a lid on things.

Wall dispensers were everywhere. Sensors picked up increased adrenalin breathed out by agitated citizens and politely but firmly offered sedation. The police force, known as the Guardians, was armed with paralyser guns and the instruction to shoot first, ask questions later. Someplace else, out of the public view . . .

Just like the historical land-based Glasgow, Greater Glasgow had an extensive Tube system. It was powered by hydro-pressure, and its pods were well stocked with sensors and dispensers in case rush-hour delays got on a citizen's nerves. Trains of spherical pods floated through a complicated system of transparent reconstituted algae-plast tubes, a little like an old-fashioned marble run, up, down, round and at every conceivable angle, and about a third full of water. It was an *amazing* feat of hydraulic engineering but, like anything you use all the time, nobody much noticed.

The Tube was crowded – the end of the working day always saw enormous shifts of people desperate to get from one sector to another. Sometimes Jay loved all that. She would pretend she was part of the important grown-up world of commuting and being anonymous and purposeful in a crowd. She would stare out through the distorting curve of the tube walls at people passing and shops and lights coming on in the Housing Sectors. Sometimes she did it for hours, just in a daze, and would come to herself in an empty pod at the Inverness station, maybe, or even the suburbs at Ullapool.

But not today.

Today the Tube was just irritating. Jay got out at the next station and wandered along, looking in at the shops. She caught a glimpse of herself in a window and slowed down.

As a fifteenth birthday present to herself, Jay had gone to the hairdresser's. She'd opted for a velvety black cap of hair, a bit like the fur of a wet otter. It hadn't been cheap, but she knew she had a nice-shaped head and sexy ears – she didn't need to disguise them under elaborate curls and padding. Not like *some* people she could name.

'If you've got it, flaunt it!' the hairdresser said, and Jay had been happy to believe him.

Heads had been in style for a while now. It was legs before that. Irritatingly, long legs went out of vogue just as she had a growth spurt and got some. They still tripped her up sporadically and she didn't always remember to duck going through doorways. And even when she wasn't falling over herself, she had a tendency to fiddle with things, and almost invariably break them, which drove her parents to distraction.

'She'll grow out of it,' they said to each other through gritted teeth. 'I'm sure she will.'

'Ooops – sorry!' said Jay. She'd stopped paying attention and bumped a young woman's arm as she passed. Fortunately, the woman just grinned at her.

'You should wake up *before* you come out!' she laughed.

That was lucky! thought Jay. The rules on respecting personal space were pretty strict. Either the woman was better at remembering what it was like to be fifteen than most adults were, or else she must have just patched. Jay suddenly saw two Guardians standing by one of the shops. They were turning their heads away, their blank-faced masks scanning another part of the promenade. Clearly they had only just stopped watching her . . .

Jay felt cold sweat break out on her skin.

Everybody knew that Guardians were just people. They were recruited from O-class Sectors at a little younger than Jay was now, trained up in segregated installations that no one who *wasn't* a Guardian ever saw the inside of, and then assigned, always away from their home city. But still, just people – people who all looked exactly the same . . . It was the masks that really spooked Jay. They were designed so that the wearers were protected from attacks on any of their senses – sight, hearing, smell, even touch and taste. Nothing got through the mask membrane that shouldn't. It covered their skulls completely, leaving the place where their faces would be blank and featureless. The masks protected them, but it also made them all look alike . . . not quite human.

You couldn't tell them apart by their voices either – an integral microphone in the mask turned tenor, baritone and bass into one horrible breathy rasp. It was as if the Guardian behind the voice was only just in control of it. Jay remembered a classmate complaining once, 'You'd think with all that technology, they'd be able to get the voice right!' But *she* knew it was no mistake. It was the perfect voice, straight from nightmare.

Suddenly Jay didn't want to be *there* any more either. She didn't want to ride the Tube or shop or meet up with friends or go to a cafe or check out the new entertainment centre or *any* of it. She *certainly* didn't want to go home and revise.

Up top! she thought to herself. *That's what I'll do . . .*

She set off through the crowds, doing her best not to be noticeable or bang into anyone. Up a few levels, over to another section of the Tube, up again – until finally she reached the part of the city nearest the surface. D-class and RD-class lived up here, so it was a good idea not to be spotted wandering about. Minders and Maintenance O-class were of course allowed into these Sectors, but Jay didn't think she could pass for anything like that. Finally, having first checked that there was no one watching, she turned down a little-used side tube. There was a ladder at the end of it, and in the ceiling, there was a hatch . . .

Jay had first started going up top about a year ago. It was a Restricted Sector, so being there unsupervised was absolutely not allowed. The old surface platforms were not all that safe any more. Before the perfecting of sub-hydro power, they'd housed solar-power panels and wave-power generators and windmills. Further back than that, they'd provided people with a place to be 'in the air', though it'd been a long time since the platforms had been used very often for that. Jay's people adapted to underwater living long ago, and didn't pine much for the sight of the sky.

If you fancied some spectacular seascape views, though, this was the place. On a clear day you could see islands as far away as Nevis and the Cuillin chain, where the seabirds bred in season and the air was filled with their screaming for space. The horrendous noise and the stink of guano – that's what she remembered from a school trip round the archipelago – hellish. But from a distance, the islands were quite pretty, with their swirling haloes of birds overhead and the white waves round their feet.

It was already getting cold again and the birds would be gone soon. Once the winter storms set in in earnest, it wouldn't be any fun at all coming up top.

Jay shivered. It wasn't that much fun *now*, except for the fact that she wasn't supposed to be here in the first place. She'd seen the view before – and she had promised her parents she'd get stuck in to her schoolwork . . . She was just about to give in and go home, when suddenly she froze. There was a sound coming from the hatch.

Guardian! thought Jay, crouching anxiously behind a box-housing for something, but it wasn't the police. It was just a man, obviously RD-class, in a peculiar coat. She'd seen him here before. He seemed very good at giving his minder the slip. She wasn't sure what he came up here *for*, but then nobody ever *did* know why an RD did things! He never stayed long, and of course he always left immediately if he saw her . . .

The hatch opening mechanism whirred again – and this time Jay hid in earnest.

'Sir! Dr Horace, sir! Come inside at once!' The minder was a middle-aged O-class woman with unconvincing hair rolls. She bustled up to her charge but was careful not to touch him. 'Running off again – you shouldn't make me worry like that!'

Jay saw the man's face as he turned towards the woman. It was a surprisingly young face, unlined and wide-eyed under his old-man hair.

'I shouldn't?' he said in mild surprise.

Jay didn't hear the minder's reply as she ushered the man back to the hatch. Then they were gone.

Jay sighed. *Better wait a while, till they're well away,* she thought. She wandered to the railing and gazed out over the swell.

That could be me, she thought glumly of the woman. *If I don't get better marks, minding some D or RD will be the only work I'll be able to get.*

It was a prospect as bleak as the scene before her, nothing but the grey end of day, the cold flinty sea, the passing of the year . . .

She was just turning away, to go in search of some warmth and light and, if possible, some cheerfulness, when it happened. She only saw it out of the corner of her eye – a completely impossible whirlpool the height of a tall man balanced *above* the surface of the sea – before it disappeared, leaving two bodies thrashing about in the icy water.

The RNLI (Robotic Naval Life-saving Initiator) deployed immediately. Sensor-directed netting shot out from the platform, snaring the targets on the first cast and winching them to safety with such enthusiasm that Jay had to leap out of the way. Two Medi-boxes opened automatically to receive them, then hissed shut and began their analysis. Jay rushed over and tried to see through the lids, but they had already opaqued. The boxes hummed busily, while giving nothing away. She would just have to wait to find out who on earth these people were and how on earth they'd ended up in the sea . . .

Which was when it struck her that she was not going to be the only one wanting to know those things. RNLI deployment would automatically set off alarms all over the place – medical staff for one, but worse than that, there were the Guardians. They'd be swarming out of the hatch before she knew it and she did *not* want *them* finding her here!

She had already started to sprint for the exit, when she remembered the man in the coat and screeched to a halt. She could blame it on him! RD-class were always pressing the wrong buttons at the wrong times . . .

Without stopping to consider the consequences, Jay turned on her heel, raced over to the RNLI instead, flipped open the control panel and punched in the standard code all O-class were taught for 'False Alarm' and 'RD Error'. She didn't think, *But now the people in the boxes are* my *responsibility* or *What if they're dangerous?* or even *What do I do if the Medi-boxes can't save them and they die?!* She just banged in the codes and ran back to see if the strangers were ready to emerge.

One of the boxes was making heavy weather of its work. *Must be malfunctioning*, she thought. The machine couldn't seem to make up its mind whether it had one or two rescue subjects inside it, or even what their *species* might be. (In the early days of the RNLI there had been instances of disconcerted seals being rescued against their will and popped into Medi-boxes, which then stalled on the Basic Limb Count.)

She went to check the other box. *It* seemed to be working properly, anyway. Jay was able to access the initial report now, with details of gender, height, weight, age, injuries, prognosis and so on. She got as far as 'Subject is male, height 165 centimetres, weight 71 kilos (estimated dry weight), approximately 15 years of age, fractured left olecranon . . .' when a sequence of frustrated beeps distracted her. It was the other, malfunctioning Medi-box, giving up the ghost. Its lid opened and a boy with beautiful fair hair climbed out.

A boy with beautiful fair hair, and an enormous rat . . .

She knew immediately that he wasn't like her. It wasn't just the big rodent round his neck. It wasn't the clothes, though they were strange – nice material, nice style, but not like anything she'd seen before. Or the stunning hair (unconsciously she put a hand up to her own cropped head). It was something else, something about the way his face was put together or a look in his eyes – something that made her overwhelmingly aware of *difference* . . .

And then he grinned, a little shakily, and she was not so sure any more.

'I don't know when I'm going to get used to this,' he said. 'I'm Eo. Where's Adom? He was trying to save us from the vortex, which was very brave, though it was actually the saint we were expecting to be given, so he may be a little confused. Well, actually, I am too. Where is this, and when is this?'

These were the kinds of question Guardians asked when they suspected you of being under the influence of over-patching. 'Greater Glasgow, 30/10/2314,' she answered promptly, 'and *you've* been acting a lot stranger than *I* have!' She didn't for an instant think he could actually *be* a Guardian . . . could he?

'What? *2314?!* That's amazing! That's really . . .' He poked a finger at the creature round his neck. 'Come on, Professor, aren't you excited?! What are you being so quiet about? At least say hello to the nice lady – her box thing saved your life and groomed your fur all by itself.'

The rat heaved a long-suffering sigh. 'Very subtle approach, Eo. Confront her with some completely unexplained strangers, throw in a linguistically superlative ferret to top things off and then watch while she screams and/or faints. *Very* diplomatic.'

The animal turned his attention to Jay. 'Allow me to introduce myself, my dear. My name is Professor Pinkerton Hurple, and could you please take us to an adult person, preferably one with a good deal of power. I would also like to ask you, as a great *personal* favour, not to scream. Or faint. Or both.'

'Well, I'll be swamped,' was all Jay could think of to say. 'That's some robot!'

'Young woman, you are mistaken,' said the rat, or – *no*, thought Jay, *more like a weasel* – 'I am *not* a robot.'

'Really? Hologram, then?'

The creature tutted.

'*No*. I am a *ferret* . . . but not an ordinary ferret. I am a ferret gifted with speech. And a rather enormous IQ.'

Jay shrugged. 'Fair enough,' she said.

There was a burst of agitated and unintelligible words from behind her. She swung round to see another boy standing beside the other box. He was shorter, stockier and not nearly as pretty as the Eo person, and he was waving one of his arms about as he came over to them.

'What language *is* that?!' exclaimed Jay. 'What's he saying?'

'Adom, there you are,' cried Eo, sounding relieved. Then he turned back to Jay. 'No, I suppose you wouldn't recognize that – I'll translate. He says he wants to know where we are, of course, but he's also saying he was absolutely *sure* he broke his arm, back on the beach,' Eo translated. 'It hurt like – it hurt *a lot*, apparently. And now . . .'

'The Medi-box fixed it,' said Jay. 'It'll have healed anything that needed it – it's not going to let him out still damaged, is it? It'll have mended any rips in his, um, smock thing too. Given him and his clothes generally a quick clean and dry.'

But why do you need me to tell you that? she wondered. *What game are you playing with me here? Where could you possibly come from that you don't know what a Medi-box does?*

'Actually, now you mention it, his skin's looking a lot

85

better too – did you notice?' the one called Eo commented to the rat. Weasel. *Ferret*. Then, 'Hey! I wonder –' and he wrenched back the sleeve of his shirt. There were three angry-looking sores on his forearm. Just seeing them made Jay suck in her breath, but he seemed resigned to them being there.

'I'm really sorry . . . I think the box you were in must have been malfunctioning,' said Jay. 'Those look like they hurt!'

Eo shrugged. 'G normally take care of healing themselves. Your box probably never met somebody like me before, and these –' he pulled down his sleeve again, covering the welts – 'well, if I can't heal them, I guess it's not surprising it couldn't. My pain blocks are holding fine, though, so never mind.'

Jay wasn't sure she understood much of what had just been said.

'I'm sorry – *who* did you say normally heal themselves?' she said.

'G,' said Eo. 'That's me. G.' He grinned at her.

'You're . . . Gee?' said Jay.

'Yes.'

'Would you care to spell that?'

'Sure. It's spelled "G".'

'But . . .' Suddenly Jay realized that time was passing, much too fast. She turned briskly. 'Come on – we really should go now. With any luck the Guardians and the Medics will accept the False Alarm I coded in, but there's bound to be Maintenance staff on their way to reset the RNLI equipment and . . .' She noticed the total absence of comprehension on her audience's faces. 'Never mind, just *come!*'

'Am I correct in assuming our present location is, in some way, out of bounds?' asked the non-robot.

'You might say so,' Jay replied drily.

'Why's that?' asked the boy.

'Perhaps it's some sort of holy site,' suggested the animal. 'Or a religious taboo.'

Jay rubbed her hand down her face. 'Let me put it this way,' she said. 'I'm leaving. You lot stick around if you want to.'

After a quick translation to the stocky boy, the strangers fell in behind her without further argument.

It only occurred to Jay later that she'd become a minder after all.

By the time she got her party of weirdos to the nearest station, it was late enough for the platform to be almost completely deserted. The few remaining commuters gave them some pretty disapproving looks, but nobody had the energy to ask questions. Jay had no trouble finding them an empty pod.

'And this will take us to a person in power?' the ferret kept wittering, but Jay resolutely chose not to hear. She was in no hurry to hand them over to *anyone*.

Thank goodness there's nobody waiting for me at home, she thought. *How lucky is that!*

'I think we'll take the quickest way,' she murmured to herself, coding in the route.

As the train set off, Adom sat bolt upright, not moving a muscle. It looked as if, on some illogical level, his brain was telling him that the only way to survive all this strangeness was to not draw its attention.

Eo, on the other hand, was fidgeting all over the place.

He was having difficulty making himself comfortable leaning into the curve of the wall. 'Things are quite *round* in your world, aren't they?' he said, waving a hand at the train of spheres moving through the cylindrical Tube.

'What? Oh, yes, that's right. Well, they would be, wouldn't they? It's the whole water-pressure thing. Spheres are the best shape underwater because the pressure gets distributed equally all the way round. Also there aren't any seams. You use a square shape, you've got floors having to meet walls and walls having to join up with ceilings – and you've got leaks just waiting to happen. Spheres you can build all in one. Here . . .' She reached across and showed him how to get a padded back to the bench to rise up from inside the seat. 'You can do what you like with the *inside*! See . . .'

But before she could show them anything else, another panel emerged. A slot in the front opened and a tray with a bit of silvery material on it slid out.

Jay made a rude face at the dispenser, took the proffered patch and stuck it unceremoniously on the underside of the bench.

'Um . . .' said Eo. 'And that was?'

'Patch dispenser. The sensor'll have picked up a raised adrenalin level.'

The others stared, first at her and then where she'd dumped the patch.

'Is that bad?' asked Eo.

Again the question came to her. *What game are you playing? Do you really expect me to believe you don't know . . . ?! There's no city on earth that doesn't monitor, that doesn't patch . . .*

'Don't mind us – if you're supposed to be, er, applying

a, um, thing, you just carry on!' said Hurple. He seemed very polite, for a rodent. He also seemed completely sincere, as far as you could tell through the fur.

I just can't believe they're lying, she thought to herself. *It feels like they really do not know! They really do come from . . . somewhere else!*

(It was at this point that something shifted permanently in her own brain. Instead of thinking, *Wouldn't it be great if these weirdos were, I don't know, aliens or something*, she was now suddenly, totally convinced that that was *exactly* what they were!)

'Sure – go ahead!' the boy Eo urged. 'We don't mind at all!'

'What? Oh no. Look, it's not like it's the law or anything!' She certainly sounded defensive, even to herself. This wasn't the bit of her world she wanted strangers to focus on too much. And she didn't want to even *begin* to explain how the Guardians always checked up on anyone who *didn't* take a patch they were offered. 'Patches are more of a . . . *suggestion.*'

'Well, as the Professor said, don't let us get in your way. Just you ignore us. You do whatever you do do . . . normally, I mean,' Eo said, with good manners but not a lot of clarity.

The dispenser stuck out its tray again. There were two more patches on it.

'Cool! For us?' chirped Eo.

Jay swore, and slapped the patches under the seat as well.

'Looks like the sensors haven't noticed you, Mr Hurdle.' She began to dig about in her bag.

'Here – put these on,' she said, extracting three gauzy

rectangles from the very bottom of her bag. She showed the boys how to put the material over their nose and mouth. When they inhaled – somewhat nervously – it instantly dissolved. A moment later the dispenser retracted into the wall.

'Adrenalin maskers,' explained Jay. 'Gets the dispensers off our backs, and the Guardians. I'm not planning on trying to explain you lot to anybody just yet!'

Eo and the ferret exchanged glances.

'So . . . not legal, as such?' the Professor asked.

Jay snorted rudely.

'How did you learn about, um, this technique?'

She shrugged. 'Kids at school. You can buy maskers easily enough if you know who to ask, but I get them from Mum's work. The surgeons prefer to work on conscious candidates when they do implants – it makes it easier for some reason – but they don't want every sensor in the place going crazy! Anyway, I know the code to the stockroom . . . Don't worry, though, these'll last for hours, and I've got more at home. If we need them.'

Every now and then either Eo or the ferret would have to stop and translate what was being said for the other boy. It didn't seem to make him any less confused, however. His big plain face was all wrinkled up with bemusement. Then, suddenly, he asked Hurple a question.

The animal chuckled.

'What'd he say?' frowned Jay.

'He was just wondering if you were a crazy person. He's never seen a basically bald woman before, and you sound – to him – like you're gibbering.'

'BALD?!' *Hey!* she thought. *He called me a woman!*

'I *like* your hair!' put in Eo hastily, but Jay ignored him.

'Well, I'm not crazy,' she said. 'I'm not talking gibberish, and I'm not bald! This style cost me a lot of credit, I can tell you – and *you* can tell *him*, he's not so drop-dead gorgeous himself – no, wait, *I'll* tell him.'

She pulled back her sleeve as if to scratch, but instead began to tap on her forearm, complicated patterns using index, middle and ring fingers, singly and in combination.

'There's something inside your arm?!' gasped Eo.

She looked up. 'My computer,' she said. 'What do you think I am – some kind of *child*?!'

'What are you doing?' asked Hurple.

'I'm accessing a language program for – what is that he's speaking? Some sort of antique Gaelic? So I can tell him to his face *my* opinion of *him*!'

'You can do that?!' The animal seemed extraordinarily excited by this.

'Well, yeah. Languages are all pretty much the same. Download some vocabulary, a bit of grammar, guide to pronunciation – the brain uses the same pathways for Swahili as it does for Mandarin. Anything *he* can speak, *I* can speak!'

'Astonishing! That it should be so easy, I mean! In my time, humans' understanding of their brains was that they were a complete jumble of incredibly complex relationships, with the simplest thing making synapses fire all over the park!'

Jay looked over at him. 'That's right,' she said. 'That's

how it *does* work. But –' and here her voice seemed to shift – 'it's no problem navigating if you've got a decent map! Isn't that true, Adom?'

'That's right,' said Adom. 'What?!'

'He *understood* you!' exclaimed Eo and Hurple.

Jay gave them a smug grin.

'I have the software for every known language, written and spoken, in this arm, and I'm not afraid to use it!'

Nobody seemed to think this was funny, but Adom might not even have heard. He'd grabbed Jay's sleeve – the one on the arm without the computer – and, eyes huge in his face, asked, no, *begged*, 'Could you do that for me?'

'Do what?' said Jay, surprised and uncomfortable with his intensity.

'Enchant my arm so that I have the gift of tongues,' said Adom, his voice low with longing.

'*Enchant your – ?!*' She paused and thought through the kind of vocabulary old Gaelic had on offer. 'Well . . . yeah, I guess. Sort of. But why?'

'It's a long story,' interrupted Hurple.

She looked down her nose at him. 'Don't think I've forgotten about *you* – setting aside you talking at *all* – how is it *you* can speak my language and his language and presumably rat language . . .'

Hurple shook his head. 'Long story.'

'Is that right? And what about *you*?' Jay turned to Eo.

'That's a long story too,' said Hurple, making it absolutely clear there were going to be no explanations.

FAQ 306: How is it that the G are so good at languages?

HURPLE'S REPLY: Languages hold no difficulties for shape-shifters, since the G brain is happy to accept imprints from the ambient electrical patterns which words and the use of words leave in the air. In the old days it was believed that language was actually **inhaled** (hence that old G expression, 'Big nose, big . . . vocabulary'), a little in the way humans once thought breathing in bad smells made them ill. Now, of course, it is understood that the G's acquisition of languages is not such a crudely physical process, and the nose has pretty much nothing to do with it!

Suddenly Jay reached over to the control panel and tapped in another sequence. Almost immediately their pod detached itself from the train, slid over into a side tube and stopped.

'Are we there?' asked Eo.

She shook her head.

'Do we get out now?' asked Hurple.

'No.'

'So . . . what's happening now?'

'*Nothing,*' Jay stated firmly. 'Nothing whatsoever of any shape or description is going to happen until *you* have told *me* exactly *everything*.'

Hurple tutted and humphed and tried to bully her into starting the pod up again, but Jay was having none of it.

'I don't care how long your stories are,' she said firmly. 'We're going nowhere until I've heard the lot.'

That was clear enough, so, with extremely bad grace on the Professor's part, they began to talk . . .

By the time they'd finished, Jay was leaning forward, elbows on knees, chin in hands, eyes wide. She made several attempts at speaking, but delighted laughter kept getting in the way.

'That is the most . . . *outrageous* story I have ever heard!' she eventually hooted.

'It's not just a story, child,' said Hurple sternly.

'Quiet!' Jay hissed abruptly, focusing over his shoulder.

Before the animal could react to her rudeness – she could see his mouth all set to start – she had reactivated the pod and swung it back into the main tube, where it attached itself neatly to the end of a passing train.

'Guardians,' she explained. 'I saw their lights at the other end of the side tube back there.'

Hurple shut his mouth again, but still looked miffed.

'Look,' said Jay impatiently, 'you do *not* want the Guardians getting their hands on you.'

'We don't?' said Eo.

'Well, put it this way, with a story like yours, it'd take a lot longer than the rest of *this* Tide to convince them to let you go again.'

She couldn't help letting a bit of a shudder come into her voice. The boys didn't pick up on it, but Hurple certainly did.

'Thank you, then, for keeping us clear of "the awful people", as I believe they have sometimes been called.'

Jay saluted cheerfully. 'Yes, *sir*, Mr Weasel, sir. Glad to be of service.'

'That's *Professor* Weasel – I mean, Hurple – to you,' huffed the ferret. 'And as we explained, we haven't got all day, so could you please *finally* take us to an appropriately powerful but *safe* adult, in the hopes that that adult will be moved to present us with a gift from this Tide?'

He watched the girl's face lose its manic chirpiness and close up.

'And now you're going to say "yes" and mean "no",' he said, with a resigned sigh.

She stared at him.

He waved a paw. 'I *have* met young creatures before, you know. So let's just skip that part, shall we, and go straight to *why* you don't want to take us to an adult.'

'I . . . um . . .' Jay seemed completely flummoxed. 'Well . . .'

Hurple just looked at her and waited.

'All right. OK. You're right,' she finally said. 'I wasn't planning on taking you to *any* grown-up. And it's not because I don't believe you. It's because I *do* believe you and your crazy story and your mad monk boy there and the shifty boy and *you* – well, if I can believe in *you*, I can believe in *anything*, right?! But the thing is, I really truly can't think of anyone older than me who would. Not anybody O-class anyway, and I don't *know* anybody else.'

There was a pause while Eo tried to bring Adom up to speed on the conversation. Jay kept lapsing into English, and besides, many of the words she was using had no Gaelic equivalents.

'Look, I'm not just making this up. Things like you really do not happen any more, you know. It's not just the Guardians. There is no grown-up I could take you to who wouldn't want to study you for the next decade – and besides, even if there were – I have no intention of letting you go!' She didn't know exactly when she'd decided she was going with them, but it felt as if had been forever. This was *her* secret, *her* unbelievable adventure, and there was no way she was going to let anybody else get their hands on it, for better or worse.

Hurple groaned. 'No, no, *no*. Don't you *see*? This isn't a game! This is *serious*! Didn't you understand anything we've been telling you? When the boy opened the way between the worlds, he condemned himself to almost certain death. And when he took on the Wager, he included everyone in his universe in the same danger. The same fate.'

Jay looked at Eo. The colour had drained out of his face and he looked as if he were going to be sick.

'All *right*!' she cried. '*I get it*! Leave him alone. But what *you* don't seem to get is, *I can help*! Equipment? Technology? General all-round knowledge? I've got it all. You said wisdom was one of the things you were looking for, and I've got access to *centuries* of information you couldn't possibly know about!'

'So give that to us,' said the ferret gently. 'Let that be the Gift. Can't you see how much more use that would be than, well, you?!'

In her mind, Jay knew he was right, but it just made her even more stubborn.

'You took *him*,' she said sullenly, pointing at Adom.

'We didn't ask for him! We were trying to be offered the help of a great man, a powerful man. Adom just . . . happened.'

'Did you force him to come?'

'No!'

'Did you trick him into coming?'

'I told you, no.'

'So,' said Jay slowly. 'Adom is with you not because you tricked him into coming, or forced him into coming, but because he offered himself. Voluntarily. Like . . . a gift.'

Hurple stared at her for a long moment. 'Very clever.'

Jay took a deep breath. 'I'll tell you what I think,' she said. 'I think I've just made you an offer you can't refuse.'

There was a silence, then,

'I think she's got a point there, Professor,' muttered Eo.

Hurple chewed uncertainly on a paw. 'But surely it's the technology we need from here?' he said in a last attempt. 'And – wait a minute – if you're the Gift, won't that mean Adom can't have his arm enchanted? Because then *that* would count as our Gift?'

Adom looked stricken, but Jay gave him a reassuring pat.

'You lot really aren't used to working *around* rules, are you?' she said. 'One Gift for the Challenger, yes, and that's me, because I'm offering and you can't say no. But where does it say I can't bring things of my own with me? And where does it say I can't give things to the Challenger's *other* Gifts?'

There was a pause. Hurple was not meeting anyone's eyes.

'Professor?' said Adom.

With a sigh, the ferret gave them all an acquiescent wave of a paw.

'YES!' hooted Jay, and she planted a big fat kiss on Adom's cheek, causing him to turn scarlet and forget his own name.

'Ooops – sorry!' she said.

'No kissing me!' chirped Hurple firmly.

Eo looked hopeful, but Jay just grinned at him and began to recode their route.

'Right, my friends, first things first – Adom here needs his language capability extended by about four million per cent if he's going to be properly in the loop. Luckily, when it comes to Assessment, Learning Programmes and the Glorious Greater Glasgow Way of Life – I'm your woman!' She threw Adom a reassuring look. 'In other words, one enchanted arm coming up!'

The pod detached itself, nipped along another side tube, paused a moment at the junction and then attached itself to the tail end of a train going in a different direction. It was a moment before the visitors realized what was odd about their new route . . .

'Hey! The train – the water – it's going *up*!' said Eo, pressing his nose against the transparent wall.

'But that's impossible!' spluttered Hurple. 'Everyone *knows* water doesn't just *run uphill*!'

Jay snorted. 'It does if you push it hard enough!' she said, and, as the ferret drew an eager breath to ask questions, she stopped him with, 'And if you think I know diddlysquat about hydraulic engineering or infrastructure technology, you can forget it right there. Half that stuff I haven't covered yet and the other half I slept through!'

Eo laughed, Adom looked confused and Hurple tutted, appalled.

Jay just went on grinning, and their pod sped on past the sights of Greater Glasgow.

Even though it was already late when they reached the Sector where Jay's mother worked, there were still lights on in the Neural Assessment pod.

Jay swore. 'Somebody must still be working,' she said. 'I'd hoped we'd have the place to ourselves. OK, never mind. Try not to be noticeable, and follow my lead.' She paused and looked at her companions, Adom in his medieval habit and sandals, Eo with a live animal draped round his neck. 'Well . . .' she said. 'Just follow my lead.'

She keyed in a code to open the door of the pod and

walked confidently in. A woman in a lab coat spun round, surprised.

'Jay! What are you doing here?'

'Hello, Mrs Chambers. I'm here for some stuff,' said Jay with a straight face. 'You know my mum has this conference . . .'

The woman rolled her eyes. 'I swear your mother has the makings of a D-class, the way she manages to forget things! Can you find what you need by yourself, though, dear? Only I'm late leaving already.'

Jay reassured her, and promised they'd lock up when they left. The woman was clearly uncertain what to make of Adom and Eo, though. (Hurple was safely out of sight now in the bag.)

'You've met my friends before, have you, Mrs Chambers? Amazing costumes, aren't they?' said Jay quickly, and the woman's expression cleared.

'Fancy dress party, eh? You're sure to win a prize!' she said, giving Adom a friendly shove with her shoulder as she passed.

Fortunately she was in too much of a hurry to notice his lack of reply.

'Nicely handled,' said Eo approvingly, once the technician was gone. 'You didn't actually lie and you didn't tell the truth either. Well done.'

Jay gave him a mocking half-bow, and Hurple tutted.

'The Assessor's through here. Come on,' she said, leading the way into the next room.

The Assessor was just a chair, and a kind of silver dome thing on an arm above it, and some discreet panels and keyboards to one side. As far as way-in-the-future technology went, it was pretty unthreatening-looking.

Adom, however, was having none of it. He just stood there, shaking his head, and getting more and more stubborn-looking.

'You are *not* putting *me* in *that*,' he stated flatly. 'Enchant my arm, but leave the rest of me alone.'

Jay gave a sigh of frustration. 'But I have to assess you *first*. Look – it's just like, I don't know – blood types, right? If you needed a transfusion I'd need to know what blood group you were *first*, wouldn't I, and so I'd test your blood – and this is no different.' Adom just looked at her. 'Oh. Yeah. That explanation doesn't exactly help, does it? Couple of thousand years too soon.'

'Not quite that long,' said Hurple, 'but no, I don't think that particular analogy is easing his disquietude very much.'

Jay stuck her tongue out at him, and tried again.

'Adom, you need to *listen* to me here. All I want you to do is sit in the Assessor and I'll fit the dome over your head, which will map your brain's wiring pattern. Once I know what kind of neural class you are, I'll *also* know what kind of learning package will suit you, we can get you understanding English and any other language you like, and everything'll suddenly make more sense. Wouldn't you *like* everything to make more sense?!'

Unfortunately, there just weren't the words in Gaelic for a good part of what she was trying to get across, and so English (i.e. gibberish) words kept cropping up instead. The overall effect was to just make things worse.

Jay sighed and then stiffened, eyes wide.

'Look! An eagle!' she shouted suddenly, pointing at the ceiling. As Adom's head snapped up she slapped a patch on to his hand. She just managed to catch him before he hit the floor. 'Sedative,' she grunted to the others. 'Don't stare at me like that – it doesn't make any difference to the basic assessment whether he's awake or not. Come on, give me a hand! He weighs a ton.'

With Eo's help, she got him into the chair and lowered the dome.

'What –' he began, but Hurple shushed him.

'Don't distract her,' he whispered solemnly.

Jay wasn't listening to them anyway. She adjusted the dome and then plonked herself into her mother's chair, pulled two of the keyboards over and began coding in information. A number of shapes and graphs came up on the screens around the walls. She watched them closely for a moment and then nodded her head, satisfied.

'*Now* can I ask what you're doing?' said Eo, a bit huffily.

Jay checked the progress of the shape on the screens one more time. Coming along nicely. She swung back and forth idly in the chair, making Professor Hurple's head swing back and forth in time.

'Sure,' she said. 'I'm mind-mapping. Well, the computer is. It's charting the basic wiring patterns in his brain so that I'll know what sort he's got – there's not a lot of point plugging RD-class software into him if he's got an O-class brain, now is there?!'

There was a pause.

'Perhaps if you explained a little more fully?' Professor Hurple suggested cautiously.

'Yeah,' said Eo. 'Assume we're really stupid.'

Jay refrained from making the obvious reply.

'OK. We've got some time. Let's see . . . There are

three basic wiring patterns in humans' brains – three basic classes, is what we call them. There's O-class, D-class and RD-class. O-class is the most common one. Stands for Ordinary Class. That's where you have a bog-standard right–left division of things your brain does. There's some flexibility, obviously, a range of abilities within a class, but still, we're talking pretty ordinary.'

She checked the screen again and then looked over at her audience.

'With me so far?' she asked.

The two nodded numbly.

'OK . . . Then there's RD-class – that stands for Rigid Division. An RD brain has wiring that allows the *least* flexibility of functions. RD people tend to be extremely specialized. They have huge over-development of specific skills and huge *under*-development of the rest.'

'And the third one?'

'D-class. Stands for an old word, "dyslexic". My mum told me what it used to mean but I forget. Anyway, D-class brains have the most complicated wiring of all, pretty anarchic, really, so they have the most flexible brains there are. A D-class certificate opens any door you want to mention.'

'They're the best?' Eo was struggling to keep up.

'Well, the official line is that all classes are equal – different but equal – and it's supposed to be illegal to discriminate against Os and RDs. But everybody knows employers will pick a D-class over anybody else, no matter what kind of capacity they've got. It's only natural.'

'So, D-class get the best jobs, then RD-class – what does O-class get?'

Jay snorted. 'O-class gets what's left! Technical Support,

Maintenance, Minding RDs and Ds . . . *We keep the world ticking over – there's no shame in that!*' she mimicked, making a sour face. 'The Psychs are always doing the pep talk. All about proper pride, and everybody being worthy and important *in their own way*. Makes me want to spit. Or get totally patched!'

Neither Eo nor Hurple knew what to say to this. Eo got as far as 'Um . . .' when the computer beeped.

'So!' said the Professor. 'What class is our unconscious friend?'

Jay swung back to the screen and let out a whistle.

'Well, I'll be swamped,' she exclaimed. 'The boy's a D!'

Eo and Hurple grinned at each other, looking absurdly proud. Even Jay felt pleased, in a peculiarly proprietorial sort of way. This was one of *her* weirdos, after all!

She pushed the dome back up on its arm and applied a stimulant patch to Adom's hand. Then, as he came to, she began downloading a basic D-class learning package on to a wafer.

'You don't get a full implant till you've pretty much finished growing, for obvious reasons. *Children* have strap-ons.' She didn't mention she'd only progressed from a wrist-strap model herself a few months ago. 'Our friend here is certainly *big* enough, but even if my mum were here, and willing, she doesn't do implants. Just programming.' There was a pause as she listened to what she'd just said. 'When I say "just" programming, it's not like that's *easy*. It's incredibly complicated, and she's *very good*. You don't get to go to conferences unless you're already the best!' She glared at them, but there was nothing but respect – and bemusement – on their faces.

Even the rat looked properly impressed. 'Right. OK.' She turned back to the storage panel and called up several trays of wristbands. 'Usually they let kids choose their own strap . . . Our lad here will probably be wanting something manly . . . unobtrusive . . . plain . . .'

She was interrupted by a broad, calloused hand, which reached over her shoulder and pointed.

There was a short, stunned pause.

'Are you sure?!' Jay gargled.

The wristband Adom had chosen was covered in fluffy material. Its clasp was in the shape of an unspeakably cute kitten, with flashy diamanté eyes, one of which winked on and off knowingly. And both the kitten and the fluffy material were . . .

. . . pink. *Outrageous* pink. A pink that made candyfloss pink look understated and subdued.

Jay turned and looked into the boy's eyes. There was longing there, and she had a sudden spark of insight. Adom came from a time when the palette of colours available to most people consisted entirely of variations on 'mud'.

Whatever else that wrist strap might be, it wasn't *brown*.

Without another word, she lifted the monstrosity out of the tray, inserted the wafer and strapped it gently to his wrist. He was so busy grinning and stroking all that fluffiness that he didn't notice the neural patterners making contact with his skin. Without fuss, they began to send the necessary signals to the appropriate places in his brain . . .

'Will it take long?' whispered Hurple.

Jay shook her head. 'Any minute now and we'll be

having erudite conversation in flawless English out of our antique boy!'

First words are worth waiting for. First words are the ones that get noted down by adoring parents and recited endlessly to tolerant relatives. Adom's first words in English, courtesy of his pink and fluffy enchanted arm, came out loud and clear.

'Saints and Angels,' he said. 'I'm HUNGRY!!'

The trip to Jay's home pod was uneventful.

'Right, make yourselves comfortable and I'll get us some food,' said Jay as she led them into the living area. 'If I've got the different times right, we've all been on the go for far too long. Some food, some rest – that's what we need now.'

Her guests hesitated just inside the doorway, looking uncomfortable.

'Don't be so silly! Sit!'

The room was round, like everything else they had seen in Jay's world. The walls/ceiling were still transparent, offering a view out into the dark water. All around, above and below were other pod shapes glowing, strung together by tubes at all angles like an enormous luminescent marble run. In a few of the pods they were able to catch tantalizing glimpses of the inhabitants moving about, but most had been opaqued for the night and only shadows showed on their curved surfaces. Jay touched a panel and immediately the view from their pod disappeared.

'Probably better not to let the neighbours know I've got company,' she explained. In the ride here, she'd told them of her parents' absence. None of them had seemed to think it strange, but then they were pretty much all on oddness overload still.

'Look, would you just relax?!' she said to them generally. 'Sit down – chairs can't have changed *that* much, right?'

There were things that *did* look more or less like chairs, of a round, basket sort of shape. Eo and Adom managed to sit in them, though Adom looked as if he were afraid it wanted to eat him instead. Professor Hurple jumped up on to the cushioned bench that ran round the curved walls and settled down.

'Good,' said Jay. 'That's a start. Now stay there while I get us something to eat – and don't touch anything!'

Which of course made Eo desperate to find something *to* touch. There were a number of intriguing panels on the walls . . . Fortunately, Jay was back very quickly. She pressed more buttons, and tables for each of them appeared from under the floor.

'Eat first,' she said brightly. 'Make plans later!'

The food was . . . fishy. And a bit seaweedy as well. It wasn't all that different from what Adom ate a lot of the time anyway, though it looked different on the plate – and the plates were a bit unfamiliar. It took them a moment to realize what their hostess was doing when she started eating hers, but once they gave their own crockery a nibble, they found it quite tasty.

Jay had just served them all some tea when suddenly the pod began to judder and shake. She didn't seem to notice this much, except to steady her cup, but the others were appalled. It was hard enough being so far underwater, without the walls and the floor jittering about and threatening to split.

'Earthquake!' squealed Professor Hurple, and the boys tried to find something solid to hold on to.

'What? No, no.' Jay looked at them, amused. 'They're just de-limpeting the pods! It only takes a moment – nothing to worry about.'

Her guests did not look convinced, even when the shaking *did* abruptly stop.

'Look, I'll show you.' She went to a wall panel and touched a button. At once the sphere became transparent again, and the light from the room spilled out into the water. 'See?'

Her guests gasped. Unbelievably, it was snowing out there! Hundreds of little whitish blobs pinged gently against the top of the pod and tumbled on down into the darkness below.

It was hypnotizing, a surreal underwater blizzard. Then, after a few moments it died away, and stopped.

'Lucky for us, limpets never learn,' said Jay, returning the surface of the pod to its opaque state. 'They keep attaching themselves to the spheres – we keep shaking them off – then we collect them at the lowest levels and –' she held up her cup – 'there you have it! Tea!'

There was a confused pause.

'You make tea out of shellfish?'

'Well, yeah!' snorted Jay. 'What else would you make it out of?! Drink up.'

In fact, it wasn't bad. Adom's idea of what constituted tea wasn't like Hurple's anyway, and Eo hadn't drunk much of any sort before. And it *was* warming. Then Adom caught Jay looking at him intently, and started to choke.

'W-what is it?!' he spluttered.

'Oh. Nothing – sorry,' she said, colouring a little. 'It's just, you're a bit of a surprise. I mean, we studied medieval stuff last year, and I sort of thought you'd be . . . different. The Medi-box said you were fifteen, and I thought that meant you'd be married already and have six kids, or be dead, or something.'

Adom looked confused. 'Medieval? What?'

'Medieval! You know, the Middle Ages – when you live. Lived. Used to have lived.' She thought about it for a moment. 'Though you probably didn't call it that. The *Middle* Ages, I mean. You probably called it *Modern Times*, or something!'

'We call it *now*,' said Adom simply. 'Just the way you do. Why are you all swaying?'

They weren't, of course. *He* was. He couldn't sit straight and his head ached, and he thought suddenly and with enormous longing of the abbey dormitory and his hard bed and the cold wind whistling through the window slit and the clear knowledge of everything a given day could reasonably be expected to hold . . .

'The lad's overloading,' said Professor Hurple. 'Put him to bed this minute, or suffer the consequences.'

'Oh,' said Jay, looking a touch embarrassed. 'That'll be the tea. I put just a little sedative in it, but I guess he's more susceptible than I expected . . .'

She realized she was talking to herself. Adom, Eo and Hurple were all asleep, worn out by too much strangeness and too little rest. Jay smiled fondly at them and began to tidy up. She bustled quietly about, putting the furniture they weren't using back under the floor and gathering things together that might be useful on the great adventure.

Saltwater-powered torch, Water Purifiers (they could be filled *anywhere* – they were lined with a sensitive one-way membrane which extracted anything non-potable, like salt or harmful bacteria or parasites, leaving only the purest drinking water behind), Medi-kit, a Portable Generator, a selection of Depth Gauges, Hull Pressure Gauges, Oxygen-concentration Gauges . . .

Leave a note for the parents, she thought. She knew her mum would be getting in touch at some point while she was at the conference. *What shall I say that will keep her from worrying, or worse yet, getting somebody else to check up on me . . .*

'Working on a project with friends . . .' Should she try to say what kind of project? Historical? Mythic? Alternate Interpretations of the Space Time Continuum? Better keep it simple. She set the comm to answer her mother's code when it was activated.

'Hi, Mum. I'm working on a project with some friends. I'll probably stay over – bit lonely here by myself. Have a great time at the conference. Love, J.'

That should do it.

She looked through the things she'd gathered, discarding a few and then reinstating them. She got a pocketed belt from her father's work gear and distributed the kit so that the weight was well balanced. Then she sat on the floor and looked at her visitors for a moment, enjoying the strangeness of it all until a huge yawn interrupted her. She checked the time, set a wake-up call for an hour later, adjusted the floor temperature and consistency to something toasty and soft, and fell asleep.

*

Waking up was hard for all of them. Jay plied them with more hot drinks with something in to help. Then they headed out into the city night. Jay coded in a round-about route that would take them away from the places where people would still be around – clubs and bars and theatres – and instead past empty workplaces and sleepy home pods.

They were cutting it fine. As the minutes ticked by, her band of weirdos was becoming more and more uncomfortable.

'We'll *get* there – don't worry!' Jay insisted, though she was feeling a bit sick herself. 'It's not a problem.' She paused as a thought struck her. 'Hey! What would actually happen if you *didn't* go and meet the whirlpool thing?'

'If we didn't go to it, it would come to us,' said Professor Hurple. The ferret hunched his shoulders and shivered as he looked out at the homes they were currently passing. 'The Traveller has immense destructive power.'

Jay shuddered too. 'Forget I asked,' she said. 'Anyway, we're here.' They left the train pod, hustled down the side tube and up the ladder to the hatch . . .

It was cold on the platform. There was a mean, biting wind, and the flat glare from the lights blotted out any view of the night sky. Jay redirected the housing for one of the lights till it was pointing at roughly the same place that the Traveller appeared before. The sea heaved and churned, inky black and revealing nothing. Fingers of spume seemed to be reaching blindly towards the lights.

Something wasn't right! It made the hair on the back of Adom's neck stand up. Something was *wrong* . . .

'The tide!' he yelped. 'Why isn't it lower? It should be practically on the turn – *low tide!* – but the water hasn't dropped.' He grabbed her sleeve in a panic. 'What's happened? You've tricked us – you've made us miss the Tide – we're trapped here forever!'

Jay detached him from her sleeve. 'Stop that! You forget, our pods aren't rigid. They're designed to rise and fall with the tides. The water's lower – and so are we!'

Adom stepped back from her abruptly. 'I . . . of course . . . I'm sorry.'

Jay gave him a half-grin and rubbed her arm. 'Forget it. Nothing wrong with us all that a piece of patch won't fix . . .' Her voice died away as she realized, with a cold horror, what she'd forgotten to bring.

Patches!

You couldn't get more than your immediate needs from the wall dispensers but she knew where her father kept the supplies he took with him to work out in the forest. She'd completely forgotten! How did she think she was going to manage without patching?!

'I have to go back!' she cried, but Hurple shook his head.

'No time,' he said.

'Now, you won't be able to feel my hand, but I'll still be there so don't let go,' said Eo in a rush.

'What do you mean? Why won't I be able to feel your hand? What –'

'There's no time to explain – just trust me!'

Jay made a rude noise. 'Yeah, like I'm really going to trust somebody who says, "Trust me."'

'She's right, you know,' Hurple commented. 'That's just what I say. Smart girl!'

Eo rearranged the Professor forcibly round his neck and glared at Jay. 'Just hold on,' he grunted.

'It's almost here,' said the ferret in a strangled voice. 'Can't you feel it?'

Jay stared wildly about, seeing nothing, then . . .

'Urg!' she groaned, clutching the sides of her head. 'My ears!'

Eo pulled at her arm. 'We need to hold hands,' he said urgently.

Adom's eyes were squeezed shut and he appeared to be praying.

'Come on, boy!' Hurple barked at him. 'Wake up and grab hold – unless you want to get left behind!'

Adom's eyes snapped open and he grabbed frantically at Eo's hand. Jay quickly took the G's other hand.

'Now what?' she tried to say, but a sudden silence ate her words – just before the Traveller exploded noiselessly out of the sea. It took them where they stood, and disappeared.

It was a moment before the lighting sensors on the platform realized they were no longer serving a purpose. They shut themselves down, and then there was nothing left – no trace under the dark, distant sky.

7 *The Throw of Market Jones*

The G couldn't make up their minds whether the Second Tide was going to be a success or a failure. The revelation that Eo had ended up with just some unknown boy from the First Tide, rather than the formidable skills of a demon-slayer and saint, had been bitterly disappointing.

'Maybe there's more to him than he looks,' suggested Interrupted.

'He *looks* like a yokel,' grunted Market.

'But maybe he's a *famous* yokel?'

The three G searched their memories for any reference to 'Boy Wonder Adom' or 'Young Adom the Demon Destroyer'. But they didn't find anything.

The Gift of the First Tide was *exactly* the way he looked . . . just another boy.

So . . . would the situation improve this time round? Could the Kelpie Queen *possibly* have been too clever for her own good and sent the boy (the boys) to a place and time so advanced or powerful or wise that equipping them for the Final Challenge would be a doddle? Hope flared any number of times as the hours passed – even the fact that Eo and Adom had met up with any people still alive at *all* was a bonus.

It was a bit disconcerting, though, the way everything seemed to be taking place *underwater*.

As the darkness deepened on the beach, the G built themselves a fire, for light and warmth, but even more so for comfort. The world of the future was coming across as a very confusing place. They didn't recognize many of the things they were seeing, and they weren't all that sure what was being talked about a good part of the time, especially when Eo's attention wandered – which it did rather frequently. He seemed to be randomly focused on the most unuseful items, like food and interestingly complex but obviously firmly attached wall panels. There certainly seemed to be a *lot* of technology about, though.

'There's bound to be *something* to kill Kelpies with among it all, don't you think?' muttered Market Jones.

'Should he be spending so much time with the young female?' worried Interrupted. 'Surely nothing really powerful would be *available* to a child like that?'

'On the other hand, a child might be willing to *give* him something, when a more cautious adult might not,' said Hibernation.

'He's barely even *met* any adults!' snorted Market. 'Does the boy think he's looking for *playmates*?!'

It was maddening.

It was hard to tell what the Queen herself thought of her throw and its outcome. She spent most of the Tide staring into her personal viewing disc. The way she was standing – weight on one leg, one hip relaxed, head hung down – seemed very peculiar, until they remembered she was part equine.

'*That's* what it is – she's standing like a horse!' whispered Interrupted at one point.

'They can sleep like that too, can't they – horses, I mean?' said Market – not quietly enough.

The Queen's eyes swivelled round. Without shifting her stance, she gave them an evil sidelong stare, drawing her lips back a little over her teeth.

It was the G who looked away first.

The hours wore on, the confusing images and unrevealing words passed before them as they bent anxiously over the disc and the weight of worry grew greater all the while.

Finally, according to the Tide Turn Calculating Device, time was almost up. The girl of the future led Eo and Adom back up to the surface, ready for the return of the Traveller – and still the G couldn't tell *what they had been given*!

'I'm sure we don't need to worry – even the most basic bit of kit from a time like that would do the trick,' said Interrupted.

'That's right. If the girl's understood *any* of what she's been told she'll realize how important it is,' said Hibernation. 'She seems bright enough . . .'

'I like the way she's done her hair,' murmured Interrupted.

'Are you kidding? She's practically *bald*!' snapped Market Jones. 'Anyway, that's *hardly* relevant!'

'No . . . but I do anyway. Like it, I mean.'

The tide was fully low again, and from where they were standing on the shore, the G could see the white line of the waves showing a long way off. The moon appeared and disappeared behind racing clouds, pushed by winds high in the sky. Down at the level of the beach, however, the air was dead, and the giant vortex still made its presence felt.

Market Jones's head ached. He moved away from the fire and stared into the night, needing to think, needing to make up his mind what he should do. The others had both had suggestions about what time he should aim the Traveller at, and whether champions, equipment or wisdom was what the lad needed most if he were to stand even a *chance* of saving them all. His own inclination was to have another try at finding a hero or heroine who could take over the mission – practically *anyone* would do – anyone with more credentials than a sixth-century nearly novice and a G child who clearly didn't have the sense he was born with. How hard could it *be*, finding someone to fit that bill?

The Western Isles had produced any number of fighters, over the ages, who had routinely made short work of encroaching demons. It had to be so – otherwise the fabric between the worlds would have been ripped to shreds long, long ago. It *had* to be possible that they were going to win. It *had* to be. Didn't it?

'Interesting, don't you think,' the Queen's voice sounded in his ear, 'how every age has its weapons against us, and yet – *we're still here.*'

Market lurched back with a strangled squawk. She was so *sneaky* – he hadn't heard her coming at all! 'What – have you found a way to read my mind?!' He tried to make it sound like a joke. He didn't really succeed.

The Queen didn't answer, but her teeth glinted briefly

in a bit of moonlight before the clouds obscured it again. It was still covered when the Traveller reappeared and sped to her hand, flying like a white ghost through the darkness. Market braced himself for tricks, but the Queen made the handover at once in a way that was almost tender.

'She's psyching him out,' murmured Interrupted, watching from beside the fire. 'Shouldn't we help?'

'I'm right, aren't I?' the Queen was saying. 'All those champions, all those eons, and what have you achieved? You haven't won yet. You aren't looking at all likely to win now. We're always there, just out of reach, just around the corner, ready to come in the instant your back's turned. You'll never win. Never.'

The Traveller in his hands was becoming heavier and heavier with each word. Market could feel his courage seeping away and his worst fears gaining strength. There was only so long you could hold off despair with jokes and smart-aleck remarks. There was only so long . . . what *was* that noise?

It was the government of his people.

The Head of the G and the Designated Companion were *dancing*, prancing about the fire like happy idiots, singing, 'I say I say I say!' When they were sure of their audience's attention, they stopped and turned to face one other.

'Did you hear the one about the two G who walked into a bar?' said Hibernation.

'No – tell me the one about the two G who walked into a bar,' said Interrupted.

'Two G walked into a bar,' said Hibernation. 'The third one ducked.'

'Ah, but what do you get if you cross a shape-shifter and a blender?' said Interrupted.

'I don't know – what *do* you get if you cross a shape-shifter and a blender?' said Hibernation.

'A G Whiz!' shrieked Interrupted.

'OK, but where does a G keep his armies?' countered Gladrag.

'I don't know – where *does* a G keep his armies?'

'Up his sleevies!' said the Head of the G.

'Boom-boom,' said Interrupted.

Market couldn't help himself – he started to snigger. Then he caught sight of the outraged expression on the Kelpie Queen's face and he burst out laughing . . .

Hibernation scooped up the Calculating Device, took one look at the dial and cried, '*Now!*'

Market Jones made his throw with a light heart and a smile.

Inside the Traveller . . .

I want to scream – why can't I scream? – am I screaming? – just a bad patch – hang on, then – everybody knows, you just wait out a bad patch – they don't last forever – everybody knows that – just a bad patch – just a bad . . .

8 *The Third Tide*

Two figures stumbled along the rough coastline, scratched by gorse, tripped up by heather roots and hidden rabbit holes. Were they lost? No more than most of the other English soldiers combing the west coast of Scotland for the rebel prince. Were they deserters? Not necessarily. By chance or by choice, it was easy to become separated from your regiment when the mists came down or the thick woods hid one red jacket from the next. Were they bounty hunters? Of course. Since the collapse of the Glorious Rebellion, Bonnie Prince Charlie was the prize every foot soldier dreamed about – but short of that, any Scot would do.

Dead or alive.

At the end of this particular day, the two men made themselves a camp in the lee of some rocks by the shore. The dark night pressed in around them as they dozed, waking from time to time to feed the fire. The hours passed. There were no stars to be seen, and the moon appeared and disappeared behind flying clouds.

'Smells like rain,' grunted one, as he tried to get more comfortable.

'It always smells like rain,' grumbled the other. 'God's Teeth, I hate this place.'

That was when they heard the noise from the beach. The two men were instantly on their feet. They reached for their muskets and, peering intently into the blackness, began to load.

They crept away from the fire. As they came closer to the pebbly beach, the noise separated out into voices, complaining bitterly, and the sound of someone being sick. Whoever the newcomers were, they were making no attempt to be stealthy. It was hard for the soldiers not to make a lot of noise themselves on the pebbles of the shore, but their prey wasn't paying attention, and the rain had also arrived, helping to mask the sound of their approach.

'Oh, that's *all* we needed – that's *perfect*! First we go on the world's worst excuse for a holo-ride and then we get dumped out in the dark in some smelly mud and *then* – it rains! But of course – what was I thinking? It *always* rains on amazing adventures. So why can't we have an adventure indoors? At least it doesn't *rain* indoors . . .' The voice was young and shrill, like a girl's. '*And* I landed awkwardly and it feels like at least two pockets' worth of stuff is broken already!' she wailed.

'Oh, shut up,' said another voice. 'You were the one who insisted on coming! Anyway, it's worse for Adom – at least the Traveller doesn't make you sick every time.'

'He wasn't sick last time,' grumbled the girl.

'Yes, I was,' said a third voice. 'Your machine, um, dealt with it.'

'I suggest heading for some dry land!' Yet another voice, chirpy and odd. 'Off we go!'

The soldiers crouched down behind some rocks, judging the progress of their quarry by the sounds of squelching, stumbling and complaining.

'See? What did I tell you? The torch is broken.'

'Are you sure you saw a fire? *I* don't see a fire.'

'Yes, I'm sure – it was up there under the trees. You can't see it from here because the rocks are in the way.'

'I'm *soaked*!'

'Let's try not to scare them, whoever they are. We want to be making friends here, remember.'

'*Now!*' hissed one of the soldiers.

Just as they leapt out, the clouds parted and the shore was lit up in the harsh glare of the moon. It glinted on musket barrels as the two men yelled, 'In the name of the King!'

Three white faces swung round in astonishment and someone screamed. Then everything was happening too fast – the muskets swung wildly and at the same time something detached itself from one of the children and leapt through the air, shrieking like a fiend from hell. The soldiers reeled back, yelling, and the muskets flowered into a roar and a flash, once, twice. The first shot whined and sent up a stinging spurt of sand; the second made a thud. The devil became an army of sharp-toothed demons attacking the soldiers, biting and screeching and inflicting sudden excruciating pain on legs, ears, hands. In fear for their souls as well as their lives, the men dropped everything and crashed away into the night, the devil on their tails.

At first there was nothing. Then Eo shifted, just a fraction, and the pain took him over. It grabbed him in its mouth and shook him savagely, back and forth, again and again, so that he couldn't find room to breathe, and then couldn't remember *how* to breathe. And then stopped breathing completely. The pain kept on at him, battering, savaging, but gradually it didn't seem to matter any more. *Breathing*, he thought, *that's the key. That's what does it. If you don't breathe, it can't hurt you*. Eo felt mildly pleased with himself for working that out, and then that feeling ebbed away as well and there was only . . .

Adom could see Jay on her knees, whimpering, and Eo seemed to have fallen over in the excitement.

'Jay?' Adom said. 'Are you all right?'

He sounded strange to himself and there were after-lights blurring in his eyes that made it hard to see. He'd never been so close to a lightning strike before, though he'd heard stories.

'Are you injured?' He started to stumble towards her.

'No . . . What? . . . I need some light.' *Her* voice sounded strange too. 'My torch is broken. Get me a stick from their fire – a burning stick. So I can see . . .'

Adom was pretty sure the blurry light thing would pass off soon, but he didn't fancy an argument with her just then. He went to do as he was told.

*

Jay's mind was racing.

She'd heard the thud as the musket ball hit Eo in the chest and the tiny gasp of surprise he made as he was flung on to his back. There was a Medi-kit in one of her pockets, as long as it wasn't broken too, and there was medical information in her implant – but she was too shocked to think how to make use of either.

Exit wound. Exit wound. Where had she learned about exit wounds? she wondered wildly. Must have been some old movie. *I know it's important . . .*

The last thing she wanted in the world was to touch him, but she did it anyway. As gently as she could, she levered him on to his side – but it was too dark to see anything properly with the moon half-hidden in cloud again, and his clothes were all soaked with seawater anyway, so how could she tell if there was something else staining his shirt, if there was blood?

I need light.

Where was Adom? And where was the wretched weasel when she needed him? He was the closest thing they had to an adult in this crazy outfit, but he seemed to have completely disappeared into the darkness. Gone mad, like everything else.

She heard Adom coming back with a sort of torch. He squatted down, looking into Eo's face.

'Not *that* side! Hold the light *here*, so I can *see*,' she said, sounding brusquer than she meant.

'Oh, Jay,' he said. His voice was hushed and hoarse, but he moved over to where she wanted him. 'Did the lightning . . .?'

'What? What are you talking about?' Then she realized that of course he had no idea about guns. In his time they just hacked at each other with spears and axes and things. He was hardly going to be much help.

But at least he'd brought her some light. It flickered and spat and cast shadows, but it did the job.

If exit wounds were important to have, Eo was all set. The hole in his back was clear to see.

Adom held the torch closer. 'What are you looking for?' he whispered.

'The bullet – the thing that hit him – we have to make sure all of it came out OK, because if bits stay in his body it'll make him ill . . . There it is . . .'

She dug a metal ball out of the coarse sand. It was coated in blood. She looked at it stupidly, unable to think what to do with it now, unable to do anything else.

'But how could such a little thing have killed him?'

How to explain? 'It's not the bullet just by itself that does it – it's the force it's shot at, out of the . . .' She'd only just heard what he said. 'Killed? Who's killed?'

'Eo. He's dead.'

'Dead? What do you mean?' She seemed incapable of understanding what he was saying.

Adom pushed her gently aside and laid Eo on his back again. 'I mean he's not breathing any more, and his soul has left his body. Look at his face. See? He's not there.'

There was a rustle from the darkness, and Hurple stepped slowly into the light from Adom's torch. There were red stains round his muzzle and his sides heaved in and out. He looked at Eo and screamed.

It was like the cry of a banshee and the sound grated across their nerves.

'*Stop it!*' whimpered Jay.

With a huge effort, Hurple pulled himself together.

'This is bad,' he panted. 'It's very, very bad. But not as bad . . . as you think . . . the boy's dead . . . but only here . . . and only now . . .'

He turned his back on them, fighting to regain control. Adom and Jay looked at each other in confusion, too stunned to even begin to reach towards hope. At last the ferret was able to continue.

'I'm sorry. I shouldn't have lost it like that. For a minute there I forgot where we were – what we are in the midst of. It's not as bad as it looks. I know this is strange, but then it's *all* strange, isn't it? The Rules hold, however. Whatever happens is only good for one Tide. Eo is dead, but only for the duration of this Tide. The next Tide is a clean slate.'

There was a short, incredulous pause.

'You're trying to tell us he's going to come back to life?!' shrilled Jay. 'You're trying to tell us he's dead but *he's going to get better*?!'

'That's the Rules.'

'But . . . I found *this*!' Jay held out her hand, with the bloodstained ball on it. 'I was looking for exit woun–' She choked up completely then and, dropping the ball, stumbled blindly away up the beach.

Hurple nudged the thing with his nose and shuddered. 'So this is what the Tide has given him. Pick it up, will you,' he said to Adom, 'and put it safe in his bag.' He drew a deep breath that sounded very like a sob.

'Unless . . . it's death he was given,' said Adom in a low voice as he stowed the bullet in Eo's bag. 'They gave him *that* – and freely.'

Hurple shook his head. 'No, because he won't be

taking it with him when we move on. He'll be leaving that behind.' He looked up at the boy. 'You'll have to trust me on this, even though it's not very *likely*.'

Adom stared numbly at him. 'Didn't he say before that he could heal himself? Except for those sores on his arm – that normally his people could *do* that?'

Hurple shook his head. 'Not when they die. It doesn't work like that. He can't heal if he's not *consciously* doing it.' He took a deep breath and tried to speak reassuringly. 'Come on, lad – you believe in the resurrection, don't you? That's all that's happening here. It's just a question of timing.'

'Then why did you attack those men and chase them halfway to Loch Ness?'

Hurple bristled along the whole length of himself.

'*Nobody* shoots at *my* boy,' he said, showing his teeth.

'Do you think they'll come back?' asked Adom.

'They wouldn't dare,' Hurple said flatly.

Adom nodded. It didn't even occur to him to find this statement absurd. The bigness of the Professor's personality quickly blinded everyone around him to the smallness of his body.

'Would you like me to pray for him now?'

Hurple cleared his throat, a little ferrety cough of emotion. 'Thank you. You're a good lad. I'll go and see to Jay meantime.'

After praying for a while, Adom got off his knees and went up towards the tree line, where the soldiers' fire was. It had almost burned itself out, but he salvaged the branches that were still glowing and bought them back to where Eo lay. Then he returned and collected the men's gathered wood. He built up a fire near the boy's body. All the time he was working, he was aware of Hurple's voice, rising and falling in counterpoint to Jay's tearful protests and disbelief. He didn't know just what finally made it through her distress, but something the ferret was saying to her did.

'You must be getting cold – come to the fire,' he called.

Hurple came first, and Jay followed reluctantly. She was rubbing angrily at her face, as if ashamed of her swollen eyes and blotchy cheeks. She reminded him suddenly of one of his sisters, who always hated it if anyone saw her cry. He was hit with a completely unexpected stab of homesickness so strong it made him gasp.

'What are you staring at?!' Jay snapped. She plonked herself down as close to the fire as she could get without setting herself alight, and hugged herself hard. 'This is a *lousy* adventure. In fact it isn't an adventure at all – it's a disaster! It's a fiasco! It's a . . . mess!'

Adom began to fiddle with his wrist computer. 'A calamity. A catastrophe. A bad patch,' he murmured. 'The Slough of Despond . . .'

'So you've found the thesaurus mode. Big deal. It doesn't mean you're all of a sudden smart.' The girl glared at him.

'Now, children!' said Hurple in a warning voice. 'Don't squabble.'

Jay turned on him. 'And you're not all of a sudden my mother!' she snapped.

'How true,' the ferret murmured sympathetically. 'But never mind.'

Jay caught Adom's eye and couldn't help bursting out laughing. It was a nervous reaction to all the tension, and the idea of the Professor as *anybody's* mother was just so ludicrous . . .

'Look, I'm sorry I said you were stupid, Adom. You're not – you're a better class than me altogether, and I guess I'm just jealous.'

'But I *am* stupid – Brother Drostlin tells me that ten times a day. Even the Holy Father thinks so. I can't . . . read or write and I have been trying for *months*.' His voice sank low.

'Well, of course not,' said Jay. 'No D's going to be able to lay down the connections in *that* length of time, not by themselves, no matter what system you use. What system *does* your teacher use, by the way?'

'Shout and hit?' said Adom with a shrug.

Jay stared at him for a moment. Then, 'Give me your arm,' she said.

Wordlessly, Adom stuck out his arm, the one with the pink no-longer-all-that-fluffy wrist strap.

Jay tapped in a combination, twisting his arm round a bit to get some light on to the readout panel and then nodded.

'Not yet, but not long now,' she said. 'And *definitely* before you see that bully again. The patterners are laying down pathways in your brain steadily, without you feeling a thing, and once they're there, if he tries to make out you can't read or write, *you* can hit *him*. Hard.'

Adom's eyes shone in the firelight. 'It's not just saints, then, who do miracles,' he said.

Jay coloured, and threw another branch on to the flames.

'Right. Well. What do we do now, Professor?' she asked.

'We wait. There's nothing more we can do,' he said.

'OK. That's what I thought.' She nodded. 'But this is a campfire, and if we're sitting around a campfire, then we should be telling stories. Everybody knows that. Folk wisdom and all that. You first, Professor – tell us some stories.'

'Tell us some stories about Eo,' said Adom quietly.

Jay looked across at him. 'Yes,' she said. 'That would be right, wouldn't it? Let's talk about Eo.'

And so they did. The living sat on one side of the fire and the dead lay on the other. It was as if no one wanted to sit with their back to his body, not from fear so much as not wanting to exclude him.

'Tell us about the first time you met him,' said Jay.

Hurple rubbed his nose with a paw. 'Well, of course, I knew *about* him from when he was born, but I never spend time with the babies. I prefer a creature I can converse with. But I think the first time I really became *aware* of Eo was when he was still pretty small. I noticed this little figure skulking about in the bushes. He dodged behind rocks. He snuck behind trees. Finally, I just had to know. "What are you *doing?*" I asked. And he looked up at me with those big eyes and he whispered, "Shhh. Don't tell. I'm the shadow of the doubt."'

He was met by blank expressions.

'He must have heard somebody say it, see, "the shadow of a doubt", and he didn't know what it really meant, so he decided it must mean . . . I guess you had to be there,' he concluded lamely.

'Right,' said Jay. 'OK.' She turned to Adom. 'What did *you* think, Adom, when you first saw him? Were you completely amazed, or did you think he was just some guy?'

Adom shook his head. 'No, I'd have to say I was more disappointed than amazed. When I first saw Eo, I thought he was supper.'

'What?!'

'I thought he was a dead seal. Or possibly a baby whale. I thought "Meat!" and "Feast!"' Adom grinned sheepishly.

'You greedy little . . .!'

'Well? What did you think when *you* first saw him?'

Jay blushed. 'None of your business . . .' she began, and then she laughed. 'All right, all right. I thought he was beautiful – I mean, his *hair* – I thought his *hair* was beautiful. You can't argue with that. Everybody agrees about the hair.'

Hurple and Adom nodded solemnly.

'Were you his only teacher, Professor?' Jay asked next.

'Oh no. G children have many different tutors, each with a separate speciality. We'd get together, though, and compare notes on our pupils. Eo certainly got mentioned quite a lot.' Hurple gave a wicked little grin. 'For a while there, he had his own nickname among the tutors. He was still very young, you see, and hadn't quite mastered the art of blowing his nose properly. But he was already adept at sliding out from responsibility for, well, *anything*, so we called him – perhaps I shouldn't be telling you this . . .'

'You can't not *now*!' exclaimed Jay.

'You really can't,' agreed Adom. 'What did you call him?'

'Oh well, all right. We called him "Snot my fault" – and

if you ever tell him that I'll pierce your ears for you with my teeth!'

Jay and Adom swore they would *never* betray him – and then asked for more stories.

'There was the time he handed in a note to one of his tutors, explaining why he hadn't done an assignment. It was four pages long, in rhyming couplets and iambic pentameter, and spoke at length on numerous figures from history who had also not handed things in on time, and ended with a vivid description of the alien green-eyed cat who had, in fact, ripped up all his notes and used them for litter.

'It must have taken him *hours* longer to do than the actual assignment would have.' Hurple shook his head fondly. 'I think we were all a bit jealous he hadn't written that note for *us*. There was a bit of a competition going as to who could collect the most exotic excuse from our Eo. He never stinted, and that's for certain.'

Adom put some more wood on the fire and, as the sparks flew up, Hurple added quietly, 'I'll tell you the truth about that boy . . . he's the most G person I have ever met.'

There was a silence after that for a while.

As the cold wet night wore on, they talked some more about Eo – Jay was particularly fascinated by his repertoire of homework excuses – and then without noticing they were talking about themselves, not Hurple so much, but the girl from the future and the boy from the past. And as the tide rose, and the night sky lightened towards morning, the ferret watched them turning from strangers into friends and allies.

9 *The Throw of Lackey One*

It'd been a frustrating night for Market Jones.

There was the wet, for one thing. It rained, on and off, pretty much the whole time. Gladrag and Cadence dealt with the discomfort by shifting into seals, with well-insulated bodies and waterproof fur. Since nothing seemed to be happening, they napped a good deal, which was sensible. Market Jones knew that sleep would have to be snatched whenever possible, or by the end of the Seven Tides they would all be too exhausted to think straight. But it was difficult not to resent his companions just a little, as they lay there, warm, snug and snoozing in bodies that made admirable sense. There was probably nothing in the Rules preventing *him* from shifting, yet somehow it didn't seem right. It had been *his* throw – this was *his* Tide. His responsibility. So as the long night passed, Market kept watch over the viewing disc in his human form, getting wetter and colder and more fed up with each hour that passed.

The Kelpie Queen seemed to have no problem with the rain. Occasionally she would shudder her skin, the way horses do, and the wet would fly off. But mostly she just ignored it. She may even have been *enjoying* the chilly drizzle – certainly, *something* had tickled her fancy, for she was grinning relentlessly, and Jones was sure he heard her chuckling from time to time.

Nothing he could see in their viewing disc was making *him* feel any better. In fact, there was very little *to* see and even less to hear.

'I swear she's given us a defective disc,' he muttered, more than once.

There was some sporadic moonlight but the rain and clouds here at the G beach seemed to be just as heavy in the place where Eo was. And all the moonlight *did* show, was nothing. Nothing happening. The boy just *lay* there!

'What does he think he's *doing*?!' he fumed to himself. 'Young people nowadays have no get up and go.'

There *had* been a bit of excitement right near the beginning, with some sort of flashing light display. They'd all been watching then. That was when the sound shut down.

'It'll sort itself out in a minute,' Hibernation Gladrag predicted confidently.

It hadn't.

'Should we ask *her*?' Interrupted Cadence tilted his head at the Kelpie Queen. 'Maybe she could fix it?'

She hadn't. Even though they'd asked politely.

'No sound?' she said. 'How irksome. But then these things do happen. Things die . . .'

It seemed an odd way to talk about technical difficulties.

What did she know that they didn't? They hung around for a bit, in the faint hope she might offer to share *her* disc, but the invitation wasn't forthcoming. So the rest of the night was spent in sleeping by Hibernation Gladrag and Interrupted Cadence, and in grumbling, getting wet and feeding the fire by Market Jones.

The dawn was only a suggestion in the sky when the turn of the tide came at last. Market stood up stiffly and tried to stretch some of the kinks out of his back. The others lolloped over to him and then morphed upwards into human shape.

'Your robes are wet,' said Market shortly. 'Everything's wet.'

'The sun will dry us all out in a while,' said Hibernation in her placating voice. 'And then *you* can try and catch some sleep.'

'Has anything changed? Anything happen?' asked Interrupted as he pulled the robe over his head while simultaneously trying not to let any of the cold, wet material touch his skin.

'*No.*' Market practically spat the word.

Gladrag was alternately checking the Tide Turn Calculating Device and peering into the viewing disc. 'Shouldn't he be getting up by now?' she said, sounding worried. 'I know boys that age sleep a lot, but this is hardly the time . . .'

'He's not *sleeping*. He's dead.' The Queen left her disc and slinked over to the G.

They stared at her, unable to speak.

'Of course he's dead. Surely you must have noticed he wasn't *moving* very much?!'

'We thought he was asleep!' blurted Interrupted.

'And the shooting? You didn't notice those flashing lights? At the beginning of the Tide? What did you think *that* was?' The Queen was basking in the horror on their faces.

'I can't believe it!'

'But – does that mean . . .?'

'No, no – it's just for the duration of the Tide. He's only dead *then*, not any other time,' said Hibernation.

'The poor child –'

'Did he suffer?'

'Another Tide wasted. Such a pity,' oozed the Queen.

Gladrag was just about to blow her diplomatic credentials by tearing a strip off visiting monarchy – when the Traveller suddenly flicked into sight again, ricocheted off the crest of a wave and raced towards the beach.

'Steady!' she warned.

'Look out!' yelped Interrupted.

'*Gotcha!*' cried Market Jones triumphantly. He landed flat on his stomach on the sand with his arms stuck out and the Traveller wobbling precariously between his two hands. The dive-catch may have lacked elegance, but it did the trick. Interrupted and Hibernation broke into a spontaneous round of applause.

Market grinned over at them and was about to struggle to his feet – but the Queen had other plans. With a contemptuous snap of her fingers, she summoned the miniature vortex and it leapt obediently from the G's hands to land on her outstretched palm.

'HEY!' yelled Market Jones. He scrambled upright. 'I *caught* that!'

'Is *she* throwing again?' gasped Interrupted.

'Now just a minute,' Hibernation began to protest. 'It's not your turn, for one thing, and for another thing, my Device says it's not absolute Tide Turn yet, and for *another* other thing . . .'

But the Queen ignored them all. She stalked over to the main vortex and, with one long, clawed finger, pointed into the heart of the maelstrom.

The G *knew* that anything coming from the vortex would be evil. They knew it absolutely. Yet it seemed unbelievable that the being who stepped out of it now could possibly have *anything* to do with fear or pain. He was . . . lovely. He stood, head bowed, as if deep in thought – and it would not have occurred to even the most cynical observer that he was posing, making sure there was time for him to be seen. He was fine-boned, slim, elegant, with skin so pale it was almost blue. His hair crackled about his head like thin ice round the edges of a winter pond. The three G found themselves swept with the same irresistible attraction Eo had felt at first sight of the Kelpie Queen. He was just too beautiful to be bad. This must be the one Kelpie with the heart of gold, the one led astray in his youth, ready – desperate! – to change sides, to be redeemed . . .

And then he raised his head and looked across at them, sidelong, with an expression in his black eyes so malign it made them shudder and gasp.

The Queen gave her hateful chuckle and flicked the Traveller negligently in the Kelpie's direction, like a treat to a dog. It landed precisely on a shapely, outstretched hand – and immediately changed. Its surface showed strangely crystalline now, and it made a brittle, crackling noise as it spun. When the Kelpie threw it into the air, the first rays of the sun caught it and it sparked for the briefest instant like cold diamond . . . then it dropped into the waves at no great distance from the shore and was gone.

When they looked back, the Queeen had already sent the beautiful Kelpie away. He walked gracefully to the main vortex – to it, and then straight on *into* it. The whirling wall took him and it was as though he'd never been there at all.

For a moment the three G didn't speak. Nobody wanted to say how enthralled they'd felt. Then Market shrugged.

'Wouldn't have worked,' he grunted. 'My mother would never approve of me dating somebody prettier than she is.'

The others grinned sheepishly.

'Right,' said Gladrag. She turned her back on the Queen, who was still staring at them. 'Is this disc of ours working yet?'

At first, there was nothing . . . then the view cleared – and there was sound!

'Look – I can see him!' she crowed. 'He's talking!'

'Thank goodness – the boy's alive again!' said Interrupted.

'But where *are* they?' Market fussed. 'It looks like a flipping *Ice Age!*'

'It *is* a flipping Ice Age,' said Hibernation quietly.

The others looked over at her, bemused, but before they could ask any questions, they saw the expression on her face change.

'Who *is that?* What's that pointy thing? Not another *weapon!*'

The three G drew back in horror. From her position by her own disc, the Queen gave a low, triumphant, whinnying laugh.

'Dead *again*!' she shrilled.

'Wait! Not yet! Listen!' Market turned to Gladrag urgently. 'Is that who I think it is? Big eyebrows, furs, pointy sticks? The grunty stuff? Come on, girl, is any of this familiar to you?'

Gladrag's eyes went wide. 'It's been a while . . .' she said.

'LISTEN!'

Hibernation bent right down over the disc, listening and watching intently. She stayed that way for so long, the Kelpie Queen's suspicions erupted again and she stalked over to them.

'What are you doing? You're only allowed to observe – you're not allowed to interfere –'

Gladrag lifted her head and smiled sweetly at the agitated demon.

'Interfere? Why should I want to interfere? They've just made Hurple a god!'

'WHAT?!' chorused two G and a royal Kelpie.

'Just how did *that* happen?!' yelped Market.

Gladrag seemed to be having trouble keeping a straight face. 'Well, apparently,' she said, 'the Ferret for "*impertinent bipeds*" is made up of syllables that sound remarkably like some of those used by Neanderthals.'

'So . . . they were so impressed by a ferret who could say, "*Ugh. Look. Eat.*" they decided to deify him on the spot?'

'Well, no. That's not exactly what they think he said.'

'What *did* they think he said, then?' yelled Market.

'Er, a rough translation would be, "*Worship me or die*."'

There was a short pause.

'That'll do it,' murmured Interrupted.

The Queen swore in frustration and stomped away.

'Well, *this* is going to be interesting!' said Gladrag, turning back to the viewing disc with quite some satisfaction.

'But, Gladrag . . . can I ask . . . how do you know this stuff?' Interrupted leaned closer to her and asked in a quiet voice. 'How do *you* know about *Neanderthals*?!'

Hibernation looked embarrassed. 'Long story,' she muttered. 'Tell you some other time.'

And with that, Interrupted Cadence had to be content.

Inside the Traveller . . .

In the whirling dark, there was no Pinkerton Hurple, no Professor of Human Studies. There was no store of knowledge or human memories. There was no gift of tongues, acquired over time.

In the whirling dark, there was no time, only a small animal, with a small animal's infinite capacity for fear . . .

10 *The Fourth Tide*

The surface of the sea showed like a great slushy soup in the chill light of dawn, the half-frozen water dragged sluggishly back and forth by a setting moon. The narrow shore was littered with ice-slick rocks. Steep hills, their tops obscured by a cloud of freezing fog, came down almost to the water's edge. A valley split them, where a river had cut its way to the sea.

When the Traveller emerged out of nowhere and dumped its payload, Adom and Jay were holding Eo upright on either side, and Hurple clung to the boy's neck. The G sagged like a dead weight between them. They lowered him on to the cold ground, and Jay slumped down beside him and started to wail, while Adom turned aside and was sick. Hurple climbed on to his pupil's chest and peered anxiously into his face.

He was willing the boy's eyes to open – he was *expecting* the boy's eyes to open – but that didn't stop him from falling over backwards and landing on the ground when the boy's eyes *did* open!

Eo pushed himself up on his elbows and shook his head muzzily.

'What's all the noise about?' he complained. 'Why is it so *cold*?!'

The shock of seeing Eo really, actually, truly alive again was enormous. It wasn't that Jay and Adom hadn't *believed* Hurple when he said the death was only temporary, not *exactly* – it was just, well, something else altogether to *see* Eo sitting there with his eyes open, blinking and breathing and *everything*!

Hurple let his own joy show by jumping up and down on all four legs at once, only to discover he was jumping in a puddle of ice water. With a yelp, he bounded out and shook himself, hard. In the frigid air, the Professor's wet fur froze almost instantly into spikes, so that he looked like a long, skinny, bad-hair day, all over. He was cursing in fluent Ferret, but at the sound of his companions' giggling, he switched to furious Human.

'What are you sniggering at?!' he snarled. 'What's so funny, eh? Eh?!'

The laughter stopped abruptly.

Hurple humphed, surprised, but gratified. 'That's better,' he said. 'That's more like it. That's –'

He trailed off. It was becoming clear to him that he didn't have the young people's complete attention. With a sudden feeling of dread, he turned slowly round . . . and saw a dozen stone-tipped spears levelled at Eo, Adom and Jay.

'Not *again*!' the ferret moaned.

As fast as his frozen fur would let him, he ran over and swarmed up Eo's legs, shedding tiny icicles as he went. From the boy's shoulder, the ferret opened his mouth, showed all his sharp little teeth and snarled – and the response was pretty dramatic.

The spears were instantly lowered; the spear-wielders dropped to their knees; and (in a language Hurple had learned from Hibernation Gladrag, who had acquired her knowledge from a rather embarrassing escapade in her younger life which she didn't like to talk about) their leader said to Eo,

'I am TakK. Tell the god we heard his words and do not wish to die. Tell him we *will* worship him.'

Three human types and a ferret gulped audibly.

As soon as it was clear there was no immediate danger of bloodshed, Jay had a quick whispering session with Hurple, pressed a combination of keys on her implant (her computer's knowledge came from the astonishing advances in archaeology over the centuries, which made it possible to recreate an entire language base from studying the insides of fossilized skulls), waited a moment and then transferred the language download to Adom's still-pink but rather bedraggled wrist computer.

'What *are* they?' whispered Adom to her anxiously.

'They're Neanderthals,' said Jay. 'Which means they don't live in houses, which means we get another Tide's worth of being *outdoors* with no thermostatic control *whatsoever*.' She was shivering hard. 'I'm downloading everything we know of their language for you now. I'm not surprised that thing you're wearing doesn't have it – not a lot of call for Ice Age lingo for the kiddies.'

Adom looked confused. 'Um?'

'It's an Ice Age – as in, it's cold and it lasted an age. And the Neanderthal people lived in one.'

The spear-holders, who had gone into a whispering huddle of their own, were . . . different. Even the tallest was quite a bit shorter than any of their visitors (with the exception of the Professor) and they were also a lot stockier. They were wearing clothes made of skins, and one of them had the bodies of some dead animals over his shoulder, which suggested this was a hunting party. They were all well blessed with hair, and also with an over-abundance of forehead.

Adom had never seen anything like them before. 'They're . . . *people*?' he exclaimed, louder than he meant.

'Shhh!' hissed Jay angrily. 'Don't be so rude!'

Adom blushed scarlet, but the Neanderthals showed no sign of having heard what he'd said.

'Yes, they're people.' Hurple answered his question. 'They're the strand of humans your lot are going to displace.'

Adom drew closer and whispered behind his hand, 'I don't *understand* – if they're people, why do they *look* like that?'

'Cold adaptations,' said Hurple.

'What?'

'It's quite a sensible design when you think about it. Short, well-built bodies retain heat better than tall, skinny ones. Big noses have a better chance than little ones of heating up cold air before it hits the lungs, helping keep up vital core temperature.'

Adom didn't argue, but he didn't look completely convinced either. 'And the huge eyebrows?' he asked.

'Sex appeal.'

'No wonder they died out,' snorted Eo.

'Eo!' Jay glared at him. 'Shut up!'

Adom shook his head. 'This doesn't make any sense. How can they be people and die out? If people died out, then there wouldn't be a me or an, an *anybody*!'

'Watch it!' warned Jay. 'They're coming over!'

'If the god will follow us?' It was TakK, the leader, speaking again.

Hurple gave Eo a nudge with his nose. 'Tell him that will be acceptable.'

'*You* speak Neanderthal – *he* speaks Neanderthal – why don't *you* tell him?!' Eo muttered crossly.

Hurple leaned over and delicately took a bit of Eo's ear between his teeth. He didn't exert any pressure. He didn't need to.

'OK, OK – good reason – let go – I'll do it!'

TakK received the god's message through the mouth of his slave, bowed and started inland, up the river valley.

'He doesn't actually *look* at you – did you notice?' whispered Jay. 'He doesn't talk directly to you and he doesn't look directly *at* you.'

'Well, it's understandable,' said Hurple, preening. 'I *am* pretty divine, I must say.'

'Yeah, right,' said Jay.

The hunting party set a cracking pace that left the three non-Neanderthals panting. There was no more than the suggestion of a track clinging to the edge of the river, and as they headed further up the valley into the hills, it didn't get any smoother. While the hunters practically ran up the icy incline, the children stumbled and scrambled and clung to each other on the slipperiest bits.

Over the roar of the water, Jay said breathlessly, 'They must think *we* look pretty weird. Shouldn't they be completely freaked by us?'

Hurple shook his head. 'No, they've seen people like you and Adom and . . . you and Adom before. *Homo sapiens sapiens* – that's your lot – are already about at this time, though not yet much of a threat. The Neanderthals may not think you're very pretty, of course, but they aren't bothered by you. Anyway, gods can choose any slaves they wish, and as long as they think I chose you, you should be quite safe!'

'Your *slaves*?!' Eo exclaimed.

'Well, if it keeps them from poking us with those spear things, I for one am happy in my slavery, O Great God of All Weasels,' Jay said.

'You carry him, then,' snapped Eo.

Hurple gave him an odd look and shook his head again. 'No, I don't think so. I think I need to keep you especially close. They may not be bothered by Adom or Jay, but I have a feeling they don't know *what* to make of you!'

Eo muttered something under his breath the others didn't catch, and slogged on up the valley.

They had climbed to the level of the fog-cloud now. Ice particles spangled their hair and eyelashes, and every out-breath added to the opacity of the air. The sound of voices hardly travelled at all, and the four peered around them nervously in this alien landscape. General conversation stopped. Only Eo and Hurple were still able to talk to each other easily through the blanketing mist – and they continued to mutter the whole way. The

Professor seemed to be filling Eo in on what had been happening. Judging by the way Eo's voice rose from time to time, the others could tell he wasn't very happy with what he was hearing.

'*We didn't get anything better than that?! – What do you mean, I was dead?! – What were you all doing?! – This is the Fourth Tide already?!*'

Hurple kept having to shush him.

Then, unexpectedly, they found they had climbed above the layer of freezing fog into a world made sparkling by the slant rays of the rising sun. The valley widened out and the landscape became less rocky, with winter-bare bushes and further on a stand of trees. In spite of all the tension, the sudden brightness made them want to smile. The Neanderthals seemed more relaxed here as well and paused in their upward race.

TakK approached them and spoke to Eo: 'Ask the god to give us a little while to go ahead and announce his coming to our people.'

'A breather – great!' panted Jay.

'You may tell him we will wait here for his return,' Hurple intoned pompously.

'Yeah, right,' grunted Eo. But he passed on the message anyway, and the hunting party loped off again, into the trees and out of sight.

'This divinity business is really getting up my nose, you know that?' grumbled Eo. 'I can't believe we're wasting our time on this bunch – what on earth can *they* give us that'll help? They must be even stupider than they look if they think *you're* a god!'

There was a taut silence. Hurple climbed stiffly down on to the ground and stalked away from him.

Eo kicked at a stone and hunched his shoulders in the cold air. He pulled back one sleeve to scratch and saw the sores were still there.

'Not even being dead gets rid of those!' he snarled angrily, and covered them up again.

It was a moment before he noticed nobody else was talking. He looked round to see the others all staring at him.

'Well?' he grunted. 'What's the matter with you?'

Jay squared up to him aggressively. 'That's just what I'd like to ask *you*!' she said, hands on hips. 'What's the matter with *you*? Ever since you died you've been a real pain. Well, no, I guess I mean ever since you *stopped* being dead. You weren't too bad when you were, you know, *actually* dead.'

Eo glared at her for a long moment, and then suddenly seemed to go all boneless. He slumped to the ground and wrapped his arms round his knees. He buried his head and started muttering.

'What . . . ? We can't hear you,' said Adom.

'It's not my fault!' he lifted his head and wailed. 'It's *not*! And anyway – isn't being shot enough? Can't that be enough? Professor?'

'That's not how it works, boy,' said Hurple gently. 'You know that.'

'Tell us what's got to you, Eo,' urged Jay.

'What's *got* to me?! Do you know what Tide this is? Do you?' Eo croaked at her. He couldn't have looked more tragic.

'Yeah, um . . .' Jay frowned. 'It's –'

'It's the *fourth*! The Fourth Tide! That's four out of six, and no flipping miracle yet – not that I've noticed.

But hey, I might have missed something, on account of being dead for a while. But I didn't, did I? Four out of six and who's shown up to fix this mess? A couple of kids, a useless bit of ammunition, and now what? – We're trapped with a bunch of pea-brained Stone Age morons who are going to help us how? Lend us some pointy sticks?'

'Actually, Neanderthals had, on average, *larger* brains than a modern human's . . .' Hurple began.

'And *then* you tell me they're all just going to *die*. They're a *dead end*. So now I have to be upset about *them* too. And what if they're a dead end because of one person, like maybe that's what's happening to the G, and I'm the one person, and it IS my fault, and then I got sent to find help and I didn't even do *that* right . . .' He looked round, a stricken expression on his face. 'And now I've insulted you all and you should just walk away and leave me to die *properly*!'

'That's just stupid talk,' said Adom in a firm, authoritative voice. 'Dead man talk.'

There was a new confidence in his voice. Everyone turned and stared at him. Adom stared right back.

'Well, he was *dead*!' he said. 'That's not a *little* experience. Why should he just bounce straight back from that? He won't – not without help.' He spoke directly to Eo. 'We're going to surprise you, Eo. We're probably going to surprise ourselves at the same time. We're the *perfect* combination for a job like this – we've got a crazy shape-shifter who can't shift shapes – a *genius* not-quite-novice who's too thick to read – and a bald woman technical expert who's so far managed to break pretty much every bit of technology she's brought with her. And that's not even *mentioning* the services of a god. There is no possible fashion in which we can*not* succeed . . .

'Trust me – I'm practically a monk!'

'*Never trust anybody who starts a sentence with "Trust me"!*' Hurple and Jay chorused. And for the first time in far too long, Eo gave the beginnings of a proper smile.

Adom shoved Jay with his shoulder. 'Your turn,' he whispered.

'All right – all right!' She stuck out her tongue at him and then stepped forward, as if about to make a speech. 'Eo. When you were, you know, dead, back there in the other place, the weasel told us some stories about you.'

'What?!' Eo screwed up his face. It was obvious he wasn't too sure he liked the idea.

'Yeah. It was a bit like a wake, you know?' Jay started to sound defensive. 'What did you *want* us to do – put you on hold for an entire Tide? Just ignore you? *There's Eo – he's dead. Oh, really? Shame. What's for tea?*'

Eo wriggled his shoulders. 'No, I guess not. Not when you put it like that . . . So what did the Professor tell you about me, then?'

'He told us plenty of daft stuff, and stuff that was downright cute. And I took notes on some of the stunts you pulled to get out of doing homework! But there's one thing I think you really need to know, that Professor Weasel said about you.' She took a breath. 'He said you were probably the most G person he'd ever met. And when he said that, he stopped, as if there was nothing more that anybody needed to say.'

There was a moment of stunned silence. Eo stared at

her. 'Really?' he said in a hushed voice. 'He really did?' He turned to Hurple. 'You really did!?'

'Don't let it go to your head,' the ferret humphed. He looked embarrassed, a look that deepened when Eo picked him up and kissed him.

Adom leaned closer to Jay. '*The most G person* – what does that actually mean?' he whispered.

'*I* don't know,' she whispered back, 'and *you* don't know, but what matters is that it means something to *him*.'

'Yes . . . I think you're right,' Adom nodded solemnly. Then he gave her a big smile. 'I think we're getting him back from the dead at last.'

When TakK returned, he was accompanied by a number of old men who, in spite of being obviously ancient, still travelled over the rough ground like athletic mountain goats.

'Tribal elders,' murmured Hurple. 'They'll be coming to honour *me*, of course.'

There was indeed a lot of bowing going on once they got closer. Then the god's party was led on up the valley and into the trees. Not much further on, however, the Neanderthals turned off into a side-gully. After a short, steep scramble they came to a level forecourt, and there, leading into the heart of the hillside, was the entrance to a cave.

They had come out of the wind, which helped a little, and into a solid wall of stink, which didn't.

'Peughh – what *is* that?!' gasped Jay.

'Don't *you* start being rude now,' Hurple scolded out of the corner of his mouth. 'Just be grateful it's not summertime!'

Jay turned to him angrily. 'We're standing here freezing to death and you say be grateful?! Surely even in an Ice Age it must get a *bit* warmer in summer?'

'True. Quite a bit warmer . . . and quite a *lot* smellier. Use your imagination!'

They stepped closer and looked inside. Cave-proud would not be the first word you'd use to describe the tribe. There were piles of rubbish scattered about – discarded shells, cracked bones, other things that you wouldn't want to peer at too closely. In a time without weekly rubbish collections, a quick flick over your shoulder was the accepted technique.

And then there was the tribe itself – the cave was a large high space, full of Neanderthal men, women, babies and children.

Ferrets are not known as odourless beings, but TakK and his people could certainly give them a run for their money. It was partly the lack of personal hygiene routines and partly the animal skins they were wearing.

Still, none of their visitors said no when offered cloaks of some sort of deerskin. Even Jay wrapped herself up tight and just took shallow breaths. In fact, in a surprisingly short length of time she found she wasn't really *noticing* the smell any more *and* she was starting to warm up. The skin was an excellent insulator.

There was another of the pauses that marked their interactions with TakK's people. The Neanderthal men muttered together, and the women and children carefully didn't stare at the strange beings standing around awkwardly in their doorway.

'It looks like we have a minute here,' said Hurple briskly. 'Eo, get my things out of your bag. So much has happened, I really must make some notes, and there just haven't been a lot of peaceful moments . . .'

Eo got the bundle of papers out of his bag, where it had lain forgotten for so many hours, and put it down on a conveniently flat rock. The Professor immediately started pushing the pages about with his nose and chittering at them.

Adom's eyes practically popped out. He drew Eo aside. 'What in heaven's name is he *doing*?' he exclaimed.

'What – oh, that's his manuscript,' said Eo. 'It goes everywhere with him. I'd been carrying it around for him for weeks before all this started, in case he suddenly got an inspiration in the middle of a lesson.' He noticed the blank expression. 'He's writing a book.'

Adom frowned. 'Don't be ridiculous. He doesn't have hands!'

'Ah, but who says you need hands to write a book?' Eo wandered back to Hurple, looking irritatingly smug.

Adom scowled after him.

'What's up?' said Jay, who had missed their exchange. 'I thought we'd brought him back to the Land of Cheerful?'

'Oh, he's cheerful all right, the lying Know-All,' grunted Adom. 'Telling me the beast can *write*.' Brother Drostlin's voice suddenly forced its way into his head. *A beast could write better than that!* The words tasted as bitter as the first time he'd heard them said.

'Animals can't write,' said Jay confidently. 'No opposable thumb – therefore can't hold a pen – therefore can't write. Don't worry about it – he's having you on.'

'Of course he is. The rotten little . . .'

FAQ 1,499: Is the author of these pages **really** a ferret? If so, how can an animal who has no opposable thumb manage to hold a pen?

HURPLE'S REPLY: I could answer your question with something gnomic like, 'Ah, but I am no ordinary ferret' or 'There's more than one way to skin a rabbit.' But I'll restrain myself. The straight answer to the question is an ingenious invention of the G – who frequently find themselves similarly embarrassed in the opposable-thumbs department. And that is . . . **voice-activated paper.** Pure and simple. Because, as they say, 'There's more than one way . . .'

'Right,' said Jay with half a smile. 'Look, I know I was whingeing to have a roof over my head again, but now I think the price is too high, and so are these Neanderthals. I'm heading outside for a bit of fresh air. Want to come?'

'Yes.' Adom nodded his head vigorously. 'Yes, please!'

It wasn't long before Hurple had finished his note-taking and turned his eye to the meeting of elders. He gave a fake yawn and muttered to Eo out of the corner of his mouth, 'I'm going to pretend to go to sleep now – if I go to that rock over there, I'm pretty sure I can listen in on the old boys – see if they're talking about anything that might be of help to us.'

'Do divine beings eavesdrop?' Eo whispered back.

'What would you know – you're just a slave,' muttered Hurple. 'And I'm ordering you to go and make some friends. Remember, so far what we've been given has been pretty unexpected. No reason to think it'll be different this time!'

A ferret can move fast when he wants to. In under a blink, the Professor was across the floor and curled up on a stone at convenient eavesdropping distance from the meeting of men.

Eo grinned to himself, and then looked about for somebody to talk to. He noticed a boy sitting by himself in the entrance and decided to go over and say hello.

The boy had his back to the cave, presumably to get the best light for the thing he was bent over. It looked like a leg bone of some sort of animal.

'What's that you're making?' asked Eo politely.

The boy jumped and thrust the bone behind his back.

He was a good bit younger than Eo, though it wasn't that easy to tell.

These faces are impossible to read, thought Eo to himself, and then the boy smiled, and he changed his mind.

'It's a flute,' the boy said. 'Don't tell.'

Eo hunkered down beside him. 'I won't tell.' He poked a finger at the bone. 'Aren't you supposed to, um, make flutes?'

The boy shook his head, and glanced over his shoulder. 'This is bear,' he said, as if that explained it.

It didn't.

'Bear bone is not a good thing for flutes?' Eo said tentatively.

'No – bear is *wonderful* for flutes. The notes are beautiful, pure . . . wonderful! Just not wonderful for *us* to make flutes out of.' He looked at Eo, as if waiting for understanding to dawn. He was out of luck. 'My name is MakK. So it's not going to be *bear* bones my tribe makes flutes out of, is it?'

'My name's Eo. And I'm really not getting this,' Eo admitted.

It was MakK's turn to look puzzled.

'Your name is EoO?' he said. 'What tribe is "O"?' He made it sound like a grunt, rather than a letter.

'I'm not an "O" – I'm a G, though that's not a tribe, really . . .'

'"G"? What animal . . .?'

'No, the G aren't animals – I mean, they *can* be, but . . . Anyway, I'm still too young to, um, be an animal . . .'

Mutual confusions were piling up on each other by the minute. Eo tried again.

'What tribe did you say you belong to, MakK?' he asked.

'You just said it! kK! We are the Tribe of Deer.'

'Um . . .'

Exasperated, MakK looked about and then grabbed two broken bits of antler from the rubble on the ground. He clanged them together.

'Deer!' Clack. 'Listen!' Clack.

And then Eo heard it. It was the sound of the stags clashing their antlers together during the rut, up in the high hills with the does milling round.

'I get it! You're Ma –' he took the antlers and knocked them together – 'kK! MakK!' Eo shook his head. 'You must think I'm really stupid.'

MakK put a hand on Eo's sleeve. 'No, EoG,' he said quietly. 'I think you're different.'

'Oh well, that's all right, then!' Eo laughed and stood up. Hurple had 'woken up' and was calling to him from inside the cave. He turned away, not hearing what the other boy said next.

'No, it's not,' MakK murmured sadly. 'It's *not* all right.'

Whatever the elders had been discussing, it seemed they'd made up their minds. A delegation was standing in front of Hurple's rock.

'Come on, boy,' the Professor called. 'I need my ears-and-mouth man!'

Again it was TakK who acted as spokesman for the Neanderthals, but this time he dragged another, extremely nervous-looking man forward with him. He bowed in Hurple's general direction, and then said to Eo, 'Tell the god that this is NorekK, our carver. Tell the god he is going to make a likeness of him to take to the place of gods. This is so that we can speak to him, ask for his wisdom and thank him for his aid. Does this find favour with the god?'

It was obvious to Hurple what Eo was thinking . . . *He's right in front of you – why don't you just speak to him now!?* The judicious application of a claw to a bit of bare arm kept his slave's mouth shut, however. Instead, the god nodded his assent in as haughty a fashion a small weasel-shaped animal can manage. TakK, NorekK and the elders bowed again and then walked away, each being careful not to look the ferret in the eyes. The carver left the cave and the others settled down to another session of talk.

'That's so weird,' muttered Eo. 'Well, what did you find out? Did you find any secret knowledge they can give us, any special demon weapons?'

'I found out they're agitated,' said Hurple softly.

'Well, wouldn't *you* be, if somebody dumped a god on *you* out of nowhere?'

The ferret shook his head. 'It's not me,' he said. 'They have a mechanism for me – I'll fit with the other gods without too much of a stretch, once they get the rituals done. It's *you* they're worked up about.'

'Me?!'

'Yes. They think you don't smell right.'

Eo was irate. '*I* don't smell right – have they smelled *themselves* lately?!'

Hurple rubbed a paw over his snout impatiently. 'You are in no position to whinge – you're not getting the half of it with *that* sad little set of nostrils. But that's not the point. They aren't saying you smell wrong because you smell *bad* –'

'It's not me anyway – it's these manky skins,' Eo muttered under his breath.

'– they're *saying* you smell *different*. And *that's* bad.'

Eo looked up, startled. 'That's what MakK said – *he* said I was different too.'

'MakK?'

'Yeah – that boy over there – see, by the opening. We talked. We're friends, I think. Sort of.'

Hurple shut his eyes for a moment. 'That's not good,' he said.

'Why not?'

'I heard the men – when they were speaking of your . . . not-rightness – they said you were more wrong even than MakK.'

And suddenly, Eo found there was a shift in what he was seeing – as if someone had just sharpened the focus. Groups that had seemed random before began to take on new meaning. Round the main fire it was all boys and men, now that he looked more carefully. The other, smaller ones were the girls and women, some by the cooking fire, some working at other jobs about the place, but all in twos or threes at the least. Only MakK was alone – and he wasn't by the cave opening to catch the best of the light. He was by the cave opening because he didn't belong anywhere else.

Eo felt a flicker of dread run up his back.

'Is it . . . dangerous? If they don't think you fit in, do they do something, uh, violent?'

'No. I think *that's* what they do,' said Hurple, indicating the isolated boy with his paw. 'I think they just gradually, relentlessly, push you out.' He noticed the stricken look on Eo's face. 'That's just the way they are, lad. You're not going to change it. Where're you going?'

Eo didn't answer.

Hurple watched, shaking his head ruefully, as Eo walked back to the entrance of the cave, back to the boy who didn't fit, and sat down beside him.

NorekK the carver was a fast worker – before any of them looked for him to be done, he came back to the cave with a bundle carefully wrapped up in animal skins.

It was time to leave for the place of the gods.

The whole tribe emptied out of the living cave, minus a few of the oldest women, who stayed behind on fire duty. TakK, carrying the bundle, took the lead. He was moving very carefully, but even so, he powered on up the steep incline of the valley as if it were on the flat. Everyone, even the smallest child, seemed fitter than their visitors.

'This better not be far,' Jay panted.

It wasn't. As they came out from among a stand of trees, they stumbled to a ragged halt and stared. Instead of continuing upwards between the hills, the valley stopped. Abruptly. In a wall of white.

A glacier rose sheer before them, a fluted surface of painfully bright light. Its lower leading edge was pocked and dirtied with the rocks and trees and soil it had engulfed, scraping everything in its path forward with it. The river slid out from underneath and ran away towards the sea like a thing escaping. They could feel a whole new level of cold coming off it.

Between them and the glacier was a narrow area of broken trees, a rubbled battlefield littered with branches and rocks and ploughed-up soil. It was a battlefield where one side was clearly losing.

The Professor shuddered along the whole length of his body. 'That thing eats landscapes,' he murmured.

'Where are they going?' whispered Jay, clutching Adom's sleeve for comfort. 'It looks like they're going . . . *inside*!'

She was right.

In single file, the tribe picked its way across the broken ground to an insignificant-looking crack in the wall of ice. One by one, they disappeared inside the opening . . .

'Come on, then,' urged Hurple. 'Let's see what's in there!'

Wide-eyed, the slaves of the god did as they were told.

The entrance was narrow, and the passageway leading off it was low, even for the short Neanderthals. Bent almost in half, the children stumbled forward in the strange blue half-light, unable to see clearly where they were going and stricken to the bone by the intense cold coming off the ice that surrounded them. The passage seemed to go on for a very long time until, suddenly, they emerged, blinking, into the place of the gods.

A great cavern had been dug out of the heart of the glacier, low-ceilinged but vast. The pitch torches the tribes people held smoked and spat, leaving black smudges on the roof, but their light made the ice walls and floor sparkle. In the centre of the space an enormous ice stag had been carved. It seemed to grow out of the floor like a tree. A proud span of antlers, shed by a flesh-and-blood stag, had somehow been planted on to its head. The frost inside the temple had silvered the antlers so that they glinted weirdly in the torchlight. For a moment, the sight of the great tribal god of the kK blinded them to anything else in the temple, but then they saw the others. In niches carved out of the ice walls, other, more minor gods had their places. Statues of owl and boar, wild sheep and rabbit, half-sized bear and cat – and there, in a space newly carved from the body of the glacier, TakK carefully placed the statue of the most recent incumbent, and unwrapped it. The ferret god.

'Oh!' said Hurple. 'It's beautiful!'

The others agreed.

It was a little more than life-size, in a standing pose, with its front paws tucked under its chin and its tail curled to the side. Hurple turned in Eo's hands and looked up at him, his eyes shining.

But before he could speak, the music started. It was an old man, one of the elders, playing a flute – a flute made of a deer bone. The music made Eo feel as if his skin were crawling. Each note was sounded, and left to bend as the player's breath failed. It was like hopeless wailing that would never end, unbearably mournful to Eo's ears. It filled his mind with thoughts of how these people were going to die, and not just *these* people, but all the people like them. Dying away. Utterly gone.

Shut up, shut up, he thought, partly talking to the musician and partly to himself.

From the way he was squinting, it looked as if Hurple wasn't enjoying the concert much either, and Jay and Adom appeared to be fighting the temptation to cover their ears with their hands.

And then it was over. The last note wailed away, and the visitors unscrunched their shoulders and shuffled their cold feet, ready and eager to leave. But no one else moved. There was an uncomfortable silence, in which everyone in the tribe was staring at their little group, or at any rate, at the ice floor beside their little group. They still did not seem able to look the ferret god straight in the face.

Hurple, Eo, Adom and Jay went into a huddle.

'I think they want me to do something,' said Hurple, while trying not to move his lips. 'Something to do with the statue.'

'What – like, greet it somehow?' said Jay. 'Is that it?'

'Well, perhaps . . .'

'OK, don't be thrown by it being made of ice. Just think about if it were a *live* ferret, what would you do, then?'

Hurple rubbed his nose with a paw. 'Well, I'd probably touch noses and then grab it by the scruff and wrestle it to the ground, yipping loudly.'

The others exchanged glances.

'Not perhaps what the moment requires . . .' murmured Eo.

'*I* think they want you to *bless* the statue,' said Adom. 'Not engage it in a bit of rough and tumble.'

'It's good to have a religious expert on board, for an expedition such as ours,' said Hurple, nodding graciously at him. 'That's what I'll do, then . . . uh, now, any advice on how to bless something?'

'Look, it's not as if you've never *been* blessed,' Jay put in impatiently. 'You just have to do whatever the Columba guy did to *you*.'

Three pairs of utterly shocked eyes fixed on her.

'What? What did I say?' she asked.

'Columba was a *saint!*' said Eo. 'Is a saint. Er, will be a saint.'

'Well, he should know what he's doing, then, shouldn't he?' Jay had no time for their scruples. 'You're just going to have to wing it.'

There was a tiny pause, and then Hurple nodded. He flowed down from Eo's shoulder and lolloped over the ice, as solemnly as his cold little paws would let him. Then he made a single graceful leap up into the ferret god's niche. He leaned forward and touched his warm live nose to the statue's icy one, and then, with an almost tender touch, he placed his paw on its forehead and closed his eyes. The ice cavern was utterly still for a moment, and then Hurple jumped lightly down again and ran across to Eo and the others.

'I hope that was what they wanted,' he murmured.

Jay made sure no one was watching, then leaned down and stroked his nose. 'It was just right,' she said. 'I knew it would be.'

'Just right,' Adom agreed.

The Neanderthals seemed content as well. Each member of the tribe now came up to the statue to bow and murmur a few words. There was no polite way to leave before they had finished, so the four waited over to one side, trying not to let their teeth chatter too loudly.

Adom invited Hurple up on to his arm and then stepped away a little.

'Could I have a word?' he said quietly.

'Surely. What's your problem?'

Adom looked uncomfortable. 'It's this – you know, the glacier – it's just that there's nothing like it in my time. Not that I've ever seen or heard tell of. So, what happens between then and now?' he asked.

'The world gets warmer,' said Hurple. 'The leading edges of the glaciers will recede hundreds of kilometres as the Ice Age ends.'

'It all melts?!' said Adom. 'All this?!'

The ferret nodded.

'But . . . how will they feel, when *their gods* melt?!'

Hurple shrugged one narrow shoulder. 'I expect they'll feel abandoned.'

There was a moment's pause in which the worshippers' words could be heard whispering round the space in the icy air.

'Hurple, is that why they – the Neanderthals – is *that* why they became extinct?'

'It's *never* just one thing . . . but I don't see how it can have helped. Do you?'

'No.'

'They're leaving now,' said Eo, coming up behind them. 'Can we go too? – I'm *freezing*!'

They waited until the last of the worshippers had filed out of the ice temple and then followed. Gratefully, they walked out of the glacier's blank white wall, picked their way over its bow-wave of destruction and carried on into the trees. It was only then that they realized they had been left behind. It seemed the entire tribe had moved off down the hill without waiting for them.

'It's as if they've forgotten all about us!' said Eo, surprised and hurt.

'There's no place for you.'

It was MakK. He was standing by a lichen-covered rock, so still in his scruffy furs that he looked like a rock himself.

'I don't understand,' said Eo, so MakK explained, slowly and carefully, as if he were speaking to children.

'Now that the god has breathed himself into the statue, *it's* the god. There is no need to consider any other. Now that the slaves of the god have carried him to the place of the gods, there is no need to consider them either.'

Eo, Jay and Adom exchanged glances.

'What will happen to us, then?'

'You will go away.'

It was too close to the truth to argue about, but Jay argued anyway.

'And what if we *don't* just go away?' she said.

'They'll drive you away.'

'And if we keep coming back?'

MakK shrugged. 'You wouldn't. But I suppose, eventually, they'd have to kill you.'

'Jay,' said Adom softly, 'we're going anyway. You know that.' To MakK he said, 'Can you show us the way back to the shore? It's time we returned . . . the way we came.'

The Neanderthal nodded and, without another word, led the way downhill. They followed. Nobody seemed much in the mood for talking, but Hurple kept giving Eo worried looks.

Finally, he had to speak.

'Look, lad, it's just the way it is,' he said. 'Was. Is going to be. There's nothing you can do to change things for these people.'

Eo didn't answer for a moment, and then seemed to come to a decision.

'Maybe not for *all* of them,' he said, 'but maybe . . .' He turned to Jay. 'Here, take the Professor for a bit, will you?'

'Sure . . .' She took Hurple into her hands and draped him over her shoulder, as Eo hurried forward. 'Where's *he* going, O Divine One?'

The ferret sighed. 'Off the deep end and into left field, I suspect,' he said.

Eo caught up with MakK as the track came out from among the trees. The Neanderthal slowed down a little, courteously, and smiled.

'MakK, listen – I . . . I'm worried about you,' Eo began breathlessly. 'I think you're in danger. Some things the Professor – I mean, you know, the god – overheard . . . I think your tribe is –'

'Going to exclude me soon,' MakK finished for him. 'Yes, I know. I've pretty much always known. They give you time, my people, to grow out of wanting to change things – but I'm well past the end of my time! They've been patient, but I just never could grow up. Look, it's *not changing* that has always worked for us, as a tribe. As a people,' MakK explained earnestly. 'If we change we'd become something else. Staying the same is how we know we're *us*.'

For a moment, Eo could only stare at him. The gulf was so great . . . Then he shook himself and got back to what he'd started to say.

'I can't save your people, but maybe I can save you, if you'll let me,' he said, wishing he wasn't sounding quite as pompous as he knew he did.

'Save my people from what? From not being like me? Don't be foolish. Or do you mean you can save *me* from not being like them? EoG, don't you think others have tried? Don't you think *I've* tried?!' He gave that smile of his, and Eo suddenly saw how sad it was.

'Come with us,' he said with a catch in his throat. 'I don't care if you aren't a warrior or a saint or, or anything – come with *us*.'

MakK just looked at him. Then he held out his hand. His pipe was in it.

'This is for you,' he said simply. 'So you'll remember.'

'But –'

'You'll have no trouble finding your way back to the shore. Just follow the river down.' He spoke to the others, who had caught up with them now.

'You won't come?' Eo gave one last try.

MakK shook his shaggy head.

'Goodbye, lad,' said Hurple, a little hoarsely.

MakK bowed, but, like the others of his tribe, would not look a god in the eyes – not even a superfluous one.

Jay reached over and stroked MakK's cheek with the back of her hand. 'Goodbye,' she said.

Adom gave him a nod. The Neanderthal turned and strode back up the valley with that ground-eating pace. Eo seemed frozen to the spot, unable to go forward or back.

Jay and Hurple looked at him and then headed off down the hill to the sea. Adom moved to join them. Then, as he passed Eo, he paused and said quietly, 'That's a large soul.'

'What?'

'Your friend. He has largeness of soul.'

'Yes,' said Eo after a bit. 'That's it, isn't it? He does.'

Adom nodded again and carried on along the track. Eo stood for another moment and then, holding the bear-bone pipe tightly in his hand, started downhill after the others.

At a bend in the path, he looked back, wondering if MakK might still be there, watching them. But the slope was empty.

He was gone. And then, soon after, they were too.

11 *The Throw of Interrupted Cadence*

All G are youthful-looking, but Interrupted Cadence always, no matter what form he took, seemed to give the appearance of having only just fledged. Maybe his eyes were just that bit wider, or his skin that bit softer, or the shaping of his bones just that bit more delicate . . . Whatever the reasons, Interrupted was – and always would be – boyish in appearance. And because people saw him as younger than he really was, they tended to overlook him when adult matters cropped up.

Interrupted was used to this. In a way, he even preferred it. It is usually the less pleasant duties that fall to the adults of any population, and Interrupted was G enough to want to avoid *anything* that wasn't much fun.

But *now* . . .!

Now it was his throw. Whatever *he*, Interrupted Cadence, chose to do on this pleasant autumn afternoon could decide the fate of the G for all foreseeable ages to come – and he wasn't even sure what the choices *were*!

If he lived a thousand years, he'd never feel old enough to do this.

'What should I do? Where should I aim?' he wailed, desperate for some answers.

'Just fling the thing,' Market Jones advised.

'We haven't exactly been successful with directing it, have we?' agreed Hibernation Gladrag. 'I can't help thinking random chucks might have been a better strategy from the start.' She was looking haggard and white-faced. They all were.

Hope was leaching away with every Tide. This latest visit to the people of the Ice Age might have yielded some long-lost tribal wisdom on dealing with the eldritch dimensions . . . but somehow Interrupted doubted it.

'Here it comes!'

Interrupted squared his shoulders and planted his feet firmly at the edge of the tidemark. For some reason it seemed important to notice exactly *where* the Traveller re-emerged, but, as always, it was too sudden. In a blink it was already there and hurtling towards the beach, contracting down from the height of a man at incredible speed. The Queen plucked it out of the air with arrogant carelessness – and instead of playing about with it, as she had done before, immediately lobbed it at Interrupted. He yelped in surprise, and when the vortex made contact with his skin, he yelped again. It was *cold* – piercingly, shockingly cold. It hurt to hold it . . .

. . . and then he did something he hadn't planned to do. He cradled the Traveller in close to himself and breathed on it, as if it were a freezing bird that had fallen out of the sky, or a small animal needing warming. He wasn't sure why it seemed right to do so, or why, when he made his throw, it was with quite a gentle action. But that was how it was. Hibernation gave him a sign at the moment of the tide's turn. Interrupted threw. The Traveller arced over the wet sand, dropped down – and once again was gone.

'Best bet?' murmured Market Jones.

Interrupted nodded. 'Let's see what I've just done,' he said in a husky voice, and turned back to the disc.

12 *The Fifth Tide*

Jay was dreaming – the nightmare that kept coming back. With no body, she shouldn't have cared about the cold and the dark and the ceaseless whirling round and round – she shouldn't have even been *aware* of it – but knowing it was impossible didn't help. *Nothing* helped, not even the silent words she kept saying in her mind: *It can't go on much longer, it can't go on much longer . . .*

The end came without warning, but instead of crashing in a heap with Adom and Eo and Hurple, all together on some new shore, she was suddenly wrenched away from the others by a current of water powering in the opposite direction. She shot sideways, completely submerged, completely helpless. She started to breathe too soon, and saltwater flooded into her mouth and burned her throat, but just as she thought, *This is drowning,* the current flung her, retching and gasping, up to the surface and on to a tumble of jagged rocks.

She didn't know where she was, but she was out of

the Traveller and that was a blessing all on its own. She looked about her, trying to see where the boys and Hurple had fetched up . . .

The stark landscape of the Ice Age was gone and a more temperate scene had taken its place. The sea filled a wide channel at her back, with misty hills in the distance across the way. Before her, there was a narrow heathery shoreline with low cliffs rising from it, on up to a high rounded peak. Compared to the world she'd just left, this one seemed full of colour – russets and greens, and the sky was beautifully blue . . . It was as she was gazing up at it that she saw the girl, following a path along the bottom of the cliff.

'Hey! Hello!' Jay croaked, but her voice had no strength. She felt bruised all over and close to tears. 'Please . . .'

The sharp shells of barnacles were cutting into her hands and her throat felt raw but she scrambled higher, frantic to get the girl's attention.

'Hey! HEY!'

The girl paused and looked vaguely back up the path, then ahead again – but *not* at the rocks on the shoreline.

Whimpering with frustration, Jay made one more effort. Teetering dangerously on the rock spines, she half stood up and began to wave her arms.

'I'm HERE! Help me! HEL–'

It was one effort too many. Her foot slipped, and in trying to find her balance again she stepped back and on to a patch of slimy seaweed. Arms windmilling, Jay crashed over, hit her head on the rocks and knew no more.

'I'm extremely fed up with being wet all the time!' said Eo – more or less.

What he *actually* said was full of colourful vocabulary which Professor Hurple certainly never taught him. Squelching further up the pebbly beach, he pulled at the wet straps of his bag to let the ferret out.

'At least it's not *freezing* wet this time. You all right, Adom?' he called over this shoulder. 'Adom?' The silence made him look round. 'What's up – *where's Jay?*'

Adom was standing there, looking down at his hand, too shocked even to be sick.

'I had her,' he croaked, 'and then . . . she just wasn't there any more!' He looked over at Eo, white-faced.

'You let her *go?!*' Eo charged up to him and grabbed him by the shoulders. *'You left her in the Traveller?!'*

Adom shook his head slowly, like a bewildered beast. 'No . . . no, I'm sure we were out of it, because I remember I actually could *feel* her hand – but we were still under the water . . . and then she was just ripped away . . .'

The sound of pebbles crunching interrupted him.

'*Jay!*' the two boys cried, turning in sudden hope – just as a rough net was thrown over their heads, entangling their arms and legs until they both crashed helplessly on to the shingle.

The girl glaring down at them wasn't Jay.

'What are you *doing?*' spluttered Eo.

'Let us out this minute!' Adom commanded, though the squeak in his voice undermined the effect a little.

The girl didn't reply. Instead, she put her hands up to her mouth and let out a long, yodelling cry. It was obviously some sort of signal, and at a volume that would carry for quite a distance. And all the time she didn't take her eyes off them, not for a second, as if she were expecting them to leap up and attack at any moment.

In reality, they couldn't have successfully attacked a piece of wet bread in their current tangled state.

After some more blustering and a bit of wheedling, the two boys gave up. Their captor was *not* going to let them out any time soon, *or* chat about her reasons for packaging them, though she did give a sour little smile when Eo complained to Adom about the way his elbow was poking him in the eye.

Another girl appeared round the rocks. 'Moira?' she called. 'You all right? I came ahead – the others are on their way. What's up? Yeurch!' She gave a strangled cry and leapt back as she caught sight of the lump under the net. 'What kind of catch is *that*?!'

'Something for the Old Woman.' The one she'd called Moira spoke for the first time.

The new girl looked closer.

'Goodness – *more*!'

'What do you mean, more?' asked Eo, thrashing frantically to get the new arrival into view. 'Has anyone else been found? A girl? Is she all right?'

'Yes . . . how did you know? They're bringing her to the Lady now. She got bashed up a bit in the water and she hit her head on the rocks, but –' she'd leaned over to talk to him, so Eo could see her, but now she reared back in sudden suspicion – 'unless it was *you* – did *you* bash her?!'

Eo and Adom stared.

'What are you *talking* about?'

But the girl had turned her back on them and was speaking to Moira in a low, urgent voice.

'Cait's bringing her past here on the way to the cliff path. We thought the Lady would be at the garden, so this was the quickest route – but if these are the ones that hurt her . . . They cut off all her hair, the pigs . . .'

'Best get them out of sight, then. Here, give me a hand.'

Making no attempt to be gentle, Moira started to extract Adom and Eo from the netting.

'Hey!'

'Oww!'

'That *hurt!*'

Suddenly the shingle beach seemed full of women and girls, though there were probably no more than a dozen of them. But there was enough ill-will towards Eo and Adom to be coming from twice that number.

'Look what Moira's found –'

'They're for the Leap –'

'– and I'll push!'

'Let me get my hands on them!'

Someone dragged Eo's bag off his shoulder and began loosening the ties. The boys' handling was getting rougher by the minute. Still half-entangled in the net, they could barely defend themselves.

It wasn't clear what had sparked the crowd's fury, or how far they might go in expressing it. But then, before things could get any uglier, a voice the boys knew rose over the babble.

'Stop that! – Put me down – Stop hurting them – I said STOP! *They're with me!*'

'Jay!' yelled Eo and Adom, in the sudden silence.

And there she was, looking, well, *awful*. Her skin was

scraped and bruised. One side of her face was a mask of blood and her hair was caked with it. She was being carried in the arms of a phenomenally large and powerful-looking woman, as if she were no more than a baby.

'Please put me down, Cait,' Jay said to her again.

'All right, dearie,' Cait said. 'But only for a moment. The Lady needs to see that head of yours, and sooner rather than later.' She seemed unfazed by the furore around her and gently set Jay on to her feet, steadying her with one large hand.

The rest of the gathering was not so calm. A crowd of incredulous faces turned to Jay.

'You brought them *with* you?!' someone exclaimed. 'To the Island of Women?!'

'Yes – yes, I brought them with me.' *What is going* on *here?* she thought to herself. She tried to lighten the mood. 'You know how boys are – I could hardly leave them wandering about by themselves, now, could I?!'

Usually appealing to the Girl Mafia helped, but this time it had no effect whatsoever. The women and girls continued to stare at her as if she'd just crawled out from under a rock.

Jay was drawing breath to try again, when the woman who'd taken Eo's bag screamed loudly and dropped it.

'It moved!' she gasped. 'It's alive!'

Before anyone could respond, Hurple squeezed himself out of the top of the bag like some peculiarly furry toothpaste out of a tube.

'Ah!' he said brightly. 'Greetings, my good women – and *what* did you say the name of this place was?'

Jay closed her eyes and groaned quietly to herself.

Now *what . . . Screaming? Fainting? Getting the stakes out to burn us? Oh, please – not Hurple the god again . . .*

The reaction he actually got was not at all what she'd expected.

A chorus of voices broke out.

'Oh *no* – not *another* one!'

'Oddy's bad enough –'

'How can you say that?! Oddy's lovely!'

'Is someone talking about *me*!?'

Jay opened her eyes and looked round just in time to see a large brown dog with a plumy tail bound on to the scene, bounce up to her and stand on her feet. 'Hello – you smell new – crikey –' its voice suddenly dropped down into a growl, as it swerved wildly sideways – 'those ones are *men*!'

'And they've got a talking animal with them – what do you think of *that*, then!' It was Moira. It appeared she liked this dog as little as she liked the boys.

The dog snuffled violently, without taking his eyes off Eo and Adom.

'I expect the Lady would like a new pet, don't you think?' Moira continued. 'She's probably tired of you after all this time.'

The girl who had spoken up for him before threw herself down on the shingle and hugged him.

'Don't listen to them, Oddy – we all know it's *you* the Lady loves best.'

The dog turned his head just enough to give her face a swipe with his tongue, his eyes swivelling wildly to keep the boys in view.

'Don't fear, females,' he said. 'Odysseus will protect you. If you could all just back away quietly, I will be able to rip their throats out more conveniently.'

179

He had a peculiarly clipped voice, as if each word was being bitten off from the next. This – and the fact that the dog was talking at *all* – distracted Eo and the others for a moment from what he'd just said. Then it sunk in.

'Wha–?!'

'Hey!'

'Now, just a *minute*!'

Then Hurple lolloped up to him and, despite being smaller than anyone in the place, effortlessly become the centre of everyone's attention.

'*Odysseus*,' he practically purred. 'Now *there's* a name to conjure with! And I'd really like to say, you know, that that was a fabulously convincing display of ferocity just now. Produced a definite frisson among the troops, I can tell you! I'm Pinkerton Hurple, by the way. Perhaps we might step aside for a moment and give the bipeds a bit more time to get acquainted – and we can have a *proper* chat . . .'

Looking as utterly gobsmacked as only a dog can, Odysseus disentangled himself from the kneeling girl and trotted after Hurple. As the ferret passed Jay, he looked up at her, eyes twinkling, and said in a loud stage whisper, 'What a *handsome* animal!' The dog's trot took on a new bounce and the plumes of his tail waved complacently.

Jay and the kneeling girl exchanged glances.

'He's very vain,' the girl said apologetically.

'It's a boy thing,' replied Jay with a shrug.

Without warning, the world started to go fuzzy, and immediately Cait was there to steady her.

'Time to go,' the big woman said, but Jay grabbed

her sleeve and pleaded. 'No – I'm fine – I'm just . . . *confused*! I don't understand why you're all so mad at Adom and Eo. I don't understand where we are, or when –'

'And who is the Lady?' put in Eo.

'Is she the Old Woman you spoke of?' said Adom innocently.

Mouths dropped open.

'Is it *possible* they don't know?' someone murmured.

'Don't be stupid – *everyone* knows about the Island of Women.'

'Maybe they're all, you know, *simple*?'

'Look, *I* don't know and I don't care,' interrupted Moira. 'If I had my way, they'd be straight for the Leap, but it's not *my* island. I say we let the Lady deal with them – What are *you* sighing about, Jeannie?'

'Nothing . . . it just seems a shame, that's all. That one's so *pretty* . . . such *beautiful* hair – don't you just wish –'

'Don't you let the Lady hear you talking like that!'

'It just seems a waste, that's all,' Jeannie insisted.

'Oh, do shut up!' was the general chorus.

Then Moira took charge.

'Right . . . Cait, you take the girl to the garden. Janet and Una, you keep an eye on *those two* –' it was amazing how much venom she got into her voice – 'and the rest of you, GET BACK TO WORK!'

'But . . . what are *we* supposed to do with them?' whined Janet. 'We've got an entire flock back at the cave to check over and dip today – we can't just sit around here, *watching*!'

'*I* could,' murmured Jeannie, but everyone ignored her.

'Take them along and put them in the holding pen in the cave, then – just get *on* with it.'

'But why can't they come with me?' asked Jay.

There was another of those appalled pauses.

'*Take* men *to the* sacred garden?!'

Suddenly she felt too tired to argue any more.

'Jay, you look awful. Go and get that head seen to,' said Adom. He sounded concerned. 'Don't worry about all this – we'll be fine.'

'Yeah, and if you can find out anything useful, maybe get some help for you-know-what, that'd be good too. And meantime, I promise we won't do any, um, leaping, before you get back, so you won't miss a thing,' said Eo, striking a silly, one-legged pose for her, until Janet gave him a shove towards the cave path.

'Oddy, you're with me,' Cait called as she scooped Jay up again.

'Hurple?' Jay quavered.

The ferret waved a reassuring paw. 'Don't worry. I'll look after them!' he called, lolloping after the boys.

Jay sighed. She'd been hoping he would come and look after *her* . . .

There were five or six women in the group heading for the sheep cave, ranging in age from not much more than a child to one who looked like somebody's grandmother. Eo tried to get the old one to smile at him, without success.

'What did the dog tell you?' Adom spoke quietly to Hurple, who was once more on Eo's shoulder.

'Well,' the Professor began, 'I found out we're on the Island of Women, which is called that because only humans of the female persuasion are allowed to live here. Not only are men not popular here, they tend to be sacrificed upon arrival –'

'Tell your pet to shut up!' snarled Una threateningly.

'Look!' Eo was definitely starting to lose patience. 'I keep telling you – we're *strangers*! We don't *know* about an Island of Women! And what's "the Leap" you keep going on about?'

'If you don't know already you'll find out soon enough,' said Janet, but the old woman decided to fill them in. She dropped back alongside the boys and grinned up at them disconcertingly. Eo had never seen anyone who wasn't a baby with so few teeth before.

'You want to know about the Leap?' she said. 'I'll tell you. It's a finger of rock which reaches out from the cliff-side way, way up there.' She pointed back in the direction they had come. 'Near the Lady's shrine. Handy, like. And don't worry – there's no hard work involved for you. Oh no. Two, maybe three strides is all you'll have to take, and then, nothing but thin air until you hit the water.' She chomped her gums together enthusiastically. 'Sometimes the bodies wash back on to the shore. But mostly, the Old Woman is hungry . . .'

'The Old Woman?'

'Corrievrechan. The whirlpool. When she's hungry, you can hear her voice for leagues.'

'Some people call her the Sea Hag,' another woman joined in.

'Some people call her the Swallow of the Sea,' said another.

But the oldest woman had the last word.

'We call her . . . retribution,' she said.

'You make them do *what*?!' Jay couldn't believe what Cait was telling her.

The big woman shrugged. 'It's a clean death,' she said.

'Please, Cait. I really need you to explain *all* of this to me. Slowly. From the beginning.'

At first Jay had been all tensed up, trying to weigh as little as possible. It soon became clear, though, that carrying her was not taxing the big woman at all. The dog had peeled off almost at once, following his nose roughly in the same direction as they were going but covering at least twice as much ground. They were free to talk in private.

'Tell me how all this began,' Jay said.

'Well,' said Cait, resettling Jay in her arms, 'not so very long ago there was nothing here. Nobody lived on the island then. When a girl was in trouble in those days, there was no place for her to go for help. There was only the Old Woman.'

'The Old Woman?'

Jay could feel a shudder run through Cait.

'The whirlpool. Out there in the strait. Most of the time there's nothing to see, but sometimes, when she's hungry, the surface of the water begins to eddy and judder and surge, like a pot coming to the boil. Then, from deep, deep below, the whirlpool begins to form and it's like a great throat that wants to suck you down, and it roars and groans and . . . And that's where we're sent.'

'Why?' breathed Jay. 'Why are you sent?'

Cait's voice was cold and flat. 'You can marry the man your father chooses, or you can go to the Old Woman. You can take another beating, or go to the Old Woman. You can be born a boy and be well valued, or be born a girl – *another* girl – and be sent to the Old Woman in a basket. Or if you get pregnant when you shouldn't . . . The Old Woman tidies us all away. Some of the men think she's less likely to take their boats if she's fed regularly with the cast-offs, so it's good news for them when another unwanted girl comes available.'

'But, Cait, that doesn't make sense . . . how could they possibly not want *you*?! You're lovely, and you're also stronger than any man I ever met!'

'And you expect them to *like* that?' There was a look on her face that Jay couldn't read. It made her feel inexperienced and too young. Much too young.

'Anyway, then the Lady came. No one knows how or why. But somehow, the word got out that if only you made it this far, to the island, there was someone here who was on our side. You couldn't believe it could *possibly* be true, but then you'd get here, and the Lady would look at you, and you knew you were *safe*. She's so wonderful, Jay, you'll see! She heals us, and finds out what we're good at, and sets us doing it. We've practically a village on the east side, and some boats for fishing from, and some fields and some flocks. I'll show you it all – you'll like it here!'

Jay shifted uncomfortably. 'I won't be staying that long,' she said.

Cait smiled gently. 'Lots of us say that. It's hard to

get used to at first. But you will, don't worry. And once you accept that there's nowhere else to go – that you can never go back – well, it all gets easier then.'

She looked out over the strait.

'It's hardest for the local girls,' she said. 'The ones that can even *see* home, or their father's fishing boats hugging the other side of the strait, or the smoke rising from fires they used to stoke themselves – those are the ones who sometimes don't settle. The ones who wear themselves out with longing by day. The ones who walk off the cliff in their sleep at night.'

'Are you a local girl?' asked Jay softly.

Cait didn't answer and Jay didn't ask again.

As they stumbled along the shore path, Adom whispered to the others, 'Should we try to escape?'

One of the girls overheard.

'Try it!' she grunted. 'We're on an *island* in case you'd forgotten. Everyone knows the currents are so strong round here they even make the fish think twice! And I don't plan to tell where we keep the boat. But now you mention it, we haven't had a Hunt of the Maenads for some time. That's one of the Lady's ideas – a treat for the whole island! So if you lads fancied a chance to stretch your legs and give us a run for our money, we'd all be happy to take part!'

They walked a bit further in silence. Then, 'What's a Maenad?' whispered Eo.

'Don't ask,' muttered Hurple.

The girl grinned unpleasantly. 'Listen to your weasel, boy,' she sneered.

'Why are humans apparently unable to distinguish

between *Mustela nivalis* and *Mustela putorius furo*?' asked Hurple wistfully.

Adom sounded the Latin words out carefully, then checked with his wrist computer.

'*Mustela nivalis* is the Latin for weasel and means "least mouse-killer". But it says the Latin name for ferret is "*smelly thieving* mouse-killer"!' he whispered to Eo incredulously. 'Is that right?!'

Eo winked at him, and Hurple pretended not to hear.

'Get *on*!' growled the grandmother, and poked at them with a stick.

It was possible to hear the sheep a good while before they could see them. The cave in which they were penned opened at an angle to the strait, with a stream running past it on its way to the sea. Someone had built a temporary dam, so that the water was quite deep behind it. A cauldron of strange-smelling stuff bubbled on a fire nearby.

'What's in there?' asked Eo. 'Is it lunch?'

'Not unless you eat sheep dip,' said Janet, and the others laughed. 'The Lady provides the herbs, we add them to the water and shove in the sheep. Whatever's in there, it's poison to parasites. So maybe we *should* give you some, eh?'

'We've no time for all this talking,' scolded the grandmother. 'It's past noon already and not a beast dealt with.'

'And whose fault is that?!' snapped Janet. 'It wasn't my idea to bring them!'

'Get in!' ordered Una, giving the two boys a shove that almost knocked them off their feet. Reluctantly, they climbed over the barricade into a small sea of surging wool. The sheep – who, like sheep everywhere, were always up for a bit of recreational panic – milled and leapt and baaed loudly.

The boys found their way to the comparative safety of the back wall.

'Do you know anything about sheep?' Eo asked Adom after a moment.

'Not really,' he said. 'My family didn't keep any. Why?'

'One of them just peed on my foot.'

'I think that could be considered a compliment,' said Hurple cheerfully. 'It may even be a declaration of some sort of undying affection.'

'How flat do you think a group of sheep like this could trample something as small as, say, a ferret?' Eo said, looking at Adom.

'Now that I don't know either,' he said. 'Shall we try and find out?'

'It would be quite interesting to know . . .'

There was a baa-filled pause. Then Eo stirred restlessly.

'This isn't getting us anywhere,' he said in a low voice. 'How are we going to be given anything useful if we spend the entire Tide stuck in a cave with a bunch of stinky sheep? And what about Jay? How do we know she's all right? She looked a mess – *I* know, head wounds bleed a lot. But this Lady she's going to . . . do we trust her? What do we know about her anyway?'

'Well,' said Hurple a bit prissily, 'what *you* know about her will depend on how much you were paying attention when I taught you Greek mythology last year.'

Eo groaned. 'How was I supposed to know it would

ever *possibly* come in handy?' he muttered, not quite quietly enough.

'What do you mean, mythology?' asked Adom, distracting the ferret from his obvious intention of telling Eo off till round about sundown. 'Who is she, this Lady? *What* is she?'

'Circe.' Hurple sounded definite. 'It's the only possible identification. Daughter of the immortal sun god and an extremely long-lived nymph of the sea, she is, of course, beautiful and also, of course, virtually immortal herself. But more importantly, she is fiercely intelligent and a gifted sorceress, with a vast knowledge of the uses of herbs to kill and to heal – probably acquired on the off chance that it might *possibly come in handy*.'

Eo made a face.

'I think you might both benefit from a summary of *The Odyssey* right about now,' said the Professor. There and then, he launched into the story of the Greek hero Odysseus. How, after the Trojan War ended, he and his men set sail for home, a journey that should have taken a few months but instead lasted for *ten years*. How interfering gods, terrifying monsters, a descent into the Underworld, encounters with mythological beings of horror and wonder, all conspired to keep them from finding the way back. And especially, he told them about the time Odysseus landed on the island of the sorceress Circe, who turned his men into pigs but fell in love with him . . .

From time to time, one or other of the girls would stop work for a while and listen in, but Hurple didn't manage to hold their attention for long.

'We've heard it all before,' they said. 'From the dog.'

*

FAQ 226: How could it possibly have taken Odysseus ten years to get from Troy to Ithaca? I know there were storms and contrary currents and a certain amount of divine intervention, but still – ten years to go about 1,000 kilometres?

HURPLE'S REPLY: There have been many attempts to chart Odysseus' route over the years. (Research that forces you to spend time sailing around in the Mediterranean is bound to be attractive.) Any number of sun-drenched islands have been suggested as the Blessed Isle to which Circe was banished. It is also a possible explanation that Odysseus sailed through some of the thin places between worlds which we have spoken of, and that her home was in another universe. But it is perhaps slightly **more** possible that he sailed out of the Mediterranean in **this** world. Eccentric enthusiasts have charted a route, based on their understanding of his ship's capabilities and the sorts of currents and winds on offer, which would have the Greek trickster arriving in the Hebrides at about the stage Circe enters the story. Worth a thought, anyway.

After a while, Cait and Jay came to a fold in the hillside where the path split. A noisy stream raced past, then dropped off the edge and plunged down to the sea. One part of the path crossed a rough bridge and carried on along the cliff-top, skirting round the central mountain that formed the Island of Women. The other turned inland. It was little more than a track, and quickly disappeared round a curve and out of sight.

Cait seemed uncomfortable. She set Jay down and rubbed her hands together, and then mumbled something Jay couldn't hear over the plashing of the water.

'What's wrong?' said Jay. 'Why are we stopping?'

Cait glanced sideways at the track leading inland, and then away again. 'That leads to the sacred garden,' she said, only slightly louder than before. 'Moira told me to take you there, but I'm . . . afraid.'

Jay waited to see if there was anything more coming, but that was it.

'It's not far, is it?' she asked.

Cait shook her head.

'And is there any chance of getting lost on the way?'

She shook her head again. It seemed to make her uneasy even to talk about the place.

'You know,' said Jay, 'I'm feeling a lot better already. There's no reason I can't just go the rest of the way by myself.'

Cait looked at her with an expression made up partly of guilty embarrassment and partly of relief. Jay knew so well what that felt like.

'Then that's what we'll do,' she said firmly. 'You've already been really kind to me, Cait, and I *know* you have more to do than carry me about! I'll take it from here.'

She set off cheerfully, before the woman could feel obliged to argue them both out of it, calling back, 'Thank you!' as she went.

The noise of the water drowned out Cait's reply. 'But, Jay – you do know, don't you? You mustn't go *in* the garden . . .'

The little valley the stream had formed was narrow and felt shut in. A breeze blew down through the bracken, heading for the sea. It was curiously scented, and warmer than you'd expect. Though the path was perfectly gentle to walk along, Jay found her feet were slowing down of their own accord.

She passed a copse of small trees, their roots in the dampness round the stream bed. She passed between two cairns. She passed a strange pattern carved on a rock, and what must have been the skull of a sheep.

'I wish Cait were still here,' she muttered to herself, as the world blurred a little again. 'I better not pass out –' but then she realized she'd arrived. The hills fell back to reveal a rounded open space and nestled in it, in the full warmth of the sun, was a garden, surrounded by low stone walls, with benches and pergola, terraced and full to bursting with plants and trees and shrubs. The stream welled up in the midst of it all, then ran down under the wall on its way to the sea. The track led up to a stone archway. Normally, Jay would have been interested in the carvings round the lintel and supports, but she was feeling worse by the minute now and just wanted to get in and drink from the spring and sit down.

She didn't pay attention to the odd resistance of the

air as she passed under the archway, putting it down to the bump on the head. But then, once she was inside the walls, the feelings of discomfort faded and the warm scents made her feel calm for the first time this Tide.

She went to the spring, drank deeply and washed the blood off her face and out of her hair. The icy water stung her cuts and scrapes at first and then made her feel numb and clean. Still dripping, she had a wander about the garden.

She pulled an oddly fuzzy leaf off a shrub at random and sniffed it. The effect was as quick as a patch – the pounding in her head eased at once and a feeling of well-being flooded her mind.

'Whoa!' she muttered, and let the leaf drop.

Out of the blue, the dog trotted past, his plumy tail waving. He didn't seem to notice her, which wasn't surprising perhaps. With so many scents overloading his nose, he was unlikely to pick up hers. At the far end of the garden there was a small hut with a sunny patch of grass in front. The dog headed straight over to it, turned round a few times and then curled contently in the warm sun.

The sight of him made Jay smile.

There were herbs and flowers and shrubs of many sorts clustered together in groups that would have made sense to a gardener, but which seemed completely random to an underwater city dweller. Jay strolled on, touching and sniffing and enjoying.

One bush, however, was by itself. She went over and looked at it for a moment, wondering idly why that should be. She picked a leaf and sniffed it.

It was a strange, compelling scent. She closed her eyes

and breathed in again, deeply, filling her lungs. Her hand dropped to her side . . .

When she opened her eyes again the garden was the same, but everything else had changed. The sky was brassy and, in the heat, crickets and cicadas yelled incessantly. A woman and a little girl of no more than five or six were sitting on a bench in the shade.

'And this?'

The little girl wore a short linen tunic and had black hair that tumbled over her shoulders. The young woman sitting beside her was dressed in a full-length robe of white and had the same luxurious raven-coloured hair. A single glance showed that the two were close relatives, and the child was in the middle of some sort of test. The young woman kept producing leaves and flowers and herbs from a basket for her to identify.

The basket was almost empty.

'And this, Circe? It's the last . . .'

The child thought for a moment, fingering the leaf she'd been given. Then she answered, a note of triumph in her voice.

'Love's Truth!' she said. 'Hallucinatory when inhaled; poisonous when ingested. Fast-working. Untraceable. I'm right – aren't I!'

The woman didn't speak at once. She sat there, looking solemn, until the child bubbled over.

'I *know* I'm right! Medea – don't tease me!'

The young woman's face was just blossoming into a smile when the scene changed again . . .

It was the cool of dawn, before the day's fierce heat returned, but much more than a day had passed. The girl was a woman now, wearing a married woman's robes. Her face was ashen in the dim half-light, as she reached out to the shrub, Love's Truth, and gathered its leaves . . .

It was dawn still, but a different dawn, in a different, colder climate. The garden was a blackened wreck, fire-ravaged and apparently deserted. Then something moved in the shadow of a ruined wall. It was the same woman grown old, still straight but only by strength of will. The hands that reached out to the only shrub remaining were clawed, but did not shake . . .

Jay came back to herself with a shudder. The wind from the sea was salty and clean-smelling, and the sun gave off a familiar, northern warmth. Like a dream, what she had seen began fading from her memory almost at once. And like a dream, it left something else behind, a feeling of great swathes of time and tension and passion pent . . .

She stumbled over to the bench and dropped down on it, trying to think, while the dog twitched and woofled in his sleep.

'That's unusual,' said a voice.

Jay fell off the bench on to the ground and stared in astonishment at the cloaked and hooded figure standing by the wall. She was *sure* there'd been no one there a second ago.

'Where did *you* come from?' she blurted.

The figure's laugh was low, and deeper than you'd expect.

'Isn't that supposed to be *my* question? You can get up, by the way – I don't require a complete obeisance.'

Jay scrambled to her feet. She wasn't entirely sure what an obeisance was, but the mocking tone was clear enough.

As the figure uncloaked, Jay took a step back. The woman was only a little taller than she was and slightly built, but the luxurious raven-wing hair and the way she moved like a coiled spring were unmistakable. It was the same person Jay had seen in her 'dream'.

Circe. The Lady.

'No one comes here,' the Lady said. 'A powerful sorceress might pass my warnings perhaps, or a questor of great courage and determination might brave them, to trespass in my sacred garden . . .' Her voice ended on a rising note, as if she couldn't really see Jay in either of those categories.

'The dog came in,' said Jay defensively.

'He belongs,' said the Lady. 'You don't.' Suddenly her eyes narrowed. 'You didn't just trespass, did you . . . you saw things . . .'

She moved like a cat, took Jay's hand and opened it. The crushed remains of the leaf lay on her palm, and the scent rose, dangerously, again. The Lady pulled her over to the stream and scrubbed her hand vigorously in the iciness. A greenish blur bled into the water and was swept away.

'Is that a poison?' Jay stammered. 'Will it affect things downstream?' The garden suddenly felt like a dangerous place to be.

But the Lady seemed unconcerned. 'Some fish in the strait may have strange dreams tonight, but that won't be unusual for them.' She took hold of Jay's head and moved it so she could examine the wound. 'This isn't too bad. Why did they cut your hair off? What were you being punished for?'

'They? Who? Oww! I *like* my hair!'

'This isn't as bad as it might be.' Examination complete, the Lady turned Jay abruptly to face her.

'What did you see?' The question came sharp and sudden.

'I . . . I saw . . . *you*,' Jay stuttered. It didn't even occur to her to play for time or pretend she didn't know what the Lady was referring to. 'It's hard to remember – like a dream.'

'The gift of forgetfulness comes so easily to some . . . Why do I sense so much water from you? You are no Oceanid, like my mother, and yet the sea is all around you . . . The sea, which is always changing, is always the same . . .'

There was a groan from ground level. 'Lord of All Rubbish – can a dog not fall asleep for two seconds around here without you going mystical?! It's no wonder you can't keep a man, talking tosh like that!'

Jay couldn't help giggling. The dog looked a bit surprised to see her there.

The Lady looked down at him, an unreadable expression on her face.

'You're a man,' she said quietly. '*You're* still here.'

The dog snorted. 'It's an island, darling. You think I want to swim Corrievrechan just to get away from you?' He looked at her, his tongue hanging out the side of his mouth, one ear inside out – the picture of a pooch . . . until you came to the eyes.

'Odysseus,' whispered the Lady. There was such honey in her voice, as if there were no one else there.

Jay squirmed uncomfortably.

Then the dog sneezed, knocking his ear the right way out again, and the moment passed.

'Where did she come from?' he asked. 'And when did you start bringing the new girls here?'

'I didn't,' said the Lady. 'She brought herself.'

'That's unusual,' said the dog, unconsciously repeating his mistress's words. 'She doesn't *smell* like a sorceress. Not that it's easy to tell round here,' and he sneezed again.

Circe walked round Jay slowly, staring at her intently. 'No, you're right. Not a sorceress . . . or a heroine . . .' When she finished her circuit, the expression on her face hardened. She reached up and began to plait and twist together four strands of her midnight hair.

'I'll tell you what I sense here. I sense arrogance. Ignorance. I sense another world . . .'

Suddenly, Jay found she couldn't move, not even to blink, barely to breathe. The Lady looked into her eyes, on into her mind, and there was nothing she could do to stop her.

There was so much about her own world that she never thought about, all the common, everyday images. Wallpaper stuff, really – so much part of the landscape of her mind that she never considered it consciously herself. When Adom and Eo and Hurple had arrived on her doorstep, they had seemed amazed and impressed. At least that was what she assumed they'd been feeling. Now she was seeing what Circe saw, without any polite obfuscation. The high-tech pods and workplaces suddenly appeared cramped to her and restrictive, like too-small cages. The calculated ballet of traffic between sectors and levels seemed artificial and controlled, like the herded scuttling of lab rats in a maze. And everywhere, there were the Guardians. There were so many, hung round with sprayers and needlers and nets. Had she *realized* how many there were?

'Cramped, controlled, drugged, without even the awareness you are not free . . . And *that* is why you think you are superior?' The Lady sounded mildly incredulous. 'Perhaps on a more personal level . . .'

She looked deeper, and Jay had no choice but to look as well. She wouldn't have said it out loud, but she *knew* what she thought of herself. She thought she was special. That she would do great things someday. It was only a matter of time. But Circe wasn't seeing what Jay thought. She was seeing what she *did* . . .

'But that's not it!' Jay choked. 'I'm not just – and I *don't* think I'm superior! That's . . .' *true*, she thought to herself as her voice died away. *I* do*! Right from the beginning . . . there was Adom – he outclassed me, but he was shy and awkward and he didn't know one end of a computer from the other, so I told myself I was better. And Eo – he's a shape-shifter, for crying out loud, but I convinced myself he was just a child. And Hurple, who knows more than I could ever learn in my whole life – well, he's just an animal, isn't he? And the people we've met, in each Tide . . . I'm the lowest you can get in my world, but because of all the technology I was born into, that I never made and don't even understand, I thought I was better than all of them . . .*

She felt ashamed.

'In the world I come from it's the same, of course,' said the Lady. 'Except that it's being born into money there, or family, or being male, that makes you superior.

I thought you might be unusual, but after all, it's just the old story – the safe way. No need to find out what you could do if you had to – never push hard enough to find out – ride on someone else's achievements. I understand.'

'But that's not it . . . you just met me. You don't know me!' Jay cried.

The Lady shrugged. 'It's not important,' she said. 'I just wondered, that's all. So, what is it you've come to ask me for?'

Jay felt as if she'd been kicked in the stomach.

She didn't see the sly smile on the Lady's face.

Back at the cave, the boys were still trying to come to grips with what the Professor was saying.

Adom said, 'So are you trying to tell us that we are trapped on the island of the witch-sorceress Circe as described in the pagan writings of the poet Homer?'

The ferret nodded. 'Fabulous, isn't it!'

But Eo was worrying at another bit of the tale. He said, 'So are you trying to tell us that Circe, the Lady, right, named her *dog* after her *boyfriend*!?'

'What makes you think she named him *after* anyone?' Hurple ignored their stunned expressions. 'Odysseus really loved her, you know – there's more than one version of that story. They don't all end the same way.'

'She *bewitched* him?!' gasped Adom.

'Funny word, that,' said the ferret thoughtfully. 'According to everything I've read, she certainly *was* bewitching, and she certainly *did* some bewitching, but there's quite a difference. When you think about it.'

'I don't *want* to think about it,' snapped Adom. 'I want to go and make sure she isn't turning *Jay* into a duck or a bowl of fruit or something!'

'Or *maybe* Jay's convincing her to help us, right at this very moment,' said the ferret. 'Have you thought of *that*? It's not as if anyone *we've* met seems eager to give us anything.'

'Other than a poke with a sharp stick,' said Eo mournfully.

'Or a long drop off a short rock,' said Adom.

'Don't remind them!' said Hurple.

'It's not the first time I've been asked for assistance of this kind,' the Lady said, with a wry note to her voice. 'Where are they now, your companions?'

'The one called Moira said to put them in a cave of some sort. In a pen with a bunch of sheep.' Jay was still finding it hard to speak. A bad taste of worthlessness and shame kept trying to block her throat.

'They've put them in a cave with sheep? Well, that's an idea that's been used before, eh?' She glanced sideways at the dog.

The dog snorted. He *might* have just been clearing his throat.

While asking her questions the Lady was also preparing a potion, brewing herbs and leaves in a pot over a fire inside the hut. Again, she had first rearranged her long hair, made a particular plait, quickly and without fuss. Jay wondered dully what it meant.

'Here, drink this.' The Lady handed her a wooden cup of the liquid. 'I think you'll find you are fit enough then.'

It didn't seem likely she'd deem her *worth* poisoning, so Jay drank up. The stuff was slightly bitter, but not too unpleasant, and it did give her a sense of new strength and health.

The Lady carefully banked the fire and stood up, smoothing her robe and shaking out her hair.

The dog stood too and gave *himself* a shake, but the Lady put her hand on his head. 'Odysseus, I want you to stay here,' she said quietly.

'And why is that, might I ask?' The dog looked huffy.

'Dearest, you know the girls are working with the sheep just now. And you know you can't resist how their white waggly tails flap up and down. Or the way their wool bounces all over when they run. Now can you? Hmm?'

A small whimper of longing escaped from the dog, but he lay down again.

'Wait for me,' she said. 'Till I get back.'

From the entrance to the garden, Jay could still see him lying there, his head on his outstretched paws, waiting for the Lady's return.

Eo sighed and looked out to see if there was any sign yet of Jay. The number of sheep still in the pen with them had been steadily declining, as more and more of the animals were dragged out, shoved into the dipping pool and allowed to escape, yelling in indignation, from the other side. Now there was only one left, the most obstreperous of the lot. It was tough and cantankerous, and too canny by half. It took all the women to get that one beast to the edge of the dip.

Eo was feeling grubby and hungry and anxious and scared, but it was a sight that made him grin in spite of himself. He was about to pass a comment to Adom when suddenly –

– she was there. Jay was back, looking well again. And she was not alone.

A black-haired woman was standing beside her. There was something about her, something . . . *bewitching*. It was nothing like the mesmer of the Kelpie Queen, which bewildered and bemused – if anything, it made him feel he was seeing more *clearly*. For a moment, he was swept by an irrational desire to drop to his knees. Then she caught his eye, half-smiled, and put a long finger to her lips.

Eo shoved Adom, but he was already staring in the same direction.

'*The Lady*,' he breathed, and Eo gave the slightest of nods.

The women at the dip hadn't yet noticed the new arrivals. Their attention was too caught up in the last sheep, still showing no sign of a willingness to cooperate. Then the Lady took a strand of her long, loose hair and twisted it in a certain way – and suddenly the sheep stopped baaing and struggling. It trotted of its own accord into the deep water, ducked its head, swam across and came out on the other side with no more than a decorous shake of its wool. The women, wet and filthy, were also silent. They turned to the Lady and waited for her to tell them what to do.

'Those boys who came here – it seems they're gone,' she said calmly. 'They've taken the boat, and the girl, and they've gone away. Never mind. It doesn't matter.

Tell Moira and the others. And send word to Fiona we'll be needing a new boat built.'

Jay was standing right in front of the women, in plain view. To see the boys, all they had to do was turn their heads and look into the cave. But they didn't. They nodded, and a few dropped curtsies, and then, without saying a word, they all left.

Not until the last sound of their feet on the rocks died away did the Lady let the strand of hair unwind. Eo, Hurple (standing eagerly upright on his shoulder and holding on to his ear) and Adom immediately clambered over the barricade and rushed across the shallows below the dam.

'Jay – are you all right?'

'*I'm* all right – but you smell of – what *is* that?!' Jay held her nose.

'Sheep pee, mostly.'

'It's been a bit of an anxious time for them.'

'Yeah, they worry about getting dipped.'

'And they express their worry by weeing on you two?' said Jay.

They were all grinning madly.

'Oh yes. It's the Sheep Way.'

The Lady's voice cut through their reunion.

'I will speak with that one,' she said, pointing at Eo.

'I'll just come along too, then, shall I?' asked Hurple, but one look from the Lady and he immediately slid to the ground.

Jay picked him up and gave him a pleased hug. 'I'm so glad to see you again,' she whispered, but his attention was focused on Eo and the Lady. Well, just the Lady, really.

Circe was not a tall person, but Jay noticed how she'd set herself uphill from Eo, so that he was looking up at her. She was asking him questions and listening intently to what he had to say. Then he was obviously asking her something, because she kept shaking her head and gesturing with her hands.

Then, suddenly, for no reason they could guess, they saw the Lady look up. Of course *they* all looked up too, but there was nothing there to see – nothing but the sky. Nevertheless, for a long moment Circe gazed intently into the air at something only she was aware of.

Then the moment passed and her attention returned to Eo. She asked him more questions and took particular notice of the sores on his arm. She handed him something, small and wrapped up in a bit of cloth, which he put into his bag. Then she pointed behind him, further along the shore, as if explaining where something was.

'What's she showing him?' wondered Adom.

'I don't know – Hey, where's she going?' said Hurple. 'She's not *leaving*, is she?'

Without taking any further notice of them at all, the Lady turned on her heel and walked away. To Jay, it felt like a slap in the face. Another one.

'Well!' exclaimed Hurple, as Eo came back to them. 'What was *that* all about?'

Eo looked a bit shell-shocked.

'Um,' he said.

He cleared his throat and tried again.

'I, um, told her, about the Challenge, you know, and everything. But she said she couldn't help – that there were many Underworlds, each with its own rules, and her experience wasn't with the one I was talking about. Though generally speaking, she said, getting in was easier than getting out again. She muttered something about the blood of a ram and a ewe and some field of asparagus –'

'Asphodel!' corrected Hurple.

'– yeah, but how none of that really applied.'

'Well, what did she *give* you?' asked Adom. 'Was it something for the Challenge?'

'Just some herbs,' Eo answered, looking suddenly cagey. 'For my sores.'

'But what was she *looking* at, that time she was staring up at the sky?'

'No idea – but she did tell me where they keep the boat. It's not too much further down that way, in a cave she told me about. She said if we leave now, we should be in position in time.'

'Suits me,' snapped Jay. 'The sooner the better.' She hadn't taken part in any of the questioning. She didn't seem to want to talk about the Lady at all.

'At least she healed *you*, Jay,' said Adom. 'And she didn't organize a diving competition for us, so I guess we're still ahead on this one.'

Jay looked at him in amazement. 'Where did *you* learn about diving competitions?' she asked. 'I can't believe that's a monk thing!'

Adom pointed proudly at the manky remains of his wrist computer. 'Came across it in my enchanted arm,' he said, 'and did you know . . .'

As the others set off in the direction of the boat cave, Adom happily telling Jay things she already knew, Eo held back a moment to speak privately with Hurple.

He seemed troubled.

'What is it, lad?' asked the ferret.

'Well, it's – you know I said the herbs she gave me were for my arm, but that's not what really happened. When I asked if that's what they were for, to heal my sores, she gave me this strange look and said, "Only indirectly." And then she said, "They're for the girl." She said, "When push comes to shove." And then she said not to say anything. I didn't understand most of what she was saying, really. And then, when she started staring up at nothing in the sky like that – none of it makes sense.' Eo looked completely bewildered.

Hurple shrugged. 'These mythological women! Just do what she told you, boy, and look for sense someplace else.'

Eo nodded thoughtfully. But there was a little more.

'Professor?'

'Yes?'

'About that . . . You know that thing you said, about the hero Odysseus and the, you know, dog?'

'Yes?'

'I understand now. What you meant.'

'Ah,' said Hurple, and patted the boy gently on the cheek.

13 *The Throw of Lackey Two*

On the G beach, Interrupted Cadence was staring out to sea. It looked as if he were intently watching for the return of the Traveller, while considering the successfulness or otherwise of the last Tide and assessing whatever slim possibilities still remained. Actually, though, he wasn't. Instead, his mind was full of that one brief glimpse he'd had of the Lady. *She had sensed him looking at her.* They'd all been bent over the viewing disc, but she'd looked at *him.* She'd looked up and into his eyes, and he felt he *knew* her, even from that tiny moment. She seemed to him so almost G and yet so utterly alone. She needed to be surrounded with understanding, and comforted, and set free from her responsibilities even if only a little. If only . . .

He sighed. He was tired of feeling young. He tried to concentrate on the task in hand – he didn't plan on being the only one not to manage to catch the Traveller on its return!

There is a special light that falls across the islands sometimes, a little like heather honey, a little like molten gold – impossible to describe, really, but unforgettable nonetheless. This was the light that washed the end of the long afternoon, just before it merged gently with the blue dusk.

Interrupted sighed again. The beauty of the scene, like the beauty of Circe, seemed so sad.

'Courage!' murmured Hibernation Gladrag as she came up beside him.

'That's right!' said Market Jones, joining the others. 'Never let them see you bleed, Double or Nothing, that's what I always say.'

'You're an idiot, Market.'

'No doubt. No doubt.'

Hibernation shook her head at him in mock disapproval as she consulted the Calculating Device.

'Here it comes!'

They'd become almost used to the suddenness, the speed and the shrinking act, and Interrupted caught the Traveller quite neatly. In fact, it nestled into his hands almost as if it were glad to see him – then the Queen's voice shrilled unexpectedly in his ear.

'That's it, then – your last chance over – "out of your hands", is that the expression?'

'I wish you wouldn't sneak around like that!' snapped Interrupted. 'I don't mean to be rude, but it really is quite disconcerting!'

The Queen didn't answer, but he got the impression she was rather pleased. She walked away with a leisurely insolence and pointed once more into the great vortex.

FAQ 45: Is it true that if you've met one demon, you've met them all? That they're all just the same as each other, part of a sort of hive thing? And do Kelpies and other demons really have a collective consciousness, or does it just seem that way?

HURPLE'S REPLY: It's common to assume that monsters, demons and devils are all alike, without back-stories, quirks, preferences or personalities to call their own. This isn't true. The bad guys have just as much individuality per ounce as the good guys, or the guys-in-between. As the old saying goes, 'No two Manifestations of Evil are exactly alike.' Not even the ones who are twins.

One thing demons are **all** good at, however, is the ability to pick up on their leader's requirements. If that's not by some sort of collective consciousness, then how **do** they do it? The single word answer to that would have to be 'motivation'. The Pawns of Darkness **pay attention** because getting it wrong brings with it a good deal more than a mere verbal reprimand. Misguess your leader's wishes and you are likely to be meeting your own entrails face to face.

Not only does this sharpen their focus on things no end – it also explains a certain generic nervousness . . .

For some reason, the Lackey who stepped out on to the sand did not affect them the way the other icy Kelpie had done. This one was tall, perhaps too tall, and too thin. It was almost as if he'd been in the whirlpool for so long he'd become permanently stretched. He seemed to sense immediately that there was no future in playing the allure card and he ignored the G completely. Instead he fawned round the Queen, making placating gestures with his long hands until even *she'd* had enough. She took him by the ear with her razor nails and dragged his head down level with her own. Then she *stared* at him.

'What's she plotting?' muttered Market.

Interrupted found himself horribly distracted. Even from where he stood, he could see the blood that dripped from the Lackey's ear. It was *black*. It was the same colour as the Kelpies' eyes, and the sudden grotesque idea that they had been watching him all this time through eyes filled with blood made him shudder uncontrollably.

Gladrag patted him absent-mindedly without losing her focus on the demons.

The Queen now released the bleeding Lackey and, delicately licking the stain from her fingers, gestured him over to the G. As the creature approached, it was all Interrupted could do to drag his eyes away from that ripped ear. Still, he managed to hold out his hands and pass the Traveller over.

The Lackey grinned. He seemed to find the G's horror amusing, if the strange noise he was making was, in fact, laughter.

It wasn't.

Before Interrupted's revolted eyes, the Lackey hawked

up a gob of acid and let it dribble down on to the sand at his feet. The Kelpie's grin widened as he held the Traveller over the acid and began to open his strange, long hands . . .

What happened next was a bit of a jumble. Both Market Jones and Gladrag realized at the same instant what the Kelpie was about to do, and lunged forward to intervene, just as Interrupted was stepping backwards in disgust. Since the force of two G accelerating in a given direction is invariably greater than the force of one G accelerating in the opposite direction, the three of them stumbled wildly forward and knocked the Kelpie's arm, so that instead of dropping the Traveller directly into the puddle of acid spit, it landed on the sand a short distance away, and promptly disappeared.

The Queen screamed in rage. The Lackey screamed in terror. Interrupted screamed because he'd fallen heavily across the spit and the acid was eating into his shoulder. The only reason Market and Hibernation were silent was that they'd had the breath knocked out of them. They were still in the process of trying to sort themselves out when the Queen stopped shrieking, took the Lackey's neck in her two hands, and snapped it. Then, with a snarl, she flung his body on to the sand and stalked off to the other end of the beach.

In the sudden silence that followed, only Interrupted's whimpering could be heard. The Kelpie's crumpled corpse had already begun to disintegrate. The acid within it (no longer kept in check) made quick work of his remains. By the time Interrupted's wound had been cleansed in sea water and bound up, there was nothing left but an unpleasant black patch on the ground.

Interrupted looked at the other two. He was sore and exhausted and confused, and just about at the end of his patience.

'I have absolutely no idea what just happened,' he said peevishly.

'I'm almost certain the children are OK – they must be.' Gladrag rushed over to the viewing disc, peered into it, then leaned back with a shaky sigh of relief.

'They're fine,' she said. 'Well past the worst.'

'The worst of what?!' Interrupted's voice rose to a small shriek. '*What worst?!*'

'Steady,' murmured Market.

'She was planning to kill them *all* this time,' said Gladrag. 'If she'd succeeded, there was no guarantee the two humans – or Hurple – would have come back.'

Interrupted stared. 'What are you talking about? Eo died *already* and *he* got over it!'

'That's right, that's right – the Challenger must survive – but there's nothing in the Rules about the *companions*.'

'As far as I know, it's never arisen before,' added Market. 'Who knows what put the idea into her horrible head *now*. And to send them *there*. *I'd* never have thought of it!'

Before Interrupted could explode again, Gladrag hurried to explain. 'She was sending them to the beginning of earth's time. When its surface was all lava and volcanoes and the sea was a sort of hot, acidic soup and there was only ammonia and nitrogen to breathe.'

Market shook his head. 'I guess we just weren't thinking *Kelpie* enough!'

'No,' said Gladrag. 'It was only when I saw that blob

of acid that I suddenly realized. She'd already tried to drown them in the future and freeze them in an Ice Age – this time she was aiming to *incinerate* them!'

'Instead of just getting them shot, the way *I* did,' muttered Market bitterly.

'Now, now,' the other two reassured in unison.

'So *that* could have been *them*,' said Interrupted, pointing at the blackened patch, which still smoked a little. 'But it isn't. We're sure of that, right?'

'Come,' said Gladrag. 'See for yourself.'

Interrupted Cadence peered over her shoulder into the viewing disc for a long while, as if he couldn't quite believe what he was seeing. Gradually the lines of worry on his face eased away, and he breathed a sigh of relief and a single word.

'Paradise,' he said.

14 *The Sixth Tide*

'Wake up! Wake up! I think we've died and gone to heaven!' It was a female voice calling, much too loudly.

No, groaned Adom to himself. *Not more girls! Leave me alone . . .*

He was lying on a soft bed and the air was warm and he could feel the afternoon sun on his back, but what was he doing in bed in the afternoon?

He opened his eyes, shoved himself up on his elbows and peered about stupidly. There was Eo, hugging his knees and looking inexplicably delighted, and Jay, leaping about like an over-excited puppy, and Hurple, rolling over and over in the golden sand, and the air was all strange-scented and the trees were wrong . . .

'Where *are* we?' Adom croaked. He didn't even notice he wasn't throwing up, which was a nice change.

Jay flopped down beside him. 'In a tropical paradise, that's where! I take back everything I've ever said about being indoors. This is fabulous!'

'But we should be in Dalraida – in Scotland – the Western Isles!' This place felt wrong, alien. '*We're not supposed to be here!*' he wailed.

'The boy's absolutely right, of course,' said Hurple, 'but not for the reasons he thinks.' He was lying on his back with all his legs in the air now, and still managed to pontificate. 'As far as I can tell, the time we have come to pre-dates humans of any description by a fair few million years.'

Eo joined them. 'You're not serious!' he exclaimed. 'This is *pre-human*? Is that why it feels so . . .' He waved his hands about, at a loss for words to describe how delicious it all seemed.

Hurple smiled benignly at them. 'It is pleasant, isn't it?'

But Adom wasn't feeling it. 'How can you all be so happy?! What is there here for us? What can this Tide give?'

Hurple rolled over and put a paw on the boy's leg. 'There's no one here to give us *anything*, Adom. This Tide there isn't going to be a Gift. It was the Kelpies' throw and this is where they sent us, where we couldn't receive any help because there's nobody to receive it from.'

'The only thing we can do is catch our breath, gather our strength, gird our loins, that sort of thing?' said Jay hopefully. 'Please say it's true, Professor! I've heard about places like this in history classes, about beach holidays, and, oh, bonfires on the sand, and all kinds of wonderful things. I never thought I'd ever have the chance at one.'

Eo didn't say anything, but the look on his face said it all.

'Happy holiday, children,' said Hurple, and Eo and Jay immediately leapt up, hooting delightedly.

'Who's for a swim?' cried Jay.

She started to strip off without waiting for a reply. Adom looked away quickly and gulped. Eo didn't notice, as he was busy pulling his own clothes off as well. To Adom's relief, both of them stopped at underwear.

'Why is it so *hot*?!' Adom muttered.

'Could it have anything to do with a certain young lady's sudden display of skin?'

Hurple's amused comment was not helpful. Adom turned and glared. Fortunately, the others hadn't heard.

'Last one in's a rotten egg,' shrieked Jay.

Giggling madly, the two sprinted for the water, spattering sand all over Adom and the ferret.

'Don't mind them,' Hurple chuckled. 'You know what the young are like, first day of the holidays.'

Adom just looked at him. 'I don't know what you're talking about. Sometimes I don't know what *any* of you are talking about,' he said sadly. 'Honestly, half the time I haven't a clue.'

'And you think they *do*?!' Hurple looked up at him with his mad, bright little eyes. 'Don't be daft.'

'*Me*, daft?! Look around you, ferret of Scotland, at your native land! *This* –' Adom waved a hand – '*this* is daft.'

Hurple gazed around at the exotic scene. 'You're right,' he said, nodding. 'Totally crazy. But it makes a great story. Listen . . .'

So, as Eo and Jay messed about happily in the warm sea, Professor Hurple explained to Adom how the world is a changing place, slowly, inexorably, always on the move, and how once, long ago, the land that would be his home was thousands of kilometres to the south, bound by a shallow tropical sea.

Because of the wrist computer, Adom had all the vocabulary he needed to follow the ferret's explanations. What he didn't have was the blasé familiarity with wonders that let Jay and, in a different way, Eo easily accept ideas like floating continents, unimaginable lengths of time, animal kingdoms that thrived and grew and then would someday completely disappear. For Adom, it was astonishing in a whole new way and, without noticing it, the story left him ready to be enchanted by their surroundings.

There hadn't been a lot of the afternoon left when they arrived, and now the setting sun drew the swimmers back on to the beach, puffing, a bit pruny and thoroughly content.

'Look at those colours – they don't seem *real*!' said Jay, awe-struck.

The oranges and blood reds flared across half the sky, making huge twisted hook-fingered patterns against the darkening blue.

'I've *never* seen a sunset like that before,' said Eo.

'I suspect it has something to do with our location, so close to the equator,' murmured Hurple, but there was an uneasy note in his voice.

'It looks like the sky is on fire,' said Adom.

This was so exactly what it *did* look like that no one spoke for a while. And it was into this silence that a new sound came. It was a bumbling, rumbling noise, with now and then a kind of throaty trumpeting thrown in for good measure. It seemed to be coming from the left, out of sight around the curve of the beach. It seemed to be coming closer.

'May I suggest we move a little towards the tree line?' said Hurple softly.

No one argued.

They crept up the beach and, from the shelter of the trees, looked out on an amazing sight. Around the headland came a wall of enormous beasts, not shaped like anything any of them could ever truly have seen before, not hairy or furred but with skins like lizards, patterned and coloured as surreally as the sky they walked under. All sizes – small editions that skittered ponderously around the edges of the herd – huge males that eyed the interlopers by the trees and discounted them as any threat – females that flirted or fussed depending on whether their attention was on their men or their children – hundreds passing at a stately pace –

'*Dinosaurs!*' breathed Jay, and Eo gave a strangled yelp.

Adom had the word in his brain, but it didn't mean anything to him. 'What *are* they?' he whispered. *The beasts of hell* – Brother Drostlin's voice blared in his mind – *monsters of the apocalypse – see, this is what St John saw, his vision in Revelation –*

Abomination!

But Adom knew, beyond a shadow of a doubt, that Brother Drostlin was wrong. *Whatever* these creatures were, hell had nothing to do with it.

The procession lasted many minutes, as the great herd flowed past them along the beach and on round the next headland. For a long moment after they had disappeared, nobody moved. Nobody breathed. And when they did,

FAQ 943: If the dinosaurs died out long before any humans existed, why is it so many human societies have independently come up with the idea of dragons?

HURPLE'S REPLY: Makes you wonder, doesn't it?

they looked at each other shyly, as if they had just shared something unspeakably precious and intimate.

Soon after, the fiery display in the sky also was over and, with the suddenness of the tropics, all at once it was night. Adom set about making them a fire, more for comfort and light than warmth. They shared out the last of Jay's food packs and refilled the water bottles from a stream that wandered out of the trees. Adom, Eo and Hurple sighed with contentment and lay about feeling comfortably full. But Jay couldn't settle. She fidgeted and squirmed and finally jumped up.

'That fire's not big enough,' she said emphatically. 'A place like this – a night like this deserves a . . . a *bonfire*! That's what they always had on beach holidays.' She'd never seen a bonfire in real life but she'd seen pictures, and *she knew what she wanted*.

Eo and Adom groaned. Surely the fire was fine as it was? The air was like soup, and made them feel boneless and lazy, but it seemed to make *Jay* more and more energetic.

'Come on!' she cried, prodding them with her feet. 'Let's build the biggest bonfire this beach has ever seen.'

'How about the *only* bonfire this beach has ever seen?' grumbled Eo.

'Even better!' she yelped. 'Then we can dance naked around it and howl to the moon!' She laughed at the expression on Adom's face. 'Just kidding! But the moon *will* rise soon, won't it, and when it does I want it to look down on this world with no people and be *amazed*!'

'She's mad,' said Eo flatly to Adom.

'Completely,' he agreed.

But they got up anyway.

There was no shortage of fuel, though Jay still wasn't very good at distinguishing between what was burnable and what wasn't. They fed the fire until it was leaping high into the night sky, scattering trails of sparks on the warm breeze and roaring like a river in spate. Jay got them to dance round it – fully clothed – and they were so busy jumping and laughing, and their eyes were so full of the glare of the flames, they didn't see the moon rise until it was completely clear of the hills.

The Professor was the first to notice. 'Look!' he called to the others. 'What do you think? Amazement sits upon its brow!'

The moon was huge and perfectly round, and the face of the Man in the Moon as it hung over them really could *not* have looked more surprised.

'YES!' yelled Jay, punching the air. 'We did it!'

Everybody grinned, panting slightly.

'So, what now? Anybody for a walk, this fine moonlit night?'

'Not me.'

'No, thanks.'

Jay looked at them for a moment, then shrugged. 'OK. Hurple, you're with me.' And then she scooped the ferret up and draped him over her shoulder. 'See you in a while.'

'What was that all about?' said Eo, coming up on one elbow to look after them.

'No idea,' said Adom.

'Fair enough,' said Eo with a shrug, and lay back.

*

The air was like velvet as Jay and Hurple strolled quietly along the shore.

'You're missing the patches, aren't you,' said Hurple suddenly, and he wasn't asking a question.

'Don't be ridiculous!' Jay spluttered at first. '*I* don't need to patch – I'm not a saddo, you know!'

'I know,' said Hurple.

She sighed. 'Well, yes, all right. I am. But, I'll tell you something, Professor. I can't believe how much more *alive* I feel. I mean, who would *want* to feel sad or scared or sick if they didn't have to? But I've been feeling *all* those, *and* hungry and wet and cold and cross and lost . . . and I still feel like I could "leap tall buildings at a single bound" like those superheroes in the olden days! Daft, eh?'

'One might even think there was a moral in there somewhere,' said the ferret mildly.

There was a short silence. For a moment, Jay thought she might talk to him about what Circe had said to her, and how churned up it made her feel . . . but she wasn't ready to yet.

Instead, she said, 'You know what, though, you still haven't told me about *you*. *Before,* I mean, before you started living with the G – and don't try and put me off with just any old rubbish!' She shoved an imaginary microphone under his nose with her free hand. 'Tell me, Professor Hurple, tell me about *you*.'

The ferret smiled, and then licked his foot. His fur showed fabulously silver in the moonlight. His beady eyes were black pearls. They'd been through so much together that Jay had forgotten how *different* he was from her. In some ways he had more in common with the strange, impossible creatures of the world around them than he did with her. In some ways he shouldn't really exist at all. Not outside a story, anyway.

'Why are you here?' she asked softly.

For a moment, he didn't speak, and she thought he wasn't going to. But then, still not looking at her, 'Two words,' he said. 'Two words say it all.'

Two words? she wondered. *Cosmic tilt? Inescapable fate? It's just a clever disguise – no, that's more than two . . .*

'Library closures,' said Hurple.

Jay stopped walking. 'This sounds like a story I want to be sitting down for,' she said.

Hurple didn't argue, and she headed further up the beach to where a mossy log stretched invitingly on the sand.

'Right. Library closures,' she said, setting the ferret down on the log beside her. 'I'm all ears.'

For a moment, Hurple paused, gathering his memories. Then he began to talk . . . about the Librarian.

She was a short, blobby sort of woman who wore comfortable clothes.

'She had a favourite old sweatshirt with the words "So Many Books, So Little Time" printed on it – I remember that.'

Hurple didn't know how old the Librarian was, or whether she'd ever had a life before the Ardnamurchan Library and, if so, what that life could have been. Jay gathered she was a bit mad – 'three steps to the side, you might say' was how Hurple put it. He called her D. D. Hamilton, because that's what she called herself. Apparently the initials stood for Doris Delores, but Hurple spent his kittenhood assuming they were short for Dewey Decimal.

Jay let that pass, and tried to come to grips with the important stuff.

'So, you used to live with a librarian?' she said.

'Yes.'

'Who was a human. A human librarian in a library. For humans.'

Hurple nodded.

'You were her pet?'

'No. I was her colleague.'

Jay stared at him for a moment, but he didn't elaborate.

'But what on earth did *you* do in a *library*?!' she asked.

Hurple looked surprised at her surprise. 'Well,' he said, 'during the day I kept the Librarian company, and at night I read the books.'

There was a pause.

'Isn't that a bit . . . unusual?' asked Jay carefully.

Hurple shrugged. 'Perhaps. But I didn't really *know* what ferrets usually did. To begin with, I mean. Not till I'd read up on them. I hadn't ever *met* one. The Librarian was the first being I opened my eyes to. All I can think of is I imprinted on her somehow.'

'Imprinted . . .' Jay frowned. 'Like chickens that are hatched under ducks and grow up thinking they *are* ducks until they go on to the farm pond and drown? Like that?'

'Good heavens, no!' said Hurple indignantly. 'I'm an excellent swimmer!' There was a pause. 'Not, of course, that that's relevant. I just thought I'd, you know, mention it.'

'I guess we have to accept it. You're . . .' Jay paused, looking for the right words, 'kind of unique.'

'No one can be *kind of* unique, but I take your point. I am *not* an ordinary ferret.' He paused for a second. 'D. D. Hamilton always seemed to appreciate that.'

For a moment the slightly incongruous figure of the Librarian filled both their minds.

'So, did she know what you were doing? Did you talk to her?'

Hurple shook his head. 'I only discovered speech afterwards. And though I think she *suspected* I was not an ordinary beast – maybe even the fact I could read – it was as if she didn't want to look into it all too much, you know? In case it wasn't so.'

Jay nodded. She knew what that felt like.

'We were very happy. It was a wonderful library in a spectacularly beautiful place – which of course has long been underwater in your time. You'll just have to take my word for how beautiful it was. Much better suited for luxury holiday flats or a posh hotel, or so the developers thought. You could hear them grinding their teeth every time they drove by in their big cars.'

He sighed. 'But *we* didn't worry. We thought nobody could touch us. After all, what could be more important than books?' He stopped talking. He looked as if he didn't want to start again.

Jay stroked a finger down his head. 'You don't have to tell me, you know. If you don't want to –'

'No. No, I do,' he interrupted. 'It's just . . . I haven't spoken of this to very many people . . .'

She stayed still, letting Hurple gather his thoughts. Then he took a deep breath and continued.

'At first nothing happened. But it wasn't the sort of thing you can easily keep a secret. When the developers heard the government had cut off our funding they couldn't believe their luck. There was a lot of squabbling about exactly *who* was going to get our site, and that gave us a bit more time, but eventually the highest bidder rose to the top like scum, and was ready to kick us out. Problem was, we weren't ready to go.'

'But I thought you said you had no funding!'

'We didn't. But she was never a big eater, the Librarian, and I'd been catching my own rabbits for years and . . . she'd decided to gamble.

'She thought that if she refused to remove the books, the developers would never dare destroy the building. She thought that everybody *respected* books the same way she did. That they might consider hurting her, but they'd *never* consider hurting the books.'

'What happened?'

'She gambled, like I said . . . and she lost.'

As Hurple talked, Jay felt as if she'd been there herself. She could see it so clearly – the Library, and Dewey Decimal, and Hurple. And their mad plans.

'When . . . it . . . happened, she didn't seem to think of herself at all. She just yelled at me to get out.

'"Go! Save yourself!" she said.

'For a moment, I honestly didn't understand what she meant. Go? Go where? The Library was my home – the Librarian was my family! I just stood there, chittering uselessly, until she picked me up and looked me in the eyes.

'"Back wall," she said. "By the window. Where the Celtic Mythology section meets Sci-fi/Fantasy, there's a gap. It's tight, but an exceptional ferret should just fit. I'm counting on you," she said.

'And then she gave me such a look. It had hope in it, and resignation and belief and at the same time acceptance that what she was desperate to believe might very well not be true at all, and sadness, and affection . . .

'There were so many things I should have done. I should have made her come with me, somehow. I should have reassured her there wasn't a book in the place that wasn't safe in my head, and if that was the hope she was clinging to, *she was right*! I should have stayed to help her fight. I should have . . .'

He was trembling.

'What happened?' Jay asked gently.

'Fire.' He dragged in a big breath and started to talk in a strange, strained voice. 'These things get out of hand very easily. I suspect no one really *planned* to set the Library alight. An incident not without precedent, of course. Similar things have occurred – the Royal Library at Alexandria, we are told, succumbed to accidental arson . . .' His head dropped and he said with great sadness, 'I panicked, all right? I smelled fire and I'm an animal and I ran.'

Jay nodded. 'And was there a gap?'

'What?'

'A gap. Between Myth and Fantasy. Like she said.'

'Yes. Oh yes.'

'And that's how you ended up in Eo's world.'

Another nod.

'Well, thank goodness for that!' Jay exclaimed. 'Can you imagine us having to handle all this on our own!?'

Hurple snorted, a little raggedly. 'There's that, isn't there?'

FAQ 4-87: Do time travellers find that it helps, knowing that none of the things that make them sad have actually happened yet? Or that they happened much, much earlier? Do you know what I'm on about?

HURPLE'S REPLY: Yes, I understand the question. And it should help. But it doesn't.

Jay suddenly scooped him up and held him in front of her face, the length of him dangling down in surprise.

'And I think the Librarian was absolutely right to count on you, because you are without doubt the wisest wee weasel that could possibly be. Thank you for telling me.'

And she kissed him on his furry nose and set him down in a heap. 'And that's enough moonlight meandering for me,' she said. 'Let's get back and see what Eo and Adom are up to. If they've let my beautiful bonfire go out, I'll throttle them.'

But as she started to stand up, Hurple put a restraining paw on her leg. She looked at him questioningly.

'Please – if you don't mind – don't tell the boys.'

Jay raised an eyebrow.

Hurple gave a half shrug. 'Pure vanity, I admit. It's not my finest hour we've been talking about and, to be honest, I'd rather it stayed between us two. As long as the lads don't know the facts, they can make up any number of flattering pasts for me. I'm just low enough to be willing to accept admiration I don't deserve.'

Jay snorted. 'You mean you're just *human* enough!' Then she leaned down and offered him an arm to climb up. 'Don't worry, Professor. They won't hear it from me.'

But he didn't move.

'I said, don't worry – I won't tell,' she repeated, but it was as if he'd forgotten she was still there. Then, suddenly, he gripped her arm with his sharp claws.

'HEY!'

'Can't you hear it?' he hissed at her. 'There's something coming – something *big* . . .!'

She straightened up, straining her ears. There was nothing *to* hear but the waves, and the wind, and . . . what was that? Deep, almost deeper than hearing . . . it was as if she were *feeling* it, coming up from the ground through her feet . . .

'*Run!*' screeched Hurple. '*Run for the trees!*'

She grabbed him tight and ran as the herd had first come stampeding back round the headland towards them. The earth shook and the dull thunder of their pounding feet was punctuated by bellows of panic. They surged past, a great, many-backed monster in the moonlight, until, as suddenly as it had appeared, the herd was gone.

Jay stood in the shelter of the trees for a moment, breathless and stunned.

Then she was running again, frantically, back the way the herd had come, back to where they had left the boys . . .

It was hard going on the churned-up sand, but every time she fell flat she was up again in an instant, shaking the sand from her face as she ran. Surely they would have had time to . . . they would have heard it coming . . . they wouldn't just *sit* there . . .

Then, as she cleared an outcropping of rock, she collided with them both, running in the opposite direction in search of Hurple and her.

They grabbed each other's hands.

'Are you – ?'

'Did you – ?'

'What *happened*?!' they panted to each other.

'My fire!' Jay wailed, looked over their shoulders.

The bonfire had been scattered by hundreds of feet,

bits of it flickering about the beach like the aftermath of an explosion.

They scraped some of it together and huddled round. No one knew what to say. It was Adom who first noticed that Jay was crying. He nudged Eo, and the two exchanged horrified glances.

'Er . . .' said Eo.

Jay scrubbed at her face with her hand. 'I really liked it here,' she said in a strangled voice. 'I really did. It was . . . nice.'

Hurple reached up and licked her cheek comfortingly.

'I . . .' he started to say – when the earth lurched.

They scrambled to their feet, their eyes showing white.

'Did you *feel* that?!'

'It's the whatsits! They're coming back!'

'No, it was bigger than that.'

'BIGGER whatsits!'

With a groan, the ground moved again, making them all stagger.

'Earthquake,' whispered Hurple.

For a moment, that was enough strangeness. But then Eo cleared his throat.

'I don't want to worry anybody,' he said, sounding plenty worried himself. 'But don't you think the tide's a bit . . . wrong? I mean, it's gone *really* far out now. Would you say that was normal round here?'

'Could just be very shallow,' suggested Hurple.

Everyone gazed out over the expanse of wet sand and mud. Outcrops of coral reef and seaweed-draped rock threw strange shadows in the moonlight, and everything glittered weirdly.

They weren't sure they could see the line of the sea at all.

'*Way* too far out,' muttered Adom.

And then it began to snow.

It was a grey, acrid-smelling snow, neither wet nor cold. It filled the air, so that there wasn't so much left to breathe. It made the fire stutter and smoke, blurring the moon. It began to collect on their shoulders and hair.

'What is it?' whispered Adom.

Hurple delicately put out his tongue and tasted. 'Ash,' he said hoarsely. 'Volcanic ash. There's been an eruption. Somewhere. A huge eruption.'

'Some people say it was a huge eruption that wiped out the dinosaurs.' Jay's voice sounded strange and far away. 'So huge it threw ash high into the atmosphere, where the winds took it and carried it right round the world.' The moon and the stars were only faintly visible now, and the children shuffled closer to each other in the grey fog. 'Other people say an asteroid hit the earth and did the same thing – heaving tons of dust kilometres into the sky. It lasted for a long time – for years – the sun was blocked out – no light, so nothing could grow – no light – only grey . . .' A sob stopped her.

'Don't think about it now. Our time's almost up here, anyway. The Traveller's coming and then we'll be gone. Here, take my hand.' Adom reached out and held her hand with both of his, trying to be a comfort.

'That's right,' said Eo. They could dimly see him settle Hurple round his neck. 'Hold tight, Professor!' He took Jay's other hand.

There was crashing in the forest as more animals were

caught up in the strangeness and the fear. Hurple wished with all his heart he didn't have to hear those sounds. He was starting to pant and his eyes stung. He let go of Eo with his front paws and rubbed at his face, but that only made the stinging worse. A tiny part of his brain was still able to consider the chemical components of the gases they were now inhaling, and the possible effects these might have on patterns of perception – but no *other* part of his brain was prepared to listen. Hurple's enormous mental capacity had been overloaded by memory and emotion, in particular that all-consumer, guilt.

He kept picturing all those animals, trapped in terror, about to die . . .

They have no idea what is happening to them, no idea what to expect. How could they? And yet they could be saved so much suffering if they had someone to tell them what to do. Guide them through the dangers. Show *them. A leader. I could save them – not all of them, of course not, but* some. *It's what D. D. Hamilton would have done. D. D. Hamilton. It's strange how much that bush over there looks like her . . . just like her. Bless me, it's* her –

'D. D.!'

In the bell of silence, no one heard his cry.

Hurple launched himself with all four paws and hit the ground running.

'– ?!' Eo started to turn, not understanding what was happening.

'*Hurple, NO!*' Jay shrieked silently, keeping tight hold of the G's hand. '*Come back!*'

Then the Traveller was there, and took them.

15 *The Travellers' Return*

This time, instead of shrinking as it approached, the Traveller streaked across the exposed sand and seaweed and on to the G beach at full size – and exploded in mid-air, soaking everyone and flinging three bodies hard on to the sand. Eo was up at once, spitting grit out of his mouth, throwing himself at the Queen.

'*What have you done to my friend?*' he screamed. '*Where is he?!*'

Even in his frenzy he stopped short of touching her. Nevertheless, the Kelpie rocked back on her heels a little. She was not accustomed to being menaced by filthy, wet, half-crazed boys. From the main vortex, her minions clacked and wailed in agitation till she gestured abruptly and they subsided.

'Your *friend* is where you left him. As you can see.' And she indicated the G's viewing disc, shimmering on the sand.

Eo flung himself down on his knees and peered frantically into the disc.

'There's nothing there,' he shrilled. 'I can't see him! You're lying! There's nothing – just grey, and –' He broke off and, before anyone could stop him, he'd plunged his arm, up to the shoulder, into the viewing disc.

'*Where are you?*' he grunted, groping blindly about. '*Where – are – you* – HA!' There was a jolt from an unseen source that shook his whole body, so violent it was as if he'd been knocked free of the earth's pull for a moment, so that there was nothing to keep him from being dragged down into the disc . . .

Eo's head and both shoulders had already disappeared when Adom hit him. The tackle had a lifetime of hard manual labour behind it and it dragged Eo back out of the disc with a horrible sucking sound and smashed him on the G beach. Hurple, clutched by the scruff of his neck, came too, but the crash-landing loosened Eo's grip and the ferret flew in an arc over the heaped boys. He hit the sand like a wet sock and lay there without moving.

'Is he . . .?' gasped Adom.

'Hurple!' cried Jay.

She rushed over, scooped him up and cradled him in her arms. There wasn't a great deal of dignity in his position, on his back with all four legs in the air like that, but there was no mistaking her concern. Eo and Adom stumbled over, and the adult G clustered around as well.

'Give him here, girl,' said Market, not unkindly.

'He's breathing, anyway.'

'Thank goodness for that. I wasn't looking forward to doing mouth-to-mouth!'

'Why won't he wake up?!' wailed Eo.

'How can you ask such a thing? *Collars* don't wake up. How odd, to call a collar your *friend*. An *unusual* collar, that speaks and moves and *interferes* through six full Tides, and now has excited such conjecture over its *health*!' The Queen was livid. 'You'll find that *that* is a collar that will *not* wake up. I may choose to revive the creature when our entrance to your world is established, since a conscious soul is so much more . . . tasty. Fear is by far the best sauce. Yes, I suspect I will choose to wake him then – but not before!'

Her voice had risen to a shriek on the last words, but she regained control of herself.

'Now you have another reason to regret *your* choice, *boy*. If you had paid the forfeit of your own poor soul at the start, all these others would not now be facing the consequences *when you fail* in the Final Challenge. When you *fail* to find your way through the mazes of the Dry Heart to the Centre, to the place that can shut the door –'

Behind her, the Kelpies spun faster and faster, wailing and beating their fists against the wall of water, their hunger made even more desperate now that their release into the world of the G was so close.

'Not long, not long,' the Queen called over her shoulder, never taking her eyes off Eo. 'We will play out the last act, even when the end is self-evident. *We* will not stoop to cheating.'

'What do you call that bright idea of burning them all up in lava? Or drowning them? Or letting them die of cold?' yelled Interrupted indignantly.

'Er, I think you're upsetting the children,' murmured Gladrag. And indeed, the three were looking pretty appalled.

'L-lava?' quavered Jay. 'Nobody said anything about *lava!*'

'Now, now,' said Market reassuringly. 'We were here the whole time. *And a fat lot of good it did too,*' he added in an undertone.

Eo mumbled something.

'What was that? Did it speak?' sneered the Queen.

'I said, I'm not going to fail.' Eo's voice sounded thin and desperate, but he kept it from quavering.

'That's right!' Jay came and stood at his shoulder and tried to glare at the Kelpie without entirely succeeding.

Adom came to Eo's other side. 'You are a demon. Hell is where you belong, with all the fallen angels.' He was doing his best not to look at any part of the Queen below the neck, but she was completely aware of how much she was disturbing him and smiled smugly.

'I'll consider myself warned, then, shall I?' she said, mocking them all. Then she drew herself up, tall as a storm cloud. 'It is almost time.'

There was a panicky chorus from the G.

'Hang on!'

'Just a minute!'

'Wait!'

She paused and looked at them scornfully. 'Well? What is it now?'

Market spluttered, 'Um, er, right. How do they get to the Island? The Traveller *exploded*, for crying out loud!'

The Queen smiled and gestured towards the Kelpie vortex. 'Why, with me, of course.'

'NO!' Eo, Adom and Jay yelped.

'No,' said Hibernation Gladrag, more quietly but no less emphatically.

'What's the matter, don't you *trust* me? Very well, then.' And she crooked a finger. Immediately the two viewing discs detached themselves from the beach and cartwheeled into her hands. With a flip of the wrist she combined them and set them spinning in mid-air and then, like a potter working with clay on a wheel, she shaped them up into a brother to the Traveller. 'There. The little darlings' own private transport.'

The 'darlings' didn't look much happier than they had been about entering the main vortex, but at least they wouldn't be with *her*.

'What other questions have you? What other pathetic attempts at delay?'

'Who throws it?' asked Interrupted.

'No one. There is only one possible destination this time. The Traveller knows where to go.'

'The Island.'

'Yes. And that is the last prevarication that time allows.'

Before anyone could move, she turned on her heel and flung the second Traveller directly at the children. There was just time for expressions of horror to register on their faces and then they were gone. The thing launched itself into the sky and headed north.

The three G stood on the beach, an unconscious Hurple in Market's arms. They looked as they felt: pathetic and unwell.

'I'll see you there, on the Island,' purred the Queen. 'Or not. It won't make any difference to the outcome.'

As she moved towards the main vortex, she looked back at them over one shoulder.

'Sure I can't offer *you* a lift?' she said with a sneer.

There was an audible gulp. Then Gladrag hastily got a grip. She shook her head. 'No. No, thank you. We'll, er, make our own way. Uh, see you there!' she concluded brightly.

The Queen was still staring at them contemptuously as she stepped into the vortex, and it folded round her and spun into the night.

For a moment, the three G didn't know why they suddenly felt so good. The air tasted delightful, and the night breeze was almost silky, and the sand felt wonderful under their feet. Even their hair began to relax out of those tight emergency buns.

'It was that blasted vortex, wasn't it!' exclaimed Market. 'It was spoiling everything, just by being there!'

'I'd honestly forgotten what it was like before,' murmured Interrupted.

Gladrag was taking deep breaths of the clean sea air. She nodded, and then frowned as a thought struck her.

'You know that thing the boy did – with the viewing disc?' she said, turning to the others.

'Yes?'

'Did the Queen know, do you think? That you could do that?'

'I'm pretty sure not,' said Market. 'She looked as shocked as anyone when the boy dived in like that.'

'Yes, I think so too. But . . .' Gladrag's face was troubled.

'But what?'

'She knows now.'

There was an anxious pause.

'There's no viewing disc on the Island, though, surely?' said Interrupted.

'No, no. Sufficient unto the day, eh?'

'Eh?'

But Market was frowning now too.

'Did either of *you* know you could do it?' he asked.

Gladrag and Interrupted shook their heads.

'And if we *had* known, would we have been tempted to, you know, stick anything in there?'

The G thought about those vertiginous depths and shuddered.

'That's what I thought,' said Market. 'And,' he added with a sigh, 'that's "the last prevarication that time allows", as our dear friend so sweetly put it.'

The three looked sheepishly at each other. It was so peaceful to just be on their own beach, alone with the sky and the waves.

'What about poor old Hurple?'

Market looked down at the lifeless ferret cradled in his arm.

'We can't just leave him out in the open,' said Interrupted anxiously.

So they carried Hurple to the high ground beyond the grass dunes. Interrupted made a sort of nest and they tucked him away in the shelter of the rocks. There was nothing more they could do for him now.

'Gulls?' suggested Gladrag, but the others shuddered.

'Too cruel. That's the Queen's territory!' said Market.

'What, then?'

'Oystercatchers,' said Interrupted firmly. 'I've always liked oystercatchers!'

FAQ 814: What are 'spring tides' and can you explain why they don't just happen in the spring?

HURPLE'S REPLY: Spring tides occur when the sun, the moon and the earth are in a line. They have very high high tides and very low low tides. Given that they happen all during the year it might seem foolish to call them 'spring tides', except that they aren't actually called that after the season but after the German word springen, which means 'to leap up'.

But then there's also the moon's orbit to take into account – it's more sort of oval-shaped than a tidy circle. This means that sometimes the moon passes closer to the earth (perigee) and sometimes further away (apogee). So when the **full** moon is also a relatively **close** moon, the difference between low and high tides is even greater. **But** if you want to see a truly **spectacular** range of water height what you want to get is the line-up of the sun, moon and earth being so exact that there is a lunar or solar eclipse happening **at the same time** as the moon is the closest it comes to the earth. Now **that's** exciting!

'Daft and cheerful,' Market agreed. 'Much more *us*!'

Without fuss, the three G shifted into the clown-coloured feathers of three oystercatchers and took off into the onshore breeze. They made a brief circle over their well-loved island, then moved away northwards under the rising moon on purposeful wings.

'That really *is* low, even for a spring tide,' said Market, looking down. 'It doesn't look . . . normal.'

'Well, it's a chancy time of year, isn't it?' said Gladrag uneasily. 'I'm sure Supernova Tangent would remind you of the details if she were here!'

'I could do with one of her lectures on Samhainn, spring tide and orbital perigee round about now – and I never thought I'd hear myself say *that*!' said Market.

'Do either of you know when we're due another eclipse?' asked Interrupted.

Market tried to count on his fingers, but stopped when he began to lose altitude.

'Oh, boy,' he said.

They looked anxiously up at the full moon. It was still white and clear, but as it reached its high point in the sky, the G knew that would change. The shadow of the earth would gradually fall across its face and the moon would darken to orange, then red. 'Blood Moon.' That's what it was called.

And strange, uncanny things happened under a moon like that.

The Island was in sight now, looking like a weird loaf of bread that hadn't risen properly in the oven. Towering hexagonal columns of basalt were capped by turfed overhangs, and the whole place slanted south to north

FAQ 736: What's Samhainn? Is it the same as Hallowe'en?

HURPLE'S REPLY: They belong to the same family, anyway! Samhainn begins at dusk on 31 October, which is the eve of the new year in the Celtic calendar. The Celts saw it as a gap in time, where the human world and the Otherworlds came together. The Celts thought of time as going from darkness to light, so the Celtic day started at dusk and lasted until dusk of the next. That's also why their year started at the end of summer – the beginning of the dark winter – and continued till harvest time of the next year.

like a gigantic wedge. Normally the sea broke against the jumble of ancient lava, surging into innumerable caves and crevices and leaving the black basalt scoured grey up to the high-tide mark. But this night it was different. Stretching out with the Island as its centre was an expanse of mud, rock and weed. Forests of kelp, several storeys high, majestic in their proper element, drooped now under their own weight and lay like dank hair over the rocks. Creatures not normally exposed to the air scuttled and gulped and dragged themselves away. The deepest places still held water, salt rivers and lakes between the jagged mountains and valleys of the sea bed. This was low tide as it was not meant to be.

Gladrag moaned softly to herself.

'There they are,' said Market, pointing ahead with his beak.

The main Kelpie vortex was clearly visible, a huge impossible column of water balanced on the top of the cliffs. It seemed to reach for the moon, but they knew that lifeless rock wasn't what it wanted. There were no souls to suck on the moon.

It was waiting for *them*.

Even from this far away, they could feel it. All the joy of flying, of being feathered and streamlined and strong, drained away until there was only the effort left.

The closer they approached, the harder it became to keep going.

'Do we really have to go?'

'I mean, it's not as if we're going to make any difference. It's entirely up to the children now.'

'That's right. And it's not as if we won't *know* what

happens. We'll know soon enough how it ended. They only have till dawn.'

'We serve no useful purpose just keeping watch.'

'It isn't as if we've done a lot of good *so* far, either.'

They were all in perfect agreement. There really *was* no earthly point in going to the Island.

They went anyway.

16 *Blood Moon*

The actual arrival of the three G on the Island was faster – and less elegant – than they might have wished. The dead air surrounding the Kelpie vortex offered no real buoyancy or currents to glide in on, so it was more of a collapse out of the sky than a proper landing. The humans who appeared out of the bird shapes were bruised and dishevelled and a good bit shaken. Fortunately, even though the G avoided the Island whenever possible, the place was included in their robe-distributing system.

The Queen seemed surprised at first to see them, but she recovered almost immediately into a default sneer.

'So glad you could join us,' she half-purred, half-snarled. 'And don't worry. My people wouldn't *dream* of touching you before the Tide is complete. Why break the Rules when so soon you will be a *legitimate* . . . menu item.'

The G stared at each other, bemused.

'What does she mean?' muttered Market.

'They can't touch us *anyway* – they're stuck inside the

v . . . v . . .' Interrupted's voice trailed off into silence as he realized that the maelstrom's outer wall of water was beginning to *thin* . . .

In ones and twos at first, and then in crowds, the vortex was ejecting its cargo, a violent, random birth. Within minutes, the entire top of the Island swarmed with Kelpies – horses, women, men – bucking and screaming and running as if they hadn't been free in the air for a thousand years. The G were dizzy with all the noise and the swirling motion, not to mention the wholesale mesmerizing that hit them from every side like a solid fog. There was *so much* the effect was nauseating rather than alluring. The Queen held her place at the centre of the commotion, but she shrieked and jerked convulsively, drunk with the mad expectant ecstasy of her subjects.

Looking up, the G saw that the eclipse was almost complete, and already the moon's face had turned a coppery red, as if painted with pale rust or a thin wash of blood. The vortex itself remained, as tall as ever, but transparent now and half its original circumference. Gladrag had a momentary vision of the whole enormous volume of water collapsing in on itself and washing them all away, and thought what a relief that would be . . . but it didn't happen.

The Queen screeched a command and the mad swirl of bodies around them froze. In the silence, hundreds of black eyes turned towards her as she cried,

'To the Pool!'

She moved away from the vortex, the G trailing after her and swathes of Kelpies opening before. She led them a little distance across the broken ground to a shallow depression and stopped.

FAQ 678: Why does the moon turn red during a lunar eclipse?

HURPLE'S REPLY: A lunar eclipse happens when the earth is directly between the sun and the moon, so that the earth's shadow falls across the moon's face. The blue part of the sunlight has been scattered in the earth's atmosphere (which is why the sky looks blue to us) and the remaining red light gets bent round and becomes the colour of the shadow, which then falls on the moon and gives it its coppery shade. Does knowing this make the Blood Moon seem any less weird or portentous? Not in my opinion.

The Western Isles are blessed with thousands of ponds of sharp, clear water, tinged with peat, stone-drained, icy and fresh. The Pool was not one of these. It was small, perhaps two metres across, its water blurred with algae and slime. It was probably a sort of murky lime-green colour in daylight but under the Blood Moon it showed a horrible thick grey, like mouldy soup. And it smelled, a clinging, bad smell.

'Makes you want to go away and scrub yourself with soap, doesn't it?' Market murmured.

Meanwhile, the redness of the moon had intensified – now, at its highest point in the sky, it justified its name. The Queen tipped back her head and opened her arms in welcome.

'Blood Moon,' she breathed. 'How beautiful!'

'Very nice,' said Gladrag, suppressing a shudder.

The Queen grinned at her, and her teeth glinted red in the weird light. Then, without taking her eyes off the G, she pointed into the seething crowd of Kelpies. Three emerged and stepped up to the far edge of the horrible Pool.

'Equal numbers,' the Queen explained smugly. 'One for each of your *heroes*.'

The three she had summoned stood there for a moment, to make sure the G were really taking them in. It was a disheartening sight. Two of the Kelpies were towering, strapping men, and the third, a female, was almost as tall and just as magnificently muscled. They were overwhelmingly a match for any of the heroes of old, and the idea of them in competition with three *children* was, frankly, ludicrous. But there was worse to come.

The Kelpies began to change, all at once, so that the G

struggled to keep track of what was happening. It was the same horrible *deforming* of shape they'd seen the Queen undergo, an ugly twisting of limbs and face. It looked agonizing. The end result for the two males was the appearance of a monk from Adom's time and a Guardian from Jay's. Without understanding exactly how, the G knew these were dangerous shapes and no good would come of them. But the third Kelpie, the female, seemed unable to *find* her final shape, writhing and shifting continuously – until they realized what she was meant to be. From animal to human to bird to sea creature, the Kelpie was . . .

'Of all the cheek!' exploded Market Jones. 'She's trying to be *us*!'

At which point the Kelpie became a replica of each of the G standing there before her, one after another, ending with a version of Hibernation Gladrag – but with the addition of some truly outrageous curves.

'Well, *really*!' Gladrag huffed, though her two Companions went quite quiet.

Then the show was over. The Queen clapped her hands, once, and immediately the three Kelpies walked forward to the edge of the horrid murky Pool and dived. The G gasped in horror – surely the water was only centimetres deep? – but there was no sickening sound of the demons hitting the rock bottom. Instead, they simply disappeared, hardly seeming to break the surface gloop.

There was a moment of appalled silence. Then the Queen leaned over and passed a finger through the slime at the edge of the Pool, lifting a long, green, glutinous rope of it to her mouth and licking it luxuriously.

'Bliss,' she said.

'Yuck!' said a chorus of G.

17 *The Seventh Tide*

'Where are we?' said Adom. 'Is this it? The Dry Heart?'

The Traveller had dumped them on the rocks at the foot of a cliff, on the scattered stubs of old lava flows. Immediately behind them a towering, vertical slash in the rock led into darkness, but as the three staggered to their feet, they didn't at first even notice it. Their attention was focused in the other direction.

'It's gone,' whispered Jay. 'The sea's gone!'

A weirdly coloured moon lit up an alien scene. The tide had receded beyond the visible horizon, leaving a ragged landscape of slimy puddles and deeper pools divided by exposed rock. Ridges and outcroppings of the sea bed seemed to be seething, as stranded creatures flailed and struggled to reach water again. An eerie wailing sound drifted on the breeze: whales, trapped and cut off from each other in remaining gullies of sea, calling urgently. The air was thick with the rank smell of mud and weed.

They stared, unable to understand what it could mean. Then Eo gave himself a shake.

'Come on,' he said. 'We'll worry about that later. One invigorating challenge at a time.'

For an instant he sounded just like Professor Hurple, so much so the others turned sharply to him. He looked deathly in the moonlight. They all did. They looked like three children who had been ill in bed for some time and really shouldn't be up for a good week yet. What they did *not* look like were heroes, mighty, magnificent, muscly, loins girded and weaponry on display. No lighting effect known to art or science could successfully achieve an impression of *that*.

Squaring his slim shoulders, Eo headed into the cliff anyway and, with a sigh and a shrug, Jay and Adom followed.

The cave was high as a cathedral, but no more than a few metres wide – more of a soaring crack than a cave – with a narrow ledge running along one wall. If there'd been any water it would have lapped the edge of it. As it was, the drop from the ledge was straight to the dark floor of the gully.

The moonlight penetrated only a little way in, then the blackness took over. The three felt their way forward gingerly along the ledge, waiting for their eyes to adjust.

'Well, at least there are no sheep,' said Adom, trying to sound cheerful.

'We could really do with my torch round about now,' muttered Jay.

Eo turned back to look at her, his face a pale smudge in the gloom with a white crescent at the bottom. She realized he was grinning.

FAQ 116: Why are there so many Underworlds in stories and myths? I hate caves, so you'd never catch me going into one!

HURPLE'S REPLY: There must be as many Underworlds as there are peoples who live in sunlight. There's something about the idea of a whole other world going on under our feet – one that we can't see and normally can't get to – that gets our interest sparked. Before there were alien worlds in outer space and the means to reach them, there were cave entrances that led down into the forbidden depths. And there's **nothing** like telling folk that something's forbidden . . .

Presumably, subterranean races have stories of brave, rebellious souls boldly going up into the Overworld of blinding brightness and bewilderingly agoraphobic skies.

I'm sorry to hear about you not liking caves. I must admit I find it hard to understand. Have you considered a nice snug tunnel instead?

"Yeah, it certainly has been useful – how long ago was it you broke that? First Tide?'

'I wasn't even *on* the First Tide! You boys were still on your own then.'

'And how many things did *we* break, eh?'

'Well, I broke my arm,' rumbled Adom.

'There! See? My point exactly! Ha!' – at which point Jay fell off the ledge.

It was more of a slither than an actual swan-dive, but it still knocked the breath out of her for a moment.

'Are you all right?' Eo shouted, and 'I'm coming down!' Adom called, but Jay had already scrambled to her feet again.

'No. I'm fine. Stay where you are.' She brushed herself down crossly. 'You take the high road, sort of thing. It's too steep here. Maybe it'll be easier to climb up further in.'

They continued to inch forward on two levels. The boys were soon forced to go sideways, as the ledge became even narrower. Jay crunched along below them, one hand stretched out in the darkness, the other following the line of the wall.

'You're noisy enough,' grumbled Eo. 'What're you walking through down there – bones?!'

Jay froze, one foot in the air. '*What?!*'

'Don't be daft,' Adom put in quickly. 'It's driftwood. Place like this, with the tides and the currents, it's bound to be full of old driftwood.'

Jay lowered her foot gingerly.

'Or bones,' added Eo helpfully.

'Oh, shut up!' snapped Jay.

A moment later, Eo spoke again.

'I'm sorry I said that about bones,' he said in a peculiar voice.

'Why?' said Jay suspiciously.

'Because the ledge just ran out.'

'Oh, great. Well, come on down, then – OWW!'

'What happened?' the boys called anxiously.

'I just stubbed my hand – looks like the cave just ran out too.'

'Well, mind yourself. There's nowhere we can go from up here – except down there!'

'Aren't you glad I've got all this nice *driftwood* for you to land on?'

Jay backed up, and with a certain amount of cursing and arguing, the boys slithered down to her level.

'Now what?' she said.

'I don't know,' said Eo, rubbing a scraped elbow crossly. 'I guess we'll have to go back and try to find another way in.'

'No, wait! Can't you feel that?' said Adom.

'Feel what?'

Adom moved his head from side to side for a moment and then nodded in the darkness. 'The wind. There's definitely a wind.'

He heard Jay sigh. 'Don't be a doofus. Of course there's a wind. There's *always* a wind around the islands.'

'Yes – doofus – but they don't usually come from *inside*, do they?'

'WHAT?!'

It was true. There was a definite draught coming, not from the open air behind them, but from the rock face that was currently blocking their way. They could all feel it now, and it was unsettling in a way they couldn't immediately identify. It felt . . . *wrong*.

Winds off the Atlantic can be many things – freezing, ferocious, hurricane-strong, with thousands of kilometres of uninterrupted run-up at their backs – or chirpy or balmy or foggy or tangy or sweet. But they are *always* cargoed up with water. *This* wind had forgotten what water was. Desert people would call it Mummy-maker, Sirocco, Brickfielder – but to these children of the tides it was nameless and alien, catching at the back of their throats and making their skin itch.

'Where's it *coming* from?'

They felt about in the darkness, and almost at once Eo came across a low, narrow slit in the rock. Normally it would have been below water level, accessible only at the most extreme of low tides. Like now.

'I think we can get through here. What do you think, Adom?' Eo said.

'Oh yes, make sure the fat one fits,' Adom grumbled, but it wasn't a problem. Sliding in sideways, they all fitted, just, and the tunnel on the other side of the slit was comfortably tall and wide enough. It angled steeply up before levelling off.

'Hey! I can see!' exclaimed Jay.

There was a flat, whitish phosphorescence coming from the rocks which made them look even sicklier than the moonlight had. But it was a relief not to have to feel their way.

'The wind's coming from further in,' whispered Eo.

And almost at once, the tunnel opened out into an enormous, astonishing, unbelievable space.

They had come out on a ledge overlooking a huge

circular cavern. Before them was a great terraced amphitheatre: three levels of mazes, threaded by three rivers that appeared and disappeared among the corridors and walls. There was something disconcerting about the rivers, though. They were the wrong colour for one thing – they were white, with an odd sheen to them. And they didn't *sound* right.

'It's like they're *sighing*,' said Adom, frowning. 'Water doesn't sigh.'

But Eo wasn't paying attention. 'Look at the stars!' he exclaimed. 'They're beautiful!'

The roof of the cavern wasn't a roof. It was an indoor sky, spangled with stars so bright they lit up the entire space. There were constellations and galaxies, recognizable for a moment, then spinning on into new combinations and conjunctions.

'And look there,' murmured Jay, pointing. 'That's it, isn't it?'

There was another source of light in this underworld. A moving something in the centre of the cave shimmered and scattered light without revealing what it was. The three looked longingly towards it for a moment, then returned their attention to the job in hand.

'OK,' said Eo. 'We have the brief. Thread the mazes with no path; cross the rivers with no water; find the Centre and mend the Dry Heart. Let's get finding.'

'Gotta thread before you can find,' said Jay. 'But from where I'm standing, that shouldn't be too hard!'

'What are you on about?' said Eo. He sounded a bit irritated. 'Did you bring some sort of maze-reading technology you haven't told us about?'

'We don't need technology. We can *see* the way from here!'

She was right. The whole thing was laid out in front of them, clear as day under the swirling stars: an aerial view of every step of the way.

'So, all we have to do is make, like, a diagram –'

'– or just a list of turn left, turn right –'

'– yeah, and that'll take us straight to the Centre!'

'Well, that's not much of a challenge!'

'It would be if you didn't have anything to write it down on, though.'

'That's true.'

'Or if it kept changing,' said Adom.

'Well, yes, but – *what*?!'

'The mazes,' said Adom in a flat voice. 'I just saw them move.'

They stared at him, and then looked out over the scene.

There was no arguing with it. The mazes were moving. First here, then there, all over the great labyrinth, walls shifted, corridors became corners, passages became dead ends and dead ends became new routes forward. They tried desperately to see a pattern in it all, something they could use as a guide, but in the end they had to give in.

The shape of the mazes was changing constantly, and the change was entirely random.

The mazes with no path . . .

'You know that technology I was kidding you about,' murmured Eo, 'could you bring it out now?'

Jay heaved a rueful sigh.

One by one, the three picked their way down the steps

that led to the first level. As the walls of the maze rose up around them, they did not see the Kelpies who had dived into the rancid pool above, appearing now out of a hole in the far wall, leaping on to the top of the nearest wall and starting to run along it. Grinning horribly, they began to work their way inwards.

Moving more slowly, the three children were doing the same. They took turns choosing which way to turn at each junction and let whoever had made that choice lead the way till the next time. It was as good a system as any. That was how it happened that Adom was in front on this particular bit – a corridor with very weird acoustics.

'Do you hear that?' said Adom, looking back over his shoulder to speak to the others. 'That whooshing sound just keeps getting lou–'

He didn't see the section of wall suddenly swing out until it shoved him sideways. Before he could even turn back, the configuration of the maze had changed once again, leaving him on one side of a blank barrier of stone, with Eo and Jay on the other.

They stared at each other, wide-eyed, unable to believe he was gone.

'ADOM!' they screamed, and then shushed themselves.

'I'm all right,' they heard. His voice was faint, coming over the top of the wall.

'We'll climb up! We'll get to you somehow,' Jay yelled, scouting frantically up and down the wall in front of them, feeling for handholds.

'No,' Adom called back and then, almost a whisper, 'This is for me.'

Jay turned to Eo. 'What did he say? What did he mean?' When Eo didn't answer she grabbed his arm and shook it. 'Eo! What's happening?!'

The face he turned towards her was almost unrecognizable.

On the other side of the wall, Adom found himself in a square chamber. It was clear now why the whooshing sound had been getting louder.

'So *that's* what it was,' he murmured in amazement.

A stream of whispering white powder, a few metres wide, flowed across the chamber, out from under one wall and disappearing again under the opposite one. The powder was so fine that its movement left an invisible mist in the air, a mist he could taste on his lips.

It was a river of salt.

He could hear Eo and Jay shouting to him in panic.

'I'm all right,' he called back – and froze.

He wasn't alone.

Someone was standing in the shadows on the far side of the chamber. There was no one that Adom could possibly be expecting to see in this strange place, yet the figure seemed eerily familiar. It was tall, and gaunt, and it wore habit and sandals . . . then, as it stepped forward, right up to the verge of the river of salt, he felt his heart lurch.

'*Columba?!*'

With part of his mind he heard the others calling again, saying they would come to him. Without taking his eyes off the man, he answered them.

'No,' he said. 'This is for me.'

The saint nodded as if in approval.

'I've been waiting for you,' Columba said, his voice like the voice of a deep gold bell.

Then he held out his hand.

Adom couldn't believe this was happening. It was like being given another chance. It was as if all the shame and confusion of the months at the monastery were being wiped away, and the story that started when he was a child was finding its proper ending at last. It was like an answer to prayer.

He stumbled forward joyfully, blindly, but at the last moment he tripped and fell heavily to his knees. The very tip of the fingers of his outstretched hand touched the lip of the river of salt – and something horrible began.

Before he could react, the white powder started to wick up his hand and then his arm. More and more of it swarmed over his skin and his sleeve, as if it were something alive and hungry and searching. And as soon as it made contact with him it began to harden, like an ever-thickening cast on a broken limb. When he tried to pull back, his arm was so grotesquely encased in salt he could barely lift it.

'Take my hand, boy,' said the voice of the saint. There was an edge to its music now. 'Don't make me wait any longer.'

Desperately Adom struggled to pull himself upright, but the swollen thing his arm had become kept him bent double and unable to stand. This couldn't be happening! He had a chance to make it right, to make it the way it should be, to take the saint's hand . . . and it was spoiled. He'd spoiled it. Again.

He would be nothing. Again.

As hopeless tears began to run, one by one, down his face, Adom could feel his cheeks stiffening. The dry air sucked at the moisture, leaving thickening bars of salt behind.

Even holding his head up now was becoming unbearably difficult, but with an enormous effort, he looked over to the figure of Columba one last time.

'I'm sorry . . . Father . . .' he croaked, then his words dried up too and choked him.

The saint's face had begun to twist and distort, his whole body contorting until he vomited great gobbets of scornful laughter. As Adom stared in horror, Columba lurched and twitched into another form altogether.

The Kelpie couldn't be bothered to hold to his disguise any more. He stood before Adom now in his own man-shape and gave himself up completely to a luxury of derision.

Adom let his head drop on to his chest, but nothing could block out the sound of that laughter. He was a fool. There had never been another chance at grace. Columba had never changed his mind about acknowledging him. It was only right that a creature as low as a demon should mock him, because he was so worthless and stupid. He would mock *himself* if he could only find the strength . . .

On the other side of the wall, Jay was so bewildered she could barely breathe.

Strangely, gently, the Eo she thought she knew so well was changing before her eyes. He was the same . . . but he was also broader. Shorter. The magnificent hair shortened and darkened. And when he looked at her and smiled, it wasn't a daft G grin she saw but Adom's slow, sweet smile.

He motioned to her to stay quiet, but she couldn't have spoken anyway, not to save her life. Then he rummaged in his bag and pulled out the deer-bone pipe MakK had given them.

He began to play.

The notes were tentative at first, as if he were listening to a tune in his head that he couldn't quite remember. Then they grew in confidence . . .

The music drifted softly over the wall, at first unnoticed by the Kelpie in his scorn or Adom in his despair. Then, in a pause in the laughter, it made its presence known.

The effect on the Kelpie was immediate. His stance changed dramatically, as he dropped down into the alert crouch of a hunter. He lifted his head and inhaled luxuriously, licking his lips. Then he leapt across the river and began to cast along the wall behind Adom, sniffing, trying to pinpoint the source.

'Delicious,' he purred. 'Fresh. Unsuspecting. It was only my job to secure the one, but what will the Queen say if I salt down the three!'

'No!' Adom croaked. 'It's just me you want. Me!'

'*You'll* wait. *You're* not going anywhere.'

Adom went cold. Trembling with the effort of holding up his head, he watched as the demon turned back to the river of salt and dipped in first one hand, and then the other.

'For the G brat –' shoving one handful of the horrible whiteness near Adom's face, taking pleasure in the way he strained helplessly to get away. 'And this is for the human girl.'

All the while, the music kept nagging for Adom's attention, trying to tell him something, remind him of something, but he was so far gone that it was like listening to someone calling down from the sunlight to the bottom of a deep well.

Then, abruptly, something happened inside his head.

There was one of those sudden shifts that come sometimes, when out of nowhere a picture leaps into your mind, stronger and more vivid than anything your actual eyes can see. Adom drew his breath in sharply, overwhelmed by a powerful vision of his home, his childhood, his mother humming that tune in the sunshine in front of their house, turning, smiling *at him*, with a look of not just fondness or familiarity on her face – with a look of *belief*.

Belief in him.

He remembered how that felt, and started to feel it again. And there was more. He remembered the tune from another time, on a hillside above the sea, with the people gathered to see Columba, the *real* Columba, and Eo was there and Hurple, and he, Adom, had said to them, *You don't convert demons*.

That was it. He could feel heat rushing to his face and hands and feet and the blood pounding in his head.

'You don't convert demons,' he muttered.

'What?' The creature was focused on the scent of souls – it wasn't paying attention to him.

'*And you don't let them convert* you *either!*' Adom's voice rose to a shout.

The Kelpie had only just started to turn round when the ghastly, swollen, salt-encased arm smashed into him, throwing him off his feet and into the wall so hard, the sound of his head cracking open was like a gunshot. Adom didn't stop. He lifted the shameful weight high over his head and brought it down, again and again, till the Kelpie was pulp, and the casing cracked and fell away in great jagged chunks that splintered on to the floor . . .

In the silence that followed, Adom became aware of a rasping, panting sound. He swung round, like a threatened bull – but he was the only one there. It was his own laboured breath he was hearing. The Kelpie was undeniably dead, and the music of the pipe had stopped, and he was alone.

Adom let himself crumple down the wall and sat, head hung down. He didn't even know he was crying again until the salt bars on his cheeks began to hit the ground, sliding off like icicles from a roof. He was too tired to notice when the walls of the maze moved again, leaving an opening on the far side of the chamber.

Eo and Jay rushed in.

'Adom!'

'Are you all right?'

They jumped carelessly over the river of salt.

'Ngggg,' said Adom, so appalled he could barely speak.

'What's wrong?' Jay said, seeing the expression on his face. 'What's happened?'

Adom pointed with a shaking hand at the white flow.

'That's weird. It looks like *salt*!' Before he could stop

her, Jay turned back, stuck her finger into the river and gave it a lick. 'Yep. Salt.' She made a face. 'Very *salty* salt! Well, there's our river with no water, or one of them anyway. So, tell us all about it. Hey, what's *that*?!' She'd caught sight of the mangled corpse.

'It's dead,' said Eo unnecessarily.

As they watched, the Kelpie's remains started to steam and then dissolve.

'It's the acid,' explained Eo. 'Like the stuff that burned me. I think we got taught about how it's in all their internal juices. When they're alive they somehow manage to control it, but when they die . . .' He shrugged. 'It's tidy, anyway.'

'Eugh,' said Jay, unconvinced. 'Let's get out of here. Back over the brine, eh?'

'Just don't let it touch you!' Adom warned, finding his voice again. 'I know you touched *it*, just now, but *don't do it again!*'

'OK, OK!' Jay took his hand. 'Come on, Hero Monk Man!' and she grinned at him. 'We'll jump it together.'

Eo grabbed his other hand and they all backed up as far as they could.

'On three, then . . . one . . . two . . . THREE!'

With a whoop, they ran forward and leapt the river, clearing it with room to spare.

It was Jay's turn to lead. Nobody was talking much. Adom was still shaky, and Jay was mulling over the shifty thing with Eo, and Eo was just . . . quiet. After a while, though, Jay came back to other unanswered questions.

'You haven't really said, yet, Adom, what happened

to you back there,' she said tentatively, speaking over her shoulder. The passage was narrower here and they were walking in single file.

'I don't think I can tell you.' Adom had a strange expression on his face, as if trying to work out a puzzle in his mind. Then he shook his head, defeated. 'I really can't.'

Jay frowned. 'You mean you can't remember?'

He shuddered, and swallowed hard. 'I can remember. But it seems it's the nature of this place that I can't tell somebody else what I remember. I'm not trying to be difficult – you'll understand when it's your turn.'

Jay stopped so fast the others piled into her. She swung round and grabbed Adom by the front of his habit.

'*What do you mean, "my turn"?!*' she squawked. 'There isn't going to *be* a "*my turn*"! I'm here for technical advice only, remember? I'm not here to kill things. Tell him, Eo. One of *you* can take my turn. Look, I've got loads of good stuff left you can use.' She began rummaging frantically through the pockets of her belt, spilling the contents on to the stone floor. 'See? There's still the Water Purifier, and the Portable Generator, or at least most of the pieces for the Generator, and the Hull Pressure Gauge –' The thing came apart in her hands. '*I can't kill anything!*' she wailed. She covered her face and leaned back against a part of the wall that suddenly wasn't there any more – and, with a shriek, she disappeared from sight.

'*JAY!*'

Eo already had his head stuck in the gap. 'It's goes down, like a slide.' He pulled his head out. 'To the next level, maybe. Let's go.'

Adom was trying to gather up Jay's things.

'Leave it!' barked Eo. 'There's no time!'

Adom hesitated, a piece of broken kit dangling from one hand.

'Come ON!' yelled Eo as he grabbed hold of Adom and threw them both head-first into the chute. The bit of wall that was already closing over the hole again almost caught their heels.

The ride from the outer ring to the next level had taken Jay completely by surprise. She landed in a heap, winded but unhurt, in a new gallery.

Staggering to her feet, she stumbled into the first corridor she came to, which also closed itself off behind her the moment she was inside.

If Jay had still been lying at the bottom of the slide-tunnel when Adom and Eo arrived, they could have done her some serious damage. As it was, they slid out unimpeded and bashed into the far wall of the empty gallery in a tangle of arms, legs and colourful language.

As they scrambled to their feet, it seemed as if a shadow passed over them, as if something had jumped across the open top of the corridor, from one wall to the next. They both crouched instinctively, but whatever it was, it was too fast for them to see.

And whatever it was, it wasn't them it was interested in.

'It's a fair guess it's after Jay. We need to find a way round *that*.' Eo pointed at the blank stone wall in front of them. 'But which way from here? Your turn to choose, Adom. Right or left?'

The gallery they were in stretched away in both directions without a discernible break.

Adom sighed. 'That way,' he said.

They headed off at an anxious jog.

The passageways and corridors all looked the same. After a while, the one Jay was in made another ninety-degree turn. With a sigh, she hurried round the corner – and skidded to an abrupt halt. There was something there that made no sense.

It was a Guardian, standing no more than half a dozen metres away, blocking the corridor.

The faceless, eyeless mask was turned directly towards her, but there was still that split second of uncertainty – had it, *he*, seen her? There was nothing to read, only the blank membrane giving no clues. She tried to locate a way out, moving only her eyes, trying not to breathe, trying not to draw attention to herself.

Nothing.

Part of her brain told her sternly that it was impossible for a Guardian to be there, that the thing she was seeing wasn't real. Unfortunately, everything that had been happening to her over the last few days was *also* pretty thoroughly impossible, and *also* couldn't be real. And she had memories – and bruises – to tell her just how real the impossible could be.

She also had fifteen years, give or take a few when she was a baby, of being terrified of Guardians. Of Guardian authority. Of Guardians' guns. A lot of years . . .

'Are you ready for your test, girl?'

The voice burrowed straight into the fear centres of

her brain, before she could even sort out the individual words or what they meant.

What? Wait!

But the Guardian wasn't waiting. He was already speaking again.

'As you were told –'

Told? When was I told? I don't remember – wasn't I paying attention?

'– you are to be tested and weighed today. Follow me.'

He turned and walked off down the corridor, not needing to check to know that she would follow. She didn't even hear Eo and Adom calling from somewhere else in the maze. She just whimpered and did as she was told.

'Stand there.'

They had entered a strange space. Up till then, things in the maze had been, well, organic. Obviously, rock in the wild didn't move the way the walls did, and salt didn't tend to flow a great deal, but still, you could certainly *find* stone and salt in the natural world. But here, Jay was faced with an array of objects made of what looked like synthetic fibres, steel and glass.

The sound of the wall closing up behind her, however, was entirely stone on stone.

On the floor in front of her was a set of large, old-fashioned scales, the kind with two hanging dishes and a fulcrum. The Guardian produced a small black weight and showed it to her.

'This is what the world has had to spend on your life, so far.'

It looked pretty insignificant, but when he placed it on one side of the scale, the dish clunked to the floor.

Overhead, there was a tangled mess of ropes and pulleys and gantries that blocked out the stars. They were connected to a wall of square doors, all different sizes, all made of some sort of opaque glass.

'Behind each door is a weighed measure, according to the value of the person described on the tags. You must find the tag which gives a fair description of your abilities, pull that rope and that particular door will open. Then we will know *your* value. Then we will know if you have been worth the outlay.'

Jay peered wildly about, unable to see how the system was supposed to work.

'What?' she dithered. 'I can't reach . . .'

Then the other ends of the ropes dropped down in a line, right in front of her face. Each had a label attached to it, with words printed on it.

Jay stepped closer to one, squinting at the writing. '*Athlete and mathematical genius, D-class,*' she murmured.

'You have begun,' the Guardian rasped. 'Fifty-five seconds remaining.'

'WHAT?! No, wait! I was just . . .'

The Guardian paid no attention. He was focused on the timing device he held in one grey-gauntleted hand.

Jay dropped the tag and grabbed another, and then another, searching desperately for one that described *her*.

Musician and hydroponicist, D-class
RD-class epistemologist
Engineer and plankonologist, D-class
'No . . . no . . . no . . .'

She worked her way along the line, becoming more and more frantic with each unsuccessful match.

'Ten seconds.' The Guardian's voice cut across her panicked brain like a whip.

Computational cartographer, RD-class

D-class physicist and animator

She grabbed hold of the final rope. The tag said just one thing: *O-class*. Nothing more.

'I must have missed it!' she muttered, looking wildly back along the line, then down at the tag in her hand again. 'This can't be *it*?!'

The Guardian looked up from his timing device.

'Time's –'

With a despairing wail, Jay pulled the last rope.

'– up.'

The elaborate pulley system lurched and one of the doors, a small one on the left-hand side, flipped open. A dribble of tiny shells spurted out and, making an incongruous tinkling sound, trickled down to the scales. As the shells dropped into the container, Jay stared hopelessly at the other half of the scale.

It didn't budge, not even when the Guardian walked over, fastidiously retrieved one final minuscule bit of mollusc and dropped it into the dish.

'And that's the best you can do,' he said. It wasn't a question.

Jay threw herself into a frenzy of rechecking all the labels on all the ropes, but nothing had changed. The tags slipped through her fingers. She just stood there, head drooping, defeated.

Which is when the little packet of leaves flew over the wall, landed on the rock floor and burst. Immediately the chamber was filled with a pungent, overpowering scent that made the Guardian snort and choke. There was a moment of displacement in Jay's mind and then the memory clicked into place: Love's Truth, and Circe's cool, considering voice. *I thought you might be unusual, but after all . . . just arrogant and ignorant . . . never push hard enough to find out . . .*

And suddenly it was all *too much*. Too much scorn and being dismissed and deemed valueless and a waste of space. If there hadn't been all that from Circe, the Guardian's weighing and testing would have got it just right, just the right amount of dis, but coming on top of what the Fifth Tide had given her . . . inside herself she hit a wall – and rebounded.

'*I'll show you!*' she sobbed, breathing in the scent and watching as Circe's face floated before her eyes. 'You said I'd never push hard enough. Maybe, maybe not, *but you just watch me* pull!'

She lunged along the line, grabbing hold of every rope at once and, throwing her whole weight into it, *heaved.* The Guardian, caught completely off-guard, took a moment to realize what she was doing. When he did, he screamed and turned to run, but it was too late. Every door in the place flew open and an avalanche of shells thundered out. The weighing scales were smashed. The Guardian was swept up and slammed against the far wall. His shrieking stopped abruptly. The shells pounded relentlessly, without letting up for an instant, battering him and burying him at the same time.

Some instinct tightened Jay's grip on the ropes as the tidal wave of shells knocked her feet from under her and laid her out horizontally, like a windsock in a force-ten gale. The noise was deafening and the power of the river without water threatened at every second to sweep her away, but she held on. Grimly. Triumphantly.

Out in the corridors, Adom was having a difficult time. They'd taken every turn that seemed to head in the right direction, until Eo said suddenly, 'Stop.' Just like that. No more. He'd not said why, or for how long. He'd just stood there, staring at the wall in front of them and fiddling with his hair in a weird way. Then he'd rummaged in his bag for a moment, pulled something out – and chucked it over the wall!

Jay was gone. Eo was acting like a madman, and . . . and . . .

'What's that noise?' It was Eo asking. He looked back to normal, as far as Adom could tell. 'Is it another river of salt?'

Adom's heart lurched, even as he shook his head. 'No. No, it sounds like something different. Something clinkier?'

The wall beside him split and an avalanche of tiny shells exploded through, slamming into the opposite wall and then surging away down the corridor. They caught a brief glimpse of something mangled and battered in the midst of it all before the river swept it round a corner and out of sight. For one horrible moment, they thought it might have been Jay – until she appeared, safe and sound, surfing the shell tide feet-first.

'Grab hold!' she gargled, flailing her arms about wildly, and they snatched at her hands and hauled her in like a great fish.

They ended up in a huddle on the floor, too relieved

at being together again to do anything else. Then Adom frowned.

'Was that a . . .' he began, then swallowed hard. 'There was a thing got swept off that way and we were scared it was you. Was that a Kelpie too?'

Jay nodded. 'But how are they *finding* us?' she panted. 'This place is *huge*, so how do they know just exactly where we are all the time?'

'Smell,' said Eo. 'They can smell souls.'

'Don't be revolting,' she snorted. '*My* soul doesn't smell, thank you very much!'

The river of shells showed no sign of slowing down. It seemed quite settled in its new bed, but this was a place of change, so as soon as they'd caught their breath, the three moved off in the opposite direction.

They'd seen what a river with no water could do.

Eo was in the lead when they found the stairs.

'This beats the last time!' said Jay as they trotted sedately down.

'Yeah, maybe this is where things start getting easier!' said Eo.

No one bothered to comment. Nevertheless, the next part of their journey passed without incident. That didn't mean they weren't all as edgy as cats, startling at imagined dangers at every turn. But as they worked their way further and further through the final level, it was hard not to let the tiniest flicker of hope begin . . .

. . . which was, of course, the moment the maze changed again.

Adom and Jay were a few paces ahead when it happened, but this time, when it was over, the three could still see each other. Instead of a wall dividing them, this time it was another river. And a wall of sound.

The river looked like sand, and if they had known any of the noises moving sand can make in a desert, they would have said it *sounded* like sand as well. A broad river of glittering sand running from under one wall, cutting across the corridor they were in and disappearing again under the opposite wall.

'Can he jump it?' shouted Jay, looking over at Eo.

'No. And we have no idea how deep it could be. Or what would happen if he touched any of it,' Adom yelled back at her.

Eo seemed to have come to the same conclusions. He shrugged resignedly across at them and then acted out a mime of 'I'll go this way, you go that way, and if you keep turning right, and I keep turning left, we should be able to meet up again.'

As the others waved ruefully and turned away, Eo sighed and headed back the way they had come. They'd passed a corridor leading off to the left not too long before and he wondered if it was still there.

It was. He followed it for a time before another left turn presented itself. Now, with any luck, he and the others might be moving towards each other again. The thought quickened his steps and he jogged along the passageway at a brisk pace, until he had to stop. The corridor had come to an end and there, in the wall, was a door . . .

. . . or not. One minute it was there and the next it was blank stone again. As Eo moved closer, however, the now-you-see-it-now-you-don't act slowed down and stopped. He hesitated, and then put out a hand to the handle, wary of being bitten or burned or electrocuted . . . but nothing happened. It was just a handle. He turned it and the door swung inwards. Eo let out his breath in a whoosh, and stepped forward into what could only be described as a room. (At which point, the door behind him flicked out of sight again.)

Unlike the other spaces they'd been in in the mazes, this one had a ceiling. Instead of the starlight he'd become used to, the place was lit by the same flat white phosphorescence they'd come across in the entrance tunnel. It was a good size and all along three sides of it there were more doors that appeared and then disappeared in an irregular pattern. Only the fourth wall, directly facing Eo, behaved in anything like a normal fashion. It just stood there, with two doors in it, side by side. They weren't moving at all. Weirdly, that made them seem much more significant.

Suddenly, Jay arrived through one of the other on–off doors.

'Adom?' she quavered, looking over her shoulder, but the door had already vanished. Then she saw Eo. 'There you are!' She rushed over to him. 'Come on, let's go. If we hurry we can catch up with him! My turn to choose –' She swung round wildly and caught sight of the non-moving doors. 'That'll do,' she grunted and started forward, grabbing Eo by the sleeve.

'NO!'

She stopped and stared at him. 'Why not?' she said.

She seemed so honestly amazed that Eo had a lurch of doubt. Then he looked at the two doors and was sure again.

'The two doors are important,' he said firmly.

'*How* important?' Jay almost wailed. 'We're wasting *time*!'

'Can't you see it? They're not just a couple more doors. They're, what's the word – mythic!'

'Mythic. Right,' said Jay. 'If you say so.'

'Can't you see it?' asked Eo again.

'No! No, I can't, and can't *you* see?! There hasn't been a mythic moment in the whole thing! Can't you see it's all been *random*?! Stuff just *happens*! And the thing I want to have happen now is we find Adom.'

Eo didn't answer. He just stood there, looking sullen.

She tried again. 'It's not your fault, you know,' she said. 'None of it, not *any* of it, start to finish. All the stuff with the moon and the tide and the thin places between the worlds – something weird was *going* to happen. *You* didn't make any difference.'

Eo stared at her. Hadn't she understood *at all*?!

'Jay, haven't you been paying attention?' He tried to explain. 'If I can't find the way to mend the Dry Heart, then everything will stay the way it is *now* – at the turn, at Samhainn, at eclipse, with the walls between the worlds permanently at their thinnest and the rip I made unhealed. The Kelpies will come, and they will suck the G world dry. And that could be only the *beginning*. That could be all they need to make them strong enough to break into another world and then another. *I don't know* – but it'll be my fault too if they do. It's my responsibility. Not yours. Not Adom's. Mine.'

'I can't *believe* that's right,' she exclaimed impatiently. 'It's not *fair*! Some stupid little thing, you hardly notice it, and then you turn around, and *bingo!* Armageddon.

It's hardly cause and effect, is it? Anyway, if it's anybody's fault, I think it's the Kelpies'.'

'How do you make *that* out?' Eo wondered why he was sounding so defensive. Why he was *feeling* so defensive, as if he *wanted* it all to be his fault!

'Well, if there *weren't* any Kelpies, then it wouldn't matter what you did.' She smiled brightly at him. 'Oh, let's stop talking about it. Let's just go. *That* door looks good.' She pointed at random at one of the non-moving doors.

'No. I think this is my test. You know, like what happened to you and Adom?'

Jay put her hands on her hips and shook her head emphatically.

'I really don't see how it *can* be,' she said. 'If it were, *I* wouldn't be here.'

A tiny alarm bell went off in Eo's mind and, at the exact same moment, Adom arrived. He staggered in abruptly from one side . . . and he wasn't alone.

For a brief second, two identical Jays stared at each other, mirror reflections of each other. Then the one standing beside Eo rushed over and threw herself at the new Jay, tripping her up and punching at her until they were rolling about on the ground in an indistinguishable tangle of arms and legs. The boys were frozen in shock for an instant and then leapt forward to break it up, but by then it was too late. When they'd dragged the combatants apart, Eo had no idea which of the two dishevelled girls was the one he had just been speaking to and which was the one who'd come in with Adom.

'Wha . . .?' Adom was completely befuddled, looking

back and forth between the two Jays like a man at a tennis match.

'Don't be stupid! It's *me*!' exclaimed one Jay. 'I just came *in* with you. I've been with you the whole time we've been trying to find Eo. Don't you *remember*?'

'You're lying. Adom, don't listen to her. You know it's me. *I'm* the one who knows what we talked about, right?'

'We didn't talk about anything,' said Adom, looking even more bewildered.

'But *she* didn't know that!' snapped the two Jays in exasperated chorus.

They turned on Eo then, but Adom got in first.

'Tell me what's happening!' he yelled at no one in particular.

'I think I know,' Eo answered slowly. He pointed at the two girls. 'One of you is Jay. One of you is a Kelpie. The one who was with me, first, I mean, seemed pretty keen on getting through one of the doors over there. The ones that aren't all flickery. Which door did you want me to go through?'

He looked at one of the Jays, who immediately pointed at the right-hand door.

'That one,' she said.

'Don't trust her!' the other Jay squealed. 'If she says take that door, you know there's going to be something wrong with it!'

'So you say I should take the other door?' said Eo.

'I don't know – YES! If it's not the door she chooses, then that's the door *I* choose!' That Jay looked a bit bewildered as she ran through what she'd just said in her mind, to see if it in fact made sense. Apparently it did, because she then nodded her head emphatically. 'That one,' she stated, pointing to the door on the left.

'Well, *obviously* we're going to choose opposite,' argued the other Jay. 'What do you expect?! If I'm the good guy and she's the bad guy, there's no other way *to* do it.'

'Eo?' Adom had come over to stand beside him, as if looking for some comfort. 'What are we going to do?' he half-whispered, half-whimpered.

For a long moment, Eo didn't answer. He seemed to be working something out in his mind. Then he nodded.

'We're going to play it by the Rules,' he said.

Neither of them was quick enough to see the tiny sly smile on one of the Jay's faces.

'What does that mean?' she asked at once.

'Yeah, what?' The other Jay wasn't quite as quick off the mark, but Eo shook his head.

'I'm not going to explain,' he said. 'Three Questions. That's my choice.'

Adom made an uneasy movement of protest, but Eo put up his hand.

'I'm not going to argue, and I'm not going to explain,' he said, and Adom subsided. To the two Jays he said, 'Do you accept, and do you agree to be bound by the results?'

The two girls nodded.

'Of course!'

'I've got nothing to lie about!'

Eo took a deep breath. 'OK, then. First Question: what did the Sixth Tide give us?'

One of the Jays answered him immediately. 'Nothing!' she crowed. 'You can't trick me!'

The other Jay nodded. 'She's right. It was nothing.'

'Easy for you to say, after I've already told you,' snapped the first one, but Eo nodded, as if satisfied.

'Second Question,' he continued. 'What happened to me in the Third Tide?'

'YOU DIED!' the two Jays answered at exactly the same time.

Adom felt as if his brain was going to explode, but Eo ploughed on.

'The Third Question is for everyone.'

'What – what are you doing?' whispered Adom. 'We already *know* who *we* are!' He pulled back suddenly and stared at Eo in alarm. 'Don't we?' But the G ignored him.

'What do we have in our pockets,' he said, '*that the Sixth Tide gave us?*'

There was a stunned silence. Then both Jays began talking at once.

'What are you *doing*?'

'We already answered that!'

'You've wasted the last question!'

'I WANT TO KNOW!' Eo bellowed. 'Every one of us, put your hand in your pocket and bring out what's there!'

One Jay responded immediately. She made an elaborate show of reaching into her pocket, bringing out a clenched fist and opening it to show them all what was in it.

Nothing.

She looked as sorrowful as the real Jay would have, at the thought of a wasted chance, but Eo ignored her.

'Now the rest of us. All together!' In an undertone, he added, 'Trust me.'

So they did. They put their hands into their pockets, drew out their clenched fists and slowly opened them . . .

. . . and let the sand trickle through their fingers.

Three players with sand from a prehistoric beach in their pockets and one without.

The Kelpie didn't change. It stayed as Jay. It walked over to the right-hand door and pulled it open. Just before it stepped through, it looked back at them and said, 'Say goodbye to the Professor for me, will you?' in a voice so full of sorrowful Jay-ness, they were *all three* swept with an instant of doubt. Then, still gazing at them over its shoulder, it stepped forward into the darkness and dropped from sight.

Eo walked over and peered through the doorway. A hot wind from the depths of the earth ruffled his hair. He stepped back, and quietly pulled the door to. Then, without another word, the three went to the other door and opened it. One by one they filed through into the place beyond, stopped and stared.

They had found the Dry Heart.

18 *The Dry Heart*

The Heart filled the space almost to the walls, and towered over them in a great circle of multicoloured globes and clouds of sharp-edged light that wheeled round each other in complicated orbits, trailing luminous tracks behind them, like cosmic snail trails. It was as if the internal workings of a gigantic clock had exploded and the bits had formed themselves into galaxies, dancing round each other, criss-crossing and interweaving in space. Faceted shapes passed by, over, under each other, almost touching but never colliding, and everywhere scattering shards of light.

Every time two worlds drew close to one another, a flickering translucent wall would appear, like the Northern Lights or a particularly pretty electric fence. The worlds would flirt right up to their edges but were each time turned away. They didn't break through.

The movement and light were hypnotic and bewildering, confusing the eye. Without realizing it, the three took a step closer, and another, drawn like moths to the moon – until a sharp-edged world suddenly swept past, just catching Adom on the arm. He cried out, shocked at the slit in his sleeve and the line of red that bloomed suddenly on his skin.

'Adom!'

'It's all right,' he said, as they hurriedly pressed back against the wall again. 'It's just a scratch.'

'They all say that,' muttered Jay, but when she examined the cut she saw it was true. 'All right, you'll live. It barely *touched* you, though, and that's tough cloth. That thing must have been like a razor!'

Adom grunted. The thought of getting close enough to *mend* this Heart was making him feel queasy.

Backs to the wall, they stared intently at the whirling motion.

'Doesn't *look* broken,' Jay murmured after a while.

'How would we know?' said Adom.

Eo shook his head in wonder. 'I've never seen anything like this in my whole life.'

'*I* saw a thing once,' said Jay, still not taking her eyes off the moving Heart. 'It was really old, from what used to be China, and it was a white filigree ball thing, with a pattern carved out, and inside it was another ball with another pattern carved out of that, and inside there was another, and another. That was a bit like this.'

'So, how would you fix one of the inside balls, say, if it broke?' asked Eo.

'No idea,' said Jay.

Eo sighed. 'I was afraid you'd say that.' He straightened up and stood away from the wall. 'Stay here. I'm going to have a nosey round.'

'We'll come too,' said Adom.

'No. Stay here. I'll be back soon.' Eo headed off, keeping as far away from any rogue planets as he could, and peering intently up into the Heart.

'He's changed, hasn't he?' said Jay with a sigh.

Adom gave her a sidelong look. 'Why does that make you sad?' he asked.

'Sad? It doesn't make me . . . well, I guess it does. Or maybe just lonely.' She glanced at him. 'Growing up. That's it, isn't it? You're crazy for it, and then you get it, and it just feels like stuff ending.'

There was a moment's intense silence. Then,

'I –' Adom began, but before he could say anything more, Eo had returned.

'I found it,' he said. He sounded grim. 'Round here.'

They followed him, hugging the wall, not speaking.

At first they didn't see what he was talking about. There was so much dizzying movement, it was hard to focus.

'There,' said Eo, pointing. 'Up there!'

And then they did.

A few metres in, two small worlds hung, one blue and one black, frozen in close proximity. The wall of light between them was motionless too. There was a darkened area on it, like a bruise, with a small black hole at the centre.

It was hard to imagine anything more inaccessible than this. Flickering lights and glittering clouds and the eccentric orbits of crystals and spheres swirled and danced between them and their task.

'Oh, boy,' said Jay.

'Doesn't look good, does it?' said Eo.

'Look out!' Adom shoved them all back as the razor-edged world swooped by again.

'That thing's out to get you, my friend!' said Jay with a whistle. Then she frowned. 'Do you think they're all diamond cutters in there?' She nodded at the Heart.

'Let's not try and find out, OK?' said Eo. 'Let's just assume.'

'Don't panic. All we have to do is think it through. That's what the Professor would say.' Jay slapped her cheeks, trying to get her brain into gear. 'So there's a hole. So what do you do with a hole? You plug it, right? OK, what did you tell me, Adom? You were plugging up the holes of your boats, in your time, back before you came to me, right? What were you using for that?'

'Ox tallow,' said Adom. 'Stinks like crazy. But I didn't bring any with me.'

'OK, OK. What else could you use to seal a hole? Come on, think!'

'Mud and stones, if you're a beaver,' said Adom. 'I didn't bring any of them either.'

Jay made a face at him. 'There are all sorts of sealants at home, but *I* didn't bring any, and even if I had, most of my stuff got left two levels back from here. What *do* we have?'

'This.'

They hadn't noticed Eo ratching about in his bag, but now he was holding something out to them in his hand. Lying on his palm was the small, bloodstained lead ball. The thing that had killed him, all those Tides before.

288

'That?' exclaimed Jay, but Adom nodded slowly.

'It's the last thing,' he said. 'It's all we've got left. So that must be it.'

'That's how I think it works,' Eo agreed.

Jay was not convinced, partly because the sight of the horrible little bit of metal made her skin crawl, and partly because there was one glaring difficulty with the idea.

'It's no good,' she argued. 'We can't get it there. There's no way we can *throw* it into all that, not with any hope of getting it to land in the right place. The rip's just too far in, and there's too much going on in between.'

'But maybe that's because we're looking at it from the wrong angle,' said Eo. 'Adom, let me get up on your shoulders.'

He clambered up Adom's back and balanced himself lightly on his shoulders.

Jay giggled. 'You look like the ferret!'

'Very funny. Move over a couple of steps, Adom. A little further. Stop!' He bobbed his head about, looking more like Hurple by the minute, and then hopped down.

'I'm pretty sure I can see a way,' he said. 'A straight line between the rest of all the activity.'

'But even if there is a way through, how can you possibly throw the ball as *straight* as all that?!'

'I can't. I was thinking more along the lines of a marble run.'

'But of course, just wait till I unpack mine!' snorted Jay.

'Ha ha. Here, help me lay this out,' said Eo.

'Lay wh– EO!' she squealed.

He was bald. His hands were full to overflowing with beautiful fair hair, which he was laying out on the ground in a line.

'What have you done?' rumbled Adom.

Eo looked up, surprised. 'What is it? Oh, the hair! We're going to use it to make a U-shaped channel for the ball to roll down – you know, like in a marble run – and I'm going to get back up on Adom's shoulders and feed it into the Heart, so that the far end is in the hole, and then we drop the ball on to *this* end and let gravity do the rest!'

'But, it's *hair*!' protested Adom.

'Yeah, but it's *G* hair. It's very biddable. I just lay it out the way I want it, and then I'll change its molecular structure so that it's not so floppy, and then we can shape it to make the run. Really. Trust me.'

'Oh, *Eo*!' It was all Jay could find to say, as she bent to help. At first she couldn't bear to look at his hairless head, but then, when she did, she saw something amazing. There was already a haze of fluff covering his skull.

'It's . . .' she gasped. 'It's growing again *already*?!'

Eo just grinned at her. He began laying the hair out in overlapping sections about ten centimetres wide and several metres long. Then, working with fingers and thumbs, he bent the sides up into a U shape all along the length of it. The hair held the shape of a long runnel, but was not yet completely rigid.

'I'm going to have to stiffen it as I go,' said Eo, climbing up on Adom's shoulders again and getting into position. 'Feed it up to me now, Jay, and I'll start sending it in.'

The hair was uncannily warm and felt like silk as she began to hand it up to him. Eo steadied his stance and, using his G knack to stiffen the length of hair into a run, he began to slide it into the midst of the Dry Heart. Carefully, carefully, he fed the cumbersome length forward, until . . .

'There,' he breathed. 'Jay?'

Jay reached up and handed him the bloodstained ball, then watched, open-mouthed, as Eo placed it on to the run. *Go! Go!* she whispered to it inside her head. Obediently, the ball began to roll, slowly at first, and then faster, and faster as it approached the hole in the divide between the worlds.

Just then the razor-edged crystalline world came swinging past again. They all yelped. It sliced through the run as if it were a sheet of paper. Most of the stiffened hair disintegrated, flying up into the air and hiding everything for the moment in a golden fog. The other end of the run dropped out of Eo's fingers as he scrambled down from his perch.

'Careful!' warned Adom as Eo leaned dangerously close to the perimeter of the Heart, peering intently inside. He took hold of Eo's sleeve.

'Come on, come on,' Eo muttered, but for long moments the glimmering fragments of his hair continued to spread out, screening what they were all desperate to see.

'Did it work? Can you tell?'

Jay was clutching his other arm so hard it hurt. Adom had shut his eyes and was praying again.

'I can't *see*,' Eo fumed, moving his head back and forth as if to peer between the obscuring particles. 'I can't –'

There was a small *ping*, and the ball rolled out from under the Heart and came to rest at their feet.

They all three stared at it in despair.

'It didn't work,' whimpered Jay, and then in a shout, '*IT DIDN'T* WORK*!*'

She picked it up and swung on her heel, ready to throw it away in a fit of rage, when Eo grabbed her by the wrist.

'Let me see,' he said in a peculiar, tight voice.

Jay was all at once too tired to argue. She let her fingers fall open – and there it was, lying in the palm of her hand. The rough surface of the metal gleamed in the glow of the Heart. It looked utterly insignificant, and yet they'd pinned such hopes to it. It hadn't looked like much when it came out of Eo's body either, even though it had his life's blood on it. Strange how that blood had stuck to it through all the other Tides and now, the ball looked all shiny clean and new again. Shiny clean . . .

'Where's the blood?' said Adom. 'It was stained before.'

As one, they turned and looked into the Heart. The bruise between the worlds was gone. There was no hole. A flickering translucent wall made a safe divide as the globes resumed their elliptical dance.

'It wasn't the ball we needed to seal the hole,' said Jay. 'It was the blood. Eo's blood.'

'Heart's blood. To mend the Dry Heart,' Adom agreed.

Eo didn't say anything. He made a sort of croaking noise. He reached up with one hand and rubbed the fluff on his skull. He backed up against the solidity of the wall. Then his knees gave way and he slid quietly to the floor, a small smile arriving on his face as if from a long way off.

One of his sleeves fell back a little, and the others stared down at him.

'When did *that* happen!?'

The sores were gone. Healed completely. There wasn't even a scar.

Jay pulled back his other sleeve, in case they'd somehow remembered the wounds being on the wrong arm, but there was no mistake.

'They must have closed up when the hole between the worlds did,' said Eo softly. 'They've healed. *I'm* healed.'

Adom and Jay hunkered down beside him, and they viewed the whirling of the healed Heart for a while in a curious state of numbness.

'We did it?' asked Eo.

'You did it,' said Jay, shoving him with her shoulder.

'*We* did it,' said Eo mildly.

'That's right,' said Adom. 'We did.'

There was a deeply satisfied pause. Then, 'Any food left?' asked Eo wistfully.

'No. All gone,' said Jay.

'And we should be too,' said Adom, heaving himself to his feet again. He gave them each a hand up and then they took a last look at the Dry Heart.

The cloud of gold sparks was changing. It was contracting in on itself, becoming smaller and denser. It was also moving further into the Heart, drawn to the G world, now orbiting blithely away from that of the Kelpies. The blue world and the black would pass each other again, when the times were as liminal as the place, but now there was a new partner to the dance. A new, golden globe, in a new, oblique orbit.

'I always said you had beautiful hair,' said Jay.

Walking *out* of the mazes with no path proved to be remarkably simple. The moment they thought to look for one, the three found a door leading from the Centre. It was tucked into the corner of the far side from where they'd come in, and the succession of corridors, galleries and stairs that ensued had one thing in common: at no point did they require the travellers to make any choices. The way wasn't straight, or short, but it took them steadily and unambiguously up and away.

The Island was ready for them to leave.

They were each bone-tired, too weary to talk, or even think much. But they drew comfort from the others being there. And at last they stumbled out of a final tunnel.

They had emerged at the lower end of the Island, on to a shoreline jumble of hexagonal basalt stumps, with the grass turf beginning only a few metres above and behind them. For a moment they just stood, desperately grateful to be in the open air again, with a sky high overhead and room to breathe. Only gradually did they begin to realize that, even after everything that had happened, something was still wrong.

Very wrong.

'It's the tide. It's still out. It hasn't changed.' Eo's voice was husky from all the hours of dryness. 'Look where the moon is. We've been underground for *hours*, but the water's as low as ever.'

The others looked. It was true. The eclipse was over. The moon was moon-coloured again and just lipping the horizon. Soon it would set and the first faint paling of sunrise would show in the east. The tide *should* be at the full, higher even than usual because of being a spring tide, but instead, the same exposed expanse of sea bed still stretched out before them. Between the deeper pools, grotesquely shaped rocks glinted slimily in the moonlight. Things had died in the hours they'd been stranded. Even in the cold night air there was the whiff of incipient decay on the breeze.

'It's like nobody even noticed,' said Adom dully.

'But we *did* it,' said Jay. 'Haven't they been paying attention? Everything's supposed to be *all right!*'

What more can they ask of us? thought Eo to himself, only half-aware of something in the background, nagging for his attention. He was so tired it took a moment for his senses to sort out which one was being called upon.

Noise. A big noise, growing bigger all the time.

He looked at the others. Jay was saying something to Adom, yelling it more like, but nothing could be heard over the thundering. Adom was looking back at her with a half-smile on his face, shrugging incomprehension. For a split second, Eo was *seeing* them both, more clearly than he ever had before. He knew (without knowing how) that many, many years from now, when he was an old G sitting, sunning on a rock, he'd only need to shut his eyes, and their faces would be there.

He reached out and took their hands. They both turned, looking enquiringly at him . . .

. . . when the water struck.

19 *Adom*

Back at the inlet below Devin's hall, what happened was
this . . .

'He's gone!' cried the Bard in horror – but before
Columba could reply, the boy was back again! He
reappeared out of thin air, in an enormous whoosh of
water that flung him full into the Holy Father's arms
and knocked him flat. Then the *water* disappeared, and
there was only the boy Adom and Columba in a heap,
surrounded by staring peasants and a stunned silence.

'I . . . we . . . you . . .?' stuttered the boy, before
fainting dead away.

That was what *happened*. By late afternoon, however,
the story had . . . evolved. Each witness had something
rich and strange to add.

'You should have been there – what a sight –'

'– the stink of hell –'

'– the screaming of the demons as they tried to drag
the boy away –'

'– hang on, I didn't hear any screaming –'

'– the Holy Father roaring prayers like an avenging angel, pulling on the boy with all his strength, and the demons not letting go –'

'– I didn't hear any roaring either –'

'– a great holy tug-of-war –'

'– roaring and heaving –'

'I saw it with my own eyes and *I* can barely believe it!'

The Bard watched the little knots of villagers meet, wave their hands about and part to form new groups.

'The story's spreading nicely,' he said as he turned back into his hall. They had brought the still-unconscious boy here and Columba was keeping watch over him.

Columba looked up now. 'What really happened down there, Devin?' he said. 'Do you know?'

The Bard shrugged and sat down on the bench beside him.

'The boy must be special,' he said.

Columba frowned. 'Brother Drostlin told me he was stupid. Lazy and thick-witted. Couldn't learn to read or write or speak Latin to save himself.'

'Strange,' murmured the Bard. 'The demons certainly thought he was worth taking an interest in. How long have you had him on Iona?'

Columba shook his head. 'I don't know. I haven't had time for . . . Brother Drostlin takes care of things now.'

Devin tutted. 'Since when did you rely on the likes of Brother *Drostlin*? The man's soul must be the size of a shrivelled acorn at the most! You should have bigger souls than that around you, my friend. Like this boy's maybe? Eh?'

FAQ 679: Why are there only heroes and heroines and champions and saints in the past? At the last Career Development Day I went to there was no material at all on any of these as a job prospect – and I checked everywhere.

HURPLE'S REPLY: Don't worry – it's just a question of labelling. What I mean is, we've got shy about **calling** anybody a saint or a heroine or a champion lately, but there are still plenty of people doing the jobs. You just need to keep your eyes open. (I wouldn't want this to get out, in case my idea is stolen by industrial saboteurs, but I can say that I am currently working on a design for a 'Perceptor Lens' which, when made into convenient and inconspicuous glasses, will allow the wearer to see the approximate dimensions of the souls of others. It is based on the simple rule of thumb that the more heroic a person is, the larger their soul is, and should make spotting champions of every description much easier. If you would like to keep track of my progress on this project, watch this space!)

'I thought he was just another boy.'

'You were just another boy once too, as I remember it.' Devin smiled fondly at him.

Columba grunted. 'Though, you know,' he continued slowly, 'I can't help thinking I've seen him before. Him, or someone like him.'

'Look, he's waking!'

At first Adom's eyes were as glazed as a kitten's, but then he seemed to focus on his surroundings and the men leaning over him.

'Father?' he said in a pale voice. 'I saw you. I saw you in hell. But it wasn't you. Not the true you. Bless me, Father, I have travelled far.'

He spoke in perfect Latin.

Columba reached out, a dazed expression on his face, and made the sign of the cross on Adom's forehead.

'I was told you knew no Latin,' he murmured.

'That's right, Father. But I've learned.' Adom lifted his arm to show Columba the wrist computer and realized, for the first time, that it was no longer there. 'I really *have* learned!' His smile shone.

The two men exchanged wondering glances.

'Can you tell us what happened?' Devin asked gently.

'I can try,' said Adom.

When he'd finished, it was fully evening, and his listeners were silent and amazed.

The Bard stood up, drifted to the door of his hall and looked out, out over the village and the trees, to where the sea and the sky and the islands blended their colours at the day's end. He felt the tale begin to find words for itself inside his mind, to lay itself out in shapes and rhythms, begin to become a thing that would last for maybe a thousand years.

Behind him, in the darkening hall, Columba spoke quietly.

'*Do* I know you?' he said. 'From before?'

Adom smiled at him. 'Yes, Father. I can tell you how we met, the first time, years ago, when you brought me back from the edge of death. Because that's part of the story too.'

After a while, Devin looked back at the pair in the hall. The boy was still there, asleep again, and the holy man was still beside him, keeping watch. At first glance it looked as if no one had moved. But then he saw. In one small detail, the picture had changed.

Columba had taken Adom's hand.

20 _Jay_

It was cold on the platform. There was a mean, biting wind, and the sea heaved and churned, inky black. Suddenly the lights came on, their flat glare blotting out any view of the stars.

'. . . and you _didn't_ leave anything here. But you won't take _my_ word for it. _Oh_ no . . .'

Two people emerging from the hatch had triggered the automatic lighting system. It was an old man wearing a peculiar coat, obviously a D-class or an RD, and his minder. She was providing a running commentary, in the voice of someone who is more than a little fed up.

'. . . _you_ have to see for yourself. Well, do so, please, and then let's get back in out of the wind. There, what did I tell you? Nothing. Just a black sky, a black sea, a cold wind . . .'

'And a dead girl,' said the old man.

'. . . a bunch of equipment, a – _what?!_'

'A dead girl. Over there. Oh, look, that's strange. She's throwing up.'

The minder rushed over to the sorry, sodden figure on the platform in a paddy of 'Oh my!'s and 'Dearie me!'s. The old man followed more calmly, with an air of detached curiosity.

The minder busily took off her own jacket and wrapped the girl up in it, clucking all the while. With a bit of effort, she got her standing and started to bundle her towards the hatch.

The girl was wobbly on her feet and more than a little woozy in her speech.

'The Traveller wasn't half as bad as that,' she said blurrily. 'I've got a lot more sympathy for you now, Adom. I'd like to tell you that. So much I'd like to tell you all. And now I'll never see you or hear from you again . . .' She trailed off into a sob.

The words made no sense to the minder, who was anyway quite used to ignoring strangeness, but the old man, drifting along behind, gave a little yip.

'Now *that's* interesting. Why are you speaking sixth-century Gaelic, little girl?' he said, coming alongside them with little skippy steps.

The whole party ground to a halt, there in the cold, black night.

'Was I?' said the girl, in English, now. 'Sorry. Long story.'

'Tell me.'

He spoke as if he were giving an order, as if he really expected her to do so that very minute.

The girl stared at him. She said, 'Tell *you*?!' just as the minder squeaked, 'Be reasonable, sir. She's just an O.'

The old man turned into the full glare of the floodlights. It was uncanny how young he looked, under that wild white hair. 'I want her to tell me. And my understanding of the system is, it's what I want that matters.'

For a second, there was a look of shrewdness on that unlined face, a look very much on the ball, very wide awake and not a little frightening.

The minder had seen the look before. She knew what it meant.

'As you say, sir,' she sighed. 'But not *here*!'

He smiled sweetly at her.

'What's your name, girl?' the minder asked crossly.

'Jay,' the girl said through teeth that were beginning to chatter.

'Right then, *Jay*, since the master has spoken. Let's *go* . . .'

'What's she *doing* here?'

'Does she think we don't *know*?!'

'The Ardnamurchan Reading Room is not and never will be open to Os.'

'And what possible use could it be to them if it *were*?!'

The minders and scribes and shelf-stackers whispered together in corners of the Reading Room, shaking their heads and tutting in disapproval.

'I'm afraid it's my Dr Horace's fault. He insisted. Don't ask me why,' one of the minders said, privately hoping that no one *would* ask her why. She really didn't want it generally known that her charge was so good at getting away from her, or that he went into Restricted Sectors like the surface platforms when he did. 'You know what they're like.'

The others nodded, wry expressions on their faces. They did indeed know what *they* were like.

'Do you know what she said to me?' somebody else said.

The others all leaned in close to hear.

'No. What did she say?'

'Well, *I* said, "If you're going to read that stuff you're going to need a download of Early Dalraidian Gaelic," and *she* said, "I'm ahead of you there, sunshine. Got it already. Right here, *in my enchanted arm.*"'

'She *never!*'

'As I live and breathe!'

On the other side of the Reading Room, Jay sat at a table covered in ancient manuscripts and scholarly commentaries, some of them almost as old as the texts themselves. A voice long dead droned in her ears, one of many in the last weeks.

'The name of the poet is not known for certain, though some scholars have suggested the work is by Devin of Dalraida. The fact that the poem is never included in collections or listings of his work is problematic. That the poem might have been written as a private work only, and not intended to be read or heard by the world in general, would have been an odd concept in his time . . .'

It had been a long day and she was tempted to skim, but something made her stick to it. Something made her pay attention.

'. . . includes passages which mention "the otter-haired woman", though some scholars think the correct translation is "the bald woman". She may have been a nun, though it is not known for certain whether nuns of this period had their hair cut off. However, the *tone* of the references is distinctly more secular . . .'

Suddenly Jay wasn't interested in the commentary any more. She shoved it aside, and peered intently at the thing itself – a peculiar poem of uncertain origin called 'The Journey'. The manuscript was only a copy of a copy, in tiny crabbed writing and pale ink, hard to read, and harder to understand, unless you somehow, magically, knew what it was saying already.

. . . the otter-haired woman . . . the one from the land of laughter . . . St James's talking beast . . . the men of ice . . . the beasts of Eden . . . the Seventh Tide . . . the phrases swam in front of her eyes, making her afraid to blink, in case it was just wishful thinking, seeing them there. So she didn't blink, for as long as possible, and then she did. And when her eyesight cleared, the words were still there.

Her shriek shattered the silence of the Ardnamurchan Reading Room.

'I found them!' she squealed.

All over the library, D-class and RD-class heads jerked up nervously. Minders and scribes hurried to soothe and placate, but after the first startlement had passed, D-class and RD-class smiles were seen. They recognized the Eureka moment, the joy of opening doors and arising possibilities. They recognized one of their own.

Jay looked round the room, smiling back at them. She kissed her finger, touched the pile of manuscripts on the table before her and began to dance.

21 *Eo*

Three clown-coloured oystercatchers – Gladrag, Market and Interrupted – circled high above the Isles as the tide, no longer restrained, surged back in search of its proper place. They looked down on a scene of foamy white chaos, as low-lying land was submerged and then returned to the air, battered but unmoved. Plumes of spume were thrown against the faces of cliffs and up into the sky, and dolphins freed from gullies rode the surf. Although they were in no doubt about what had happened, the birds still waited until they could see the top of the Island of the Dry Heart clearly before moving off.

There was no sign of the Queen, the Kelpies or their vortex. The door between the worlds was shut again.

'Home?' said one, and the others agreed.

The G island, some distance from the epicentre, had been a little protected. As the three oystercatchers came in to land, they saw how the beach was littered with torn-off seaweed fronds and a scattering of flapping fish, but there'd been no permanent damage done.

And there, in the midst of the mess, they saw the figure of a boy, lying on his side, curled up tight.

'Is he all right?' Interrupted Cadence half-squawked, half-said, as he morphed from bird to human while simultaneously trying to get into a soggy robe.

They rushed over to Eo as he began to stir and groan. For a moment he just lay there, peering blearily up into their anxious faces. Then, suddenly, his expression changed. He lurched forward and grabbed Hibernation Gladrag by the robe.

'Where's the Professor?' he croaked frantically. 'Is he safe? *Is he alive?*'

Gladrag tried to point while not getting throttled at the same time. 'We left him up there. On the high ground.'

Eo instantly let her go and scrambled to his feet.

'Show me!'

'Steady!' warned Market Jones, as the boy swayed a little, but Eo shook off his hand.

'Show me,' he repeated.

They led him up the beach, across the dune grass and on to the high ground. The returning water hadn't come this far, and the nest was where they'd left it, tucked in among some rocks.

And Hurple hadn't moved. He still lay there, apparently lifeless, looking like nothing more than a scruffy scrap of fur.

Eo reached out a hand as if to touch him, but then pulled back with a moan.

'No. No. Why hasn't he woken up? I did everything I was supposed to. *Why isn't he OK?*'

Then, suddenly, the Professor began to twitch. His four paws jerked and a muttering sound came out of his mouth.

'He's having convulsions!' wailed Eo, looking up at the others, stricken.

Hibernation Gladrag put a reassuring hand on his shoulder. 'No, no. Look! He's having a dream!' she said kindly. 'And if it doesn't include chasing rabbits, then I don't know my ferrets as well as I thought!'

As Eo looked down again, Hurple stopped twitching and heaved a great contented sigh.

'He caught one!' Eo whispered, smiling. 'And now he'll be ready for a *proper* sleep.' He picked up the still-unconscious ferret in his two hands and carefully decanted him into his battered bag. Then he laid the bag in the lee of the rocks and tiptoed away.

'He's going to be fine,' he said to the three G. 'And now I want my parents, please.' He sat down on the grass, took a ragged breath and burst into tears.

This disconcerted them almost more than anything that had gone before, but fortunately, help was at hand.

Two handsome gannets plummeted out of the sky, overshooting the figures on the hill by several metres. This meant that by the time they had landed and then shifted into human shape, they had also been able to acquire some robes. As they homed in on the weeping boy, one of them pulled a handkerchief out of one pocket and a small fish out of the other. There was only an infinitesimally short pause before the handkerchief was offered and the hugging began.

Hibernation Gladrag, Market Jones and Interrupted

Cadence strolled politely away, grateful to give the family group a little privacy. They headed back down the slope to the shore.

'He's got that hairstyle, did you notice? Like the girl had,' Interrupted commented. 'I do like it.' His own hair was relaxing out of its tight coil, and he ran a hand through it. 'I wonder if . . .'

Market looked sideways at him speculatively and then nodded. 'Could work.' The two fell behind their Head a little.

'You don't think I'm too, you know, *old*?'

'Nonsense! What do you think, Hibernation?'

'Hmmm? Oh yes. Very nice.'

Market winked at Interrupted, and they caught up with her.

'That was quite a kerfuffle,' Market said.

Gladrag shook her head solemnly and tutted.

'Haven't seen that much fuss since *you* were a child, Hibernation, old girl,' Market continued.

'Really?' said Interrupted. 'How intriguing – tell me more!'

Gladrag tried to chuckle carelessly, but a close observer would have noticed the faintest trace of a blush on her cheek. Market certainly did.

As they reached the water's edge, he started to laugh.

Interrupted giggled.

Gladrag muttered something under her breath and stepped abruptly forward. At the lip of the surf she melted, belly-flopped into the waves and seal-swam away. Her friends hooted even louder . . .

. . . and bubbles of answering mirth breaking the surface marked her path.

Tide Table

———

30 October
G Beach	ebb	mid-morning

First Tide (Adom's world)	ebb to full	mid-morning to late afternoon
Second Tide (Jay's world)	full to ebb	late afternoon to late evening

30-31 October
Third Tide (eighteenth century)	ebb to full	late evening to early morning
Fourth Tide (Ice Age)	full to ebb	early morning to late morning
Fifth Tide (time of Circe)	ebb to full	late morning to late afternoon
Sixth Tide (time of dinosaurs)	full to ebb	late afternoon to midnight

1 November
Seventh Tide (the Dry Heart)	ebb to full	midnight to early morning

Fast action and **wisecracking** humour in a **wild** fantasy adventure!